ALL THAT WE ARE

MELISSA TOPPEN

Copyright © 2018 by Melissa Toppen

All rights reserved. Except as permitted by U.S. Copyright Act of 1976, no part of this publication may be reproduced, distributed, or transmitted in any form or by any means, or stored in a database or retrieval system, without prior permission of the author.

The scanning, uploading, and distribution of this book via the Internet or via other means without the permission of the publisher is illegal and punishable by law. Please purchase only authorized electronic editions and do not participate in or encourage electronic piracy of copyrighted materials.

This book is a work of fiction. Names, characters, establishments, or organizations, and incidents are either products of the author's imagination or are used fictitiously to give a sense of authenticity. Any resemblance to actual persons, living or dead, events, or locales is entirely coincidental. This book is intended for 18+ older, and for mature audiences only.

Editing by Amy Gamache @ Rose David Editing

Cover Design by Pear Perfect Creative Covers

Scars remind us where we've been- they don't have to dictate where we are going.
-Joe Mantegna

Contents

Chapter One 9
Chapter Two 16
Chapter Three 24
Chapter Four 34
Chapter Five 48
Chapter Six 59
Chapter Seven 70
Chapter Eight 80
Chapter Nine 91
Chapter Ten 102
Chapter Eleven 114
Chapter Twelve 127
Chapter Thirteen 138
Chapter Fourteen 152
Chapter Fifteen 164
Chapter Sixteen 174
Chapter Seventeen 183
Chapter Eighteen 194
Chapter Nineteen 205
Chapter Twenty 217
Chapter Twenty-one 230
Chapter Twenty-two 241
Chapter Twenty-three 257
Chapter Twenty-four 268
Chapter Twenty-five 280
Chapter Twenty-six 294
Chapter Twenty-seven 297
Chapter Twenty-eight 305
Chapter Twenty-nine 313
Chapter Thirty 323
Chapter Thirty-one 331
Epilogue 340

Chapter One

Harlow

"Close your eyes. Yes, good. Now take a deep breath. Okay, and slowly let it out. Now, tell me what you see." I focus on nothing but Dr. Rothenberg's soft voice, though I don't find it near as soothing as I'm sure it's meant to be. Moments of silence pass before, "Harlow, tell me what you see."

"Nothing." I exhale, my eyes fluttering open. "I see nothing."

We've been at this for nearly forty-five minutes, and I feel like I've gotten nowhere. I know it's me. My inability to allow myself to open up. I've never been good at saying what I feel.

"Okay. That's okay." He gives me a gentle smile, displaying patience like I've never seen in my nearly thirty years on this earth. "Let's try this. What do you feel?"

"I don't feel anything either." I shrug my shoulders as I sink back even further into the brown leather sofa, silently cursing myself for actually thinking I could do this.

If I can't tell my only friend Angela how I feel, someone I've known for years, and who also happens to be the person I've been living with for the last three weeks, how am I supposed to tell a complete stranger? Hell, I'm not even sure I know how I feel.

"I think you're missing the point." He shakes his head, his salt and pepper hair swaying lightly against the movement. "Let's try again."

"I don't *want* to try again. Don't you get it? This is pointless. I feel nothing."

"It's not possible to feel *nothing*. Take for instance your posture. It says you're tense and uneasy. Both which are feelings."

"Because I am tense and uneasy," I clip.

"Well, that's something. Now tell me what else you feel."

"Irritated," I snip, crossing my arms in front of my chest. "I feel irritated."

"And what irritates you?"

"This."

"You'll need to be more specific."

"This." I gesture around the room. "All of this irritates me."

"And yet you chose to come here today. Why?"

"Honestly," I pause. "I don't really know. I guess I was hoping it would help."

"Help you do what? You, obviously had something in mind when you made the appointment. What is it that you need help with?"

"You're the shrink, you tell me." I inwardly cringe at my behavior. I've never been an aggressive person or one to take my frustrations out on someone undeserving, yet that seems to be my motto as of late.

"I can only help you if you're willing to share with me, which up to this point you haven't been. So, I'll ask again. What do you need help with?"

"Let me ask you something." I lean forward, resting my elbows against my thighs, the leather of the couch crunching beneath me. "Do you think it's possible to not have any clue who you are?"

He raises an eyebrow and studies me for a long moment.

"So you feel like you've lost yourself?"

"I don't know if *lost* is the right word."

"Okay, so let's focus on that. Tell me the events that happened before you started feeling this way."

"I guess if I had to pinpoint a time when things seemed to shift, it was after I got married. Ever since then it's like I've been watching someone else live my life through a hazy window. I know it's me, but it doesn't feel like me."

"And why do you think that is?"

"Honestly, I'm not sure."

"Do you think it has something to do with your husband?"

"Ex-husband," I correct through gritted teeth.

"My apologies. I didn't realize the divorce was final."

"It's not. But he's no longer my husband." I swallow past the hard knot forming in my throat.

Every time I think about Alan and what he put me through I'm not sure if I want to punch something, resolve into a puddle of tears, or, on the rare occasion, do cartwheels down the street because I feel so elated to be free finally.. But then reality seeps back in, and I remember the wasted years, the betrayal, what being married to a man like him reduced me to. A trophy wife. Something to stick on a mantle and pull down to show off when necessary but never more than that.

"Do you think that feeling like an outsider in your own life has something to do with your *ex*-husband?" Dr. Rothenberg cuts through my thoughts.

"I don't know." I shake my head. "I mean, yeah, I guess. I don't know how I let it go on for so long, the marriage that is. He was very controlling. I just gave and gave. Never once putting my foot down or fighting for what I wanted. It was always easier to see things his way." I let out a slow exhale, looking down to where my hand's rest, knotted in my lap. "When I found out about the cheating I was almost relieved. How awful is that?"

"It's not awful at all. Sometimes you need a solid reason. It sounds like he gave you one. And while it might not feel like it yet, it sounds like it was the best thing he could have done for you."

"Yeah, I think you're right," I agree. "I just wish he'd leave me alone. I don't understand what more he wants from me. I gave him six years of complete submission. Six years that I gave in to his every will and never once took anything for myself. You'd think that would be enough, but no, now he has to chase me out of Tuscan too."

"And that makes you angry?"

"Hell yes it makes me angry." I shift in my seat, finally letting the words flow. "Because there's nothing I can do about it. He's not violent. He doesn't cause a scene. But he's just always there. Lurking. It's like everywhere I turn he's waiting for me. He knows my next step before I make it. Moving in to cut me off. I just want to be done. I want him to leave me alone. Unfortunately, moving home, back to my dad's, seems to be my only option at this point."

"Aside from the why, how do you feel about moving home?"

Home. God, Kentucky feels so far from home I struggle to think of it that way. Yes, it's where I grew up, and it's where my dad and older brother still live, but for the last eleven years, Arizona has been my home. I went to college here. I got married here. I had a life, or lack thereof, here. It's hard to think about leaving even though there really isn't anything left for me here. Well, other than Angela, my college roommate. Ours is the only friendship that I've managed to somehow hang onto.

"A part of me is excited. I'm moving back to be close to my family, and that makes me happy. But I'm also dreading it. I left home for a reason. I don't want to be one of those people that went out searching for something more only to return home years later a failure."

"You can't look at it that way. You didn't fail; life simply took you in another direction. There's no shame in that."

"I guess." I sigh, wishing I felt that way about it.

"I tell you what, once you get moved and settled, call my secretary and we can schedule a session over video. I'm curious to see how you feel once you've had a few days to reconnect with your family and maybe some of your old friends. I think you'll be surprised how much better you'll feel once you're away from all of this."

"Time's up already?" I ask when he glances at his watch for the second time in less than thirty seconds.

"I'm afraid so. I have another patient coming in directly behind you. Unless, of course, there was something else you wanted to discuss before we wrap up our session."

"No, I'm good. I think you're right. I need to get out of here, go home, and reset."

"You'll call and schedule another appointment once you get settled?" He moves the tablet of paper from his lap to the small table next to him as he stands.

"I will," I agree, taking the hand he extends to me just as I push up onto my feet.

"Good luck, Harlow. I look forward to our next chat."

"Thanks, Dr. Rothenberg." I give him a small smile and nod before spinning on my heel and quickly exiting the office without another word.

Chapter Two

Harlow
Three weeks earlier

"So, Trey asked if I could join him in New York next week." Alan loosens his tie and drapes it across the back of the chair before turning toward where I'm sitting up in bed.

It's the same story as most nights in the Nagle household. I spend the evening alone, and Alan usually shuffles in from work shortly after I turn in for the night. It's been this way for months. The more responsibility he takes on at work, the further into the background I fade.

"Again?" I question, not hiding the distaste in my voice. "You were just in Boston last week."

"We've been over this, Harlow. You knew what I was signing up for when I took this promotion."

"At no point did you say this much traveling would be involved," I object, quickly softening my approach. "I just…it gets lonely here without you. Maybe if I found a part-time job, something small to occupy my time."

"No." He immediately shuts me down, stripping his shirt off before disappearing into the ensuite bathroom. "We made the decision when we got married that I would be the sole provider. It's how my parents did it and how I want to do it as well. You take care of the house, and I make money. That's how this works." He falls silent, the faucet kicking on seconds later.

"I just don't understand why you're so against me doing something for myself. It's not about the money, Alan. It's about having a life." I raise my voice to ensure he can hear me over the running water.

He reemerges in the doorway seconds later, his toothbrush in his hand, toothpaste foaming at the sides of his mouth.

"You have a life," he tells me, shoving the toothbrush back into his mouth.

"No, I don't," I argue. "I sit here all day with nothing to do. It's just you and me, Alan. We have no children, no pets, nothing. There's only so much I can clean. So much organizing and gardening I can do. I cook dinner every night, but five out of seven you're not even here to eat it. My life revolves around a man who's never here."

His gaze goes stern before he turns and disappears back inside the bathroom long enough to discard his toothbrush and rinse out his mouth.

"What's this really about, Harlow?" He steps into the doorway, leaning his shoulder against the doorframe.

"I'm telling you what it's really about. I need something more than this."

"Is this your way of bringing the children conversation back up? Because I've already told you I'm not ready."

"This has nothing to do with having kids." I shift on the bed, growing increasingly frustrated. "You've made your stance on that subject perfectly clear." I can't help how bitter the statement comes out.

I don't think it's unreasonable for a twenty-nine-year-old woman to want to have children with the man she has been married to for six years.

At first, it was all about establishing himself in his job. I understood that because he wanted us to be financially secure before having kids. Smart. But then he wanted a bigger house, more money, and once he accomplished that, he decided that being the manager of one of the most prestigious online security firms in the country wasn't enough. Nope, he wanted to be at the top. And even now, months after landing an executive position, he's still not willing to have a real discussion about it.

There's always an excuse anytime I bring it up, so I've stopped bringing it up. It only serves to start a fight, and honestly, I'm not feeling up for that tonight.

"Then what? What could you possibly need that I'm not giving you?" He crosses his arms in front of his bare chest.

"I want something of my own. Andrea offered to let me work part-time at the flower shop," I start, only to be cut off.

"My wife will not be working at some crappy little flower shop making minimum wage. Your job here is much more important."

"*What* job?" I demand, my hands going up in defeat.

"Caring for me and our household."

"Do you hear yourself right now? You can't really expect me to keep living like this. I'm miserable, Alan. Can't you see that?"

"I didn't realize I was making you so unhappy," he sneers.

"This isn't about you. It's about me and having something for myself."

"I think you're just looking for reasons to create problems." He shakes his head. "The answer is no." His arms fall to his sides before he stomps back into the bathroom, quickly closing the door behind him.

Angry tears well in my eyes and I have to fight back the urge to throw a slew of cuss words in his direction. Taking a deep breath in, I collapse back onto my pillow as the shower turns on.

Staring up at the ceiling, I wonder how we got here. How did we go from two college students crazy about each other to two people who barely co-exist?

I wish I could say we've grown up and apart over the years, but even that's not true. It all changed when we got married. Alan was one person when we were dating and became someone else entirely after we said 'I do.' It was like a switch flipped and the man I fell in love with disappeared right in front of my eyes.

I've spent years trying to find him again. Every once in a while I will see little glimpses – little pieces of the things I used to love the most about him. I try to hold onto those moments. The ones where I feel like his wife rather than some burden he endures or keeps around to prance in front of his fancy business associates.

Alan's phone buzzes to life on the dresser, snapping me from my thoughts. It's rare he leaves it laying around, and because of this, I can't resist the urge to see who is messaging him this late at night.

Rolling out of bed, I quietly pad across the bedroom floor, snagging the phone off the mahogany dresser.

Monica: I had such a great time tonight. Can't wait to do it again.

I blink. Once then twice, sure that it's not what it seems. Swiping my finger across the screen, I type in the password, my heart rate picking up speed when I realize he's changed it. It's been my birthday for as long as I can remember.

Pacing back and forth with the phone still in my hand, I type in two other combinations of numbers before finally getting it right on the third. Of course, he would change it to his office extension. I swear that man could not be more obsessed with work if he tried.

The instant the home screen comes up, I click on his messages. At the top is the one from Monica. I click on her name to open the thread and see that several other texts had exchanged between the two, each one more disturbing than the last.

I can't believe what I see as my eyes scan the device. Plans to meet up for dinner, drinks, and a hotel in Boston…

My stomach bottoms out.

I back out of their messages and scroll through some of the other conversations, stopping on a thread with a woman named Janice. Opening the text thread, I nearly lose the contents of my stomach as I see very similar messages being exchanged with her.

My hand instinctively goes to my mouth as I read about his plans to share a room with her while in New York next week and how he can't wait to be able to touch her anywhere or however much he wants.

I feel lost with confusion swirling in my mind and my heart pounding in my chest that I don't hear the shower kick off or Alan enter the room until it's already too late.

"What the hell are you doing?" His voice washes over me like being doused with ice water. My eyes shoot open like they've been closed for a very long time like I've been asleep for years.

"Monica had a really good time tonight. Says she can't wait to do it again." I turn, squaring my shoulders as I face my husband.

"You went through my messages?" he questions, not even bothering with denial. Not that I would buy it for a second if he tried.

"And Janice can't wait until New York, though I doubt she'd be as excited if she knew you were also fucking Monica."

"Harlow." He reaches for his phone, but I pull it back just in time.

"How many others are there, Alan?" I ask, tucking the device behind my back. "Three? Four? *Ten*? I mean at this point who's counting, right?" I let out a shrill laugh, not sure why this seems so funny all of a sudden.

"You don't understand. It's not what you're thinking," he objects, denial finally kicking in.

"Actually, it's exactly what I'm thinking. And for you to sit there and think that you're going to fool me for even one second is comical. I may have been blind for years, Alan, but for the first time in a very long time, I'm finally seeing the man you really are. And thank god I see it before it's too late." I throw his phone as hard as I can at the wall behind him, watching it knock a nice hole into the drywall before finally clattering to the hardwood floor. "Well, now you have one less woman to juggle." I take off through the house, managing to grab my keys and make it to my car parked out front before he finally catches up to me.

"Harlow, get your ass back in the house." He comes pounding down the front porch in nothing but plaid pajama bottoms.

"No thanks, Alan. I think I'll pass." I tear open the driver's side door, desperate to get out of here.

"You can't just take *my* car," he warns, closing in on me.

Leave it to him to throw it in my face that technically nothing we own is actually mine. Everything is in his name, considering he's the only one who's provided an income throughout our marriage.

"Well, then I guess you can call the fucking police and report me," I hiss, hopping into the car.

I yank the door shut, click the locks, and fire the engine to life, backing out of the driveway with a loud tire squeal and a middle finger thrown up to my cheating husband.

Moments later, I'm speeding down the road in my pajamas, with no shoes, no money, and not one damn clue where the hell I'm going.

Chapter Three

Miles

"So what's new with you? I feel like I haven't seen you in forever." Winston twists the cap off his second beer and takes a long pull as he settles back down into the recliner that's caddy corner from me.

Winston is my oldest friend. There's barely a single memory from childhood that he's not a part of. And while we aren't nearly as inseparable as we used to be, we make it a point to get together at least once every week or so to catch up and shoot the shit.

"Not much. The shop's busier than it has ever been. Business is booming." I shrug, resting the cold beer on the top of my thigh as I sink back into the couch.

"Think you've got time to squeeze in an old friend sometime in the next couple of weeks?"

My eyes dip to the tribal tattoo that wraps around Winston's forearm. It was the first tattoo I did when I started working for Dexter six years ago. At that time, I had no idea that I would one day end up owning the tattoo shop.

I originally got into tattoos as a way of therapy. It helped calm my mind after I returned home from my second tour in the Middle East. Provided me something to focus on. I've always loved art and drawing, so it came natural to me. When Dex decided to retire and sell the shop four years ago, I didn't hesitate.

INK*ed* was a pretty well established shop when Dexter owned it, but after bringing on some really talented artists and going through one hell of a remodel, I've been able to take it to an entirely different level. Our artists are so sought after that people suffer through a six-month-long waitlist just to get their ink done by us.

"That depends. What's got you itching for ink therapy?" I ask.

Having known Winston nearly my entire life and having done all but two of his eight tattoos, I know he usually only comes in when he needs to let off some steam.

"My sister's moving in with me." He blows out a breath through his nose before sucking back a long drink of beer.

"No shit? What about that big shot husband of hers?" Harlow was five years younger than the both of us. When she was in grade school, and we were on our way into high school, she would follow us around like we'd hung the moon.

Harlow always looked cute and sweet with her strawberry blonde hair and adorable freckles that peppered across her nose and cheeks, but she was anything but. As she'd gotten older and we were both preparing to graduate, everything about her, especially her attitude toward me changed.

Winston used to call her the devil, and on many occasions, I had to agree with him. That girl had a temper like no one I'd ever seen. And stubborn, my god was she stubborn.

Last I heard she was living the high life, assumingly better than us with a well-off husband.

"Left him about a month ago. Apparently, that jackass has been cheating on her for years. She was planning on staying in Arizona, but I guess Alan has been giving her a rough time, so she's decided to move home."

"Shit, man." I shake my head, feeling bad for Winston's little sister, even though she treated me like shit the last time I saw her.

Then again, I haven't seen Harlow in a decade, so I can't really say how I feel about her now. Who knows; maybe she's changed. Lord knows I have. Regardless, no one deserves to be dealt a shit hand like that. I've been cheated on before and it's not something I'd wish on anyone.

"That's messed up, man. I'm sorry to hear that."

"It's taken everything I have not to fly my ass to Tuscan and give that mother fucker a piece of my mind.

If I didn't think the blowback would land on Harlow, I would have. I never liked him. I always knew there was something sleazy about him."

"How soon she gonna be here?" I tip back my bottle, letting the cold liquid rush into my mouth.

"Next week." He sighs. "Don't get me wrong. I'm glad to have her home. And I know Dad and Jackie are over the moon. I'm just not sure what her mental state is going to be like when she gets here. You know me, I can't handle all that crying and moping shit. I don't know what to do with someone like that."

"Why isn't she staying with your dad and Jackie?" I ask, wondering why she would choose to shack up with her brother in a tiny two bedroom apartment rather than live with her dad and stepmom in the large four bedroom home she grew up in.

"I think it's a pride thing." He shrugs.

"I get that. How long you think she'll be here?"

"Hard to say. Hopefully not long. I love my sister and all, but you know me. I like living alone."

"I can understand that completely. Luckily, I don't have any siblings, so I don't have to worry about that shit." I grin as I tip the beer bottle to my lips.

"Lucky ass," Winston grumbles, mirroring my action and taking a long pull of his beer. "So, about that ink?"

"I can hook you up, but it'll have to be after hours. I'm booked solid until December."

"Shit, dude. It's only May."

"Tell me about it. Sometimes I feel like I'm never going to be able to catch my breath."

"It's a good problem to have," he points out.

"It definitely is," I agree.

"Maybe I can bring Harlow in with me. I'm sure she'd love to check out the shop, and who knows, maybe you can convince her to remove the stick from her ass and get some ink of her own."

As much as I dislike the idea, I know I can't verbalize it without likely pissing Winston off. No matter how much she drives him crazy, she's still his baby sister. While he would never admit it out loud, he's always been protective of her.

I nod, choosing not to say anything as I drain the remainder of my beer in one long pull.

"How's next Friday work?"

"I should be able to make that happen. Be at the shop at eleven and don't forget you're responsible for the beer."

"As always." He chuckles.

"Or I could charge you like I do everyone else," I jokingly counter.

"I think I like our beer trade off better." He grins.

"Yeah, thought so." I laugh. "Speaking of ink, I gotta bounce. I've got a doubles appointment at four," I say, pushing to a stand. "Thanks for the beer." I cross the open space into the kitchen before dropping the bottle into the trash can.

28

"Anytime, man," he calls from the chair, not bothering to get up. "I'll call you next week to confirm Friday."

"Sounds good." I throw up a half wave before pulling open the door and stepping out into the humid Kentucky heat.

If there's one thing I hate about summer here, it's the humidity. Mid-May and already the air is so heavy it feels hard to pull in a real breath.

Taking the stairs down two at a time, I reach my black Ducati within seconds. Snatching the helmet off the seat, I quickly slide it on before climbing onto the motorcycle.

I was never a fan of bikes when I was younger, but a buddy of mine that I'd served with had an old Kawasaki that he let me drive when I visited him after I left the army. I fell in love and purchased my first bike within a couple of weeks of returning home.

Firing the engine to life, I glance behind me to make sure I'm clear before slowly guiding my bike out of its parking spot. Having stayed a little longer than I had anticipated, I'll be lucky if I make it into the city by four.

My shop is located right across the river in Cincinnati. It's only a few short miles, but with the amount of traffic going in and out of the city late in the afternoon; it takes a lot longer than it really should.

Because of this, it's ten after four by the time I pull into the small parking lot directly behind my shop.

INK*ed* is sandwiched between Beans and Things, a hip little coffee shop, and Mike's Sub. Both of which are pretty good neighbors to have considering I don't usually have a lot of time to grab food between clients and more often than not I need caffeine to pick me up about halfway through the evening.

Pushing my way through the back door, I drop my helmet and keys on the cluttered desk in the office before making my way into the front of the shop. I nod to Chuck who's busy working on a back piece, before throwing a half wave to Bryan who barely nods before turning his attention back to the belly button he's about to shove a needle through.

Delia, my recently promoted manager-in-training, looks up from the front counter and offers me a smile the moment she catches sight of me approaching.

"Bout time you showed up." She gives me her normal dose of shit. If I walked in and she didn't bust my balls about something I'd know something was up.

"Got caught up at Winston's," I explain even though I don't need to. "My double here yet?"

"In the waiting room." She gestures to the small room at the front of the shop.

I lean to the side and catch sight of the two-early-twenty somethings standing side-by-side, admiring some of the artwork on the walls.

In addition to some of our best work framed and hung up, the room is decorated with two large black couches flanking both side walls and a large table in the middle cluttered with several generic tattoo books.

The front wall is a huge window looking out onto the busy street, the opposite a half wall that allows the people in the waiting area a front row seat to anyone getting work done. Unless the client isn't comfortable with the public display, in which, that case they can opt to have their work done in one of the private rooms.

"Should be a fun night for you." Delia leans in and nudges my shoulder, gesturing toward the two women.

"Funny," I deadpan, shaking my head.

Delia knows my least favorite tattoos are trivial pieces that have no real meaning. From what these girls sent me last week, that's exactly what I'm going to be working on tonight. Flowers. And not even cool ones.

I'll never understand why someone would go on a six-month wait list to have the most generic tattoo done that you can have done anywhere. Not to mention my prices run quite a bit higher than the competition because simply put – we offer the best quality and we can afford to charge for that.

"Oh come on, boss. Laugh why don't you?" Delia cuts in.

"Say something funny and I'll think about it." I arch my brow, fighting a smile.

"Such a dick." She crinkles her nose which has a small ring through each side.

Delia started working here a couple of years before I came on board. She's a tiny little thing, barely standing over five feet and weighing maybe a hundred pounds soaking wet, but she's also one of the toughest people I think I've ever met. No one messes with her and for a good reason. She's as crazy as they come.

She's a year older than me, is one of the most talented artists I've ever worked with and has about twice the amount of ink that I do – which is saying something considering my arms and torso are completely covered. Because of this, she knows she can give me a hard time and get away with it. Most of my other employees wouldn't dream of speaking to me the way she does. Not that I give a shit. Again, if she didn't bust my balls about something I'd be worried.

"Do me a favor." I ignore her dick comment. "Will you schedule Winston in for next Friday at eleven?"

"Another late night?" She arches a brow. "Tell me, Superman, do you ever sleep?"

"Not if I can help it," I smart, tossing her a smile before heading into the lobby to see if my clients are ready to start.

While I consider Delia, a friend, I have never opened up to her about my issues. Especially not the ones pertaining to my days in the military and the effect that still has on me today. If she only knew just how difficult sleep is for me on an average night.

Shaking off the thought, I force a smile as I enter the waiting room, not missing the way both sets of eyes hone in on me the moment I do.

"Holy shit. You're hot." The blonde smiles, both hands going to her hips.

"Thank you," I say, completely unphased.

I've grown accustomed to this type of attention over the years. Not because I think I'm something special, but because women seem to have a thing for men with beards and tattoos.

"Who's first?" I ask, chuckling when both girls hold their hands up in unison.

"I thought you were going to let me go first," the brunette whines to her friend.

"I want to go first," the other counters.

"Tell you what, why don't we head back and you two can figure it out while I get everything ready?" I don't wait for a response before spinning on my heel and taking off toward the back.

Chapter Four

Harlow

"Hey, Sis. You ready?" Winston raps lightly on the bedroom door before pushing it open.

"Um, hello. I could have been naked," I object, turning from where I'm standing in front of the closet, still trying to decide what to wear.

"You would have locked the door." He shrugs before collapsing down on top of the bed. "What the hell's taking you so long anyway? I told Miles we'd be at the shop by eleven and we need to eat before we go."

"Would you relax? It's not even eight o'clock yet. I think we have plenty of time." I slide a few hangers to the side before pulling a standard black tank top off the rack.

"Yeah, but you know how crazy the city gets on Friday nights. Besides, if we get there early, maybe he can squeeze you in."

"Winston, we've been over this. I'm not getting a tattoo," I tell my brother for the hundredth time since I arrived five days ago.

Moving here hasn't been the smoothest transition. We've lived so far apart for so long it's like we're getting to know each other all over again. He's changed a lot in the last decade, and lord knows I have too. I hardly even remember the person I was before Alan. Trying to find out who I am after him has proven to be more difficult than I ever imagined it would be. It's been so long since I've done anything for myself I'm not sure I know what I enjoy anymore.

So not only is my brother getting to know me all over again, but I'm getting to know me as well.

"Miles does some fantastic work, Low. Just check out this last piece he did." He turns his arm so I can see the massive tribal that wraps around the back of his bicep. "Man's a genius with a tattoo gun."

"Miles and genius are two things I never thought I'd hear in the same sentence." I roll my eyes, finding humor in the fact that my brother still thinks after all these years that his best friend is the end all to be all. Personally, I've never much cared for the guy.

Not that I can pinpoint any one thing I don't like about him. But there was something about him that didn't sit right with me, as we got older. Maybe it was his arrogance or the fact that he always had a different girl on his arm every time I saw him – which was quite frequently. Or maybe it's that my brother always preferred hanging out with him over me which used to drive me crazy.

"When are you going to grasp that Miles isn't the person you've always believed him to be?" Winston straightens his posture and gives me a stern look. "You don't even know him anymore. Yet, you still insist on making back handed comments like that. Do you have any idea what he's been through over the last few years?"

"Winston, I…" I start to apologize, seeing I've hit a nerve.

"He's been through more than you could imagine. Not all of us have spent the last decade living the good life. Shit changes people, Low. You need to stop being so damn judgmental and give people a chance."

"Wow." I shift, crossing my arms in front of my chest. "So that's what you think I've been doing, living the good life?" I completely ignore everything else he said and focus on that one little tidbit. "Need I remind you why I'm here?"

"I know it hasn't been perfect. I didn't mean it like that. It's just… you need to give Miles a chance. I think you'll find he's a good dude to have on your side when you need someone."

"Okay, fine." I huff, wanting to get off this conversation. "But if he turns out to be the same arrogant playboy that he was in high school, I'm out. I've spent the last several years of my life dealing with a man who thinks he's god's gift to everyone. I sure as hell don't intend to subject myself to another one willingly."

"I think you'll find pretty quickly that Miles is not the person you remember. I don't know that he's ever been that person. Manwhore, maybe. Arrogant and conceited, not a day in his life. Besides, if I remember correctly, that was more your M-O."

"I'm not conceited." My voice shoots up an octave.

"Maybe not now, but in high school, you were about as conceited as they come. Trust me when I say, your dislike for Miles went both ways."

"He didn't like me?" I say, surprised that the thought kind of hurts my feelings.

"Can you blame him? You were awful to him. You were always sneering at him. Grumbling shit under your breath anytime you'd walk through a room he was in. I never understood it. If I didn't know any better, I would have sworn you had a thing for him and were trying to disguise it with distaste."

"Now that's comical." I shake my head, turning back toward the closet that only bears about a third of my clothing – the remainder still stuffed in boxes in the corner of the room. I quickly snag a three quarter sleeve charcoal cardigan off the hanger and drop it on top of the black tank draped across the arm of the chair next to me. "Now will you get out so I can get dressed?" I turn back around to face Winston.

Looking at him still throws me for a loop every time. He's grown into the spitting image of our father. Broad shoulders, lean build, dark blonde hair with the same long forehead and dimpled chin. I'm pretty sure if I looked up some old pictures of my dad I'd find a mirror image of Winston looking back at me.

It's scary how similar the two are. And the older Winston gets the more his mannerisms mirror Dad's. The way he drinks from a can, how his eyes squint when he laughs, even the way he walks reminds me of our father. It's uncanny.

"Just don't take an eternity, yeah?" He pushes off the bed and crosses toward the door.

"I'll be done in five," I holler after him as he exits the room.

"So what you really mean is thirty?" he throws back, humor in his voice.

"Such a jerk," I grumble under my breath, crossing the room to kick the door closed, making sure to lock it this time around.

I make quick work of changing. Trading my yoga pants and tunic for skinny jeans, a black tank, black strappy sandals, and the charcoal cardigan, I plan to bring with me in case it gets chilly. May in Ohio is nothing like Arizona this time of year. It's pretty warm, but there's still a chill in the air at night, and the last thing I want is to be stuck walking around downtown freezing my butt off.

I run a quick brush through my long strawberry blonde waves, quickly pinning it up in a clip, so it hangs loosely at the back of my head.

It takes me less than five minutes to dab on a little powder foundation and apply a light layer of mascara and lip gloss. But then I spend another five staring at my reflection in the mirror.

I'm not sure what I'm looking for, but I'm so lost in thought that when a knock sounds against the bedroom door, it startles me to the point that my heart leaps into my throat.

"You 'bout done in there? You said five, and I said thirty. Thought maybe we could make it a happy medium and settle on fifteen." Winston's voice is muffled by the door separating us.

"You're worse than Dad," I tell him, jerking the door open seconds later.

When I was a teenager, my father would stand at the door and knock every two minutes until I was ready. Of course, in his defense, we were always late to wherever we were going if he let me get ready in my own time.

"And yet here you are, cramping my style," Winston teases, arching a thick brow.

"Shut up." I push past him into the hallway, his laugh following me all the way into the living room that's open to both the kitchen and dining area.

"So what kind of tattoo are you getting, anyway?" I ask, grabbing my small, over the shoulder purse off the table before stuffing my cell phone and lip gloss tube inside.

"Miles has been working on something for me this week. Guess we'll find out when we get there."

"You don't even know what you're getting?" I give my brother a questioning look.

"You look at me like that now, but just you wait." He wags a finger at me. "I'm telling you, Miles is an artistic genius. You'll see what he does for me, and soon you'll be begging him to ink you."

"Yeah, not likely." I shake my head.

Don't get me wrong. I love tattoos. My friend, Angela, has a quote from her favorite movie tattooed on her forearm and I've always admired it. But as much as I like them, I can't picture myself having one.

Then again, I don't know if that's because I don't want one or because Alan made me feel a certain way about them. He drilled it into my head for years how unattractive tattoos are on women. So much so that maybe I started to believe it.

Just the thought has me reconsidering the tattoo idea just out of spite.

"You say that now." Winston smiles, grabbing his keys off the bar that acts as a separation piece between the living room and kitchen. "You ready?"

"Yep." I slide my purse over my shoulder and follow him from the apartment.

The minute we step out into the muggy evening air my chest feels heavy. I had forgotten how humid it is here. It gets hot in Arizona, like really hot, but it's a different kind of heat. Not the kind that makes you feel like you're suffocating.

We keep the windows down in Winston's truck on the short drive over the river into Ohio. That's something I loved about growing up in Covington. Its proximity to downtown Cincinnati. I've always loved the city, especially all the festivals and outdoor concerts they offer in the summer.

Winston pulls into a small outdoor lot not far from Great American Ball Park, and I immediately know where he's taking me.

"Tacos!" I practically bounce in my seat.

"You keep talking about them. Thought maybe if I brought you you'd shut the hell up," he teases, throwing me a wink before killing the engine to the truck and quickly climbing out.

It's nearly ten o'clock by the time we exit Condado. Even though I rarely drink, Winston talked me into ordering a margarita shortly after we got there. One turned into two, and before I knew it, we were talking and laughing like we hadn't done since we were kids.

It feels good to spend this time with my brother. To reconnect to someone, I used to be so close to. I feel like I gave up so much for Alan that when I left him, a part of me worried I'd never be able to rebuild the relationships I left behind. I should have known Winston would never hold my absence against me. Even though he gives me crap, deep down I know he'd do anything for me.

We stop at a little convenience store along the two block walk to the tattoo shop so Winston can pick up a case of beer. That's how he pays for his tattoos. Kind of a weird form of payment if you ask me, but hey, at least it saves him some money. Last time I checked beer is a lot cheaper than tattoos.

I find myself getting a little nervous as we cross the street toward Miles' shop. It's been years since I've seen him and well, like with seeing anyone you haven't seen in a very long time, there are always nerves involved.

The tattoo parlor isn't anything like I expected from the outside. Tucked between a coffee shop and a sandwich place on the main strip through town, it stands out like a sore thumb. But in a good way.

Other than a small glass door on the left, the entire front of the shop is one huge window which looks to be hand painted with some intricate artwork. Not only is it incredible to look at, but it also strategically limits the view inside to anyone walking by. There's a huge lit sign above the dark awning – Ink*ed* spelled out in bold green lettering.

I haven't even stepped through the door, yet already I can tell this is the type of trendy place people want to come to. It's no wonder Miles opted to buy this place when the original owner decided to sell. You can't get a better location. It's right in the heart of all the action, yet somehow seems to be the one place your eyes gravitate toward.

Winston grabs the door, a bell sounding the minute he jerks it open and ushers me inside. The front of the shop is a casual waiting area decorated with leather couches and framed pieces of art. It's super clean and modern without seeming too sterile.

I follow Winston through the waiting area, into the main shop. There's a long counter on one side with a cash register on top and various pieces of jewelry on display on the glass shelves below. The other side is lined with three separate tattooing areas.

A large, bald man with a thick ring through the center of his nose looks up from the forearm he's working on as we enter. He gives Winston a nod before his eyes briefly dart to me.

"He's in the back," he grumbles, returning his attention to the young guy he's working on without another word.

"Come on." Winston nods his head toward the back before setting off in that direction.

I follow him down a long hallway, past four private rooms, before we end up in what looks like a back storage area with a small office in the corner.

"Knock, knock." Winston stops in the doorway of the office and holds up the case of beer. "Hope it's cool we came early."

"Yeah, I'm just catching up on some paperwork." The familiarity of his voice is almost unsettling and yet oddly comforting at the same time. It's deeper than I remember but still holds that same raspy quality it had when he was a teenager.

I hear what sounds like chair legs scratching across the floor, but Winston is completely blocking my view into the office so I can't see what's happening. Moments later, Winston steps back, and Miles appears in the doorway.

At first, I think my eyes are playing tricks on me. I blink slowly, once, then twice, trying to process the sight before me.

Gone is the lean, preppy athlete I remember. The one who always wore gym shorts and t-shirts. Miles never went anywhere without a baseball cap permanently attached to his head. There's no reminisce of that boy left. Instead, standing in his place is the epitome of a man.

His brown hair is long on top, pushed to the side like he's run his hands through it several times throughout the day. He has a dark beard outlining his full lips, and internally I shudder. God, I can't even bring myself to look him in the eye.

Instead, I let my gaze travel down to his shoulders, and across his broad chest where the material of his shirt strains against the muscles hidden beneath. Then to his thick arms peppered in various colors of ink, before finally coming back up to his face.

I know it's only been seconds since he appeared in front of me, but when my eyes finally make it to his, I feel like I've been ogling over him for hours.

During that time I could have sworn I was looking at a complete stranger. But the instant his hazel eyes lock with mine the confirmation is undeniable. He always had the most incredible colored eyes; green swirled with blue, a light yellow ring around the outside. The kind of eyes a person doesn't forget easily.

"Miles?" His name comes out a question, and my attempt at casually disguising my shock comes crashing down in epic failure.

I mean how could anyone blame me though? Miles Hollins was good looking as a teenager, but Miles Hollins, the man? There are no words. He's beautiful, in the most rugged way possible. And while beautiful feels like such a weird word to use to describe a *man* like Miles, it seems to be the only word that fits.

"Harlow." Miles nods in my direction, a smile playing at the corner of his mouth. If I didn't know any better, I'd say he knows exactly where my mind has gone and that thought alone snaps me back into reality.

So he's still as cocky as ever, I think to myself. Noted.

"Hope you don't mind that I'm crashing. Winston refused to let me stay home."

"Sounds like Winston." He chuckles, the sound vibrating me straight to my core.

What the hell?

Shifting from one foot to the other, I cross my arms nervously in front of myself.

"What's that supposed to mean?" my brother interjects; seeming completely oblivious to the physical reaction my body seems to be having toward his best friend.

"Nothing." Miles grins, clasping my brother on the shoulder as he exits the office. "Come on, since the shop closes soon we're gonna be out front." His deep, musky scent hits me like a thousand pound car as he passes and I swear the impact makes me feel unsteady on my own two feet.

Stupid margaritas. I knew better than to let Winston talk me into drinking. There's a reason I don't do it often. Alan hated that he couldn't control me when I drank. I seem to have a hard time controlling myself.

And even though the effects of the margarita feel like a distant memory, I'm still convinced it's what's responsible for my reaction to Miles. Well, that and the fact that even though I hated him when we were kids, he grew into quite possibly the sexiest man I have ever seen up close. Any woman in my position would have reacted the same, if not worse.

So, after a couple of deep breaths, I finally follow Miles and Winston who have already disappeared into the main part of the shop by the time I reach the mouth of the hallway.

"Well, this is going to be fun," I mutter under my breath before forcing myself forward.

Chapter Five

Miles

"I still can't believe this piece, man. Some of your best work yet." Winston studies the tattoo I sketched out for him a couple of days ago while I lay the outline on his right shoulder.

It's a pretty basic design; angel wings twined together with the name 'Joni.'

"I thought you'd like it." I dab more ink onto the needle before pressing it to his skin.

"Sometimes it's like you know what I want even before I do."

"Made sense. Figured it was only a matter of time before you'd want something to represent your mom," I say, briefly locking eyes with Harlow.

She's sitting in the chair to my left, positioned, so she's next to her brother, but can still watch me work.

A small glimpse of sadness washes over her face but it's gone almost as quick as it came.

Winston and Harlow's mom died in a car accident when they were kids. Even though they were young, especially Harlow, I know they felt her loss immensely. It has always been something that has tied them together beyond just being siblings. A loss like that changes people in a big way.

"It's amazing," she agrees with her brother, speaking for the first time in a while.

"Thank you." I wipe the excess ink off of Winston's shoulder with a towel, my eyes lingering on Harlow's face as I do.

She was always pretty as a teenager, but now she's a fucking lot more than pretty. My gaze has fallen to her a hell of lot more than I have intended over the last several minutes. Almost like I can't help myself.

Her strawberry blonde hair is a little darker than it used to be. With it pinned back, away from her face it puts her big, green eyes on full display. And then there are the adorable freckles that pepper her nose and cheeks. The same ones that she used to cake makeup over when she was younger but now on full display.

"It's perfect, dude. Seriously. Perfect." Winston breaks into my thoughts causing me to refocus on his shoulder quickly. "I've been trying to talk Harlow into getting one, but she doesn't seem too keen on the idea."

"Oh yeah." I chuckle, dabbing the needle in ink continuing with the outline of the left wing. "Got something against tattoos, do ya?" I briefly flip my gaze to Harlow's.

"No." I see her shake her head in my peripheral vision, but I keep my eyes on Winston's shoulder. "I just don't want one."

"That's fair. Tattoos aren't for everyone."

"Don't get me wrong. I think tattoos are amazing. Especially this one. But I don't know that it would look good on me."

"I think you could pull one off," I smirk, throwing her a wink before refilling my ink and refocusing. I can tell by the shocked reaction she tries to hide that she thinks I'm flirting with her, and maybe I am, but not because I'm into her. It's how I am with most of the women that come in here. It's almost a habit.

"All different types of people have tattoos," I quickly continue. "It's not like you have to fit into a certain mold to get a little ink done. I've tatted people you never in a million years would guess to have tattoos. Of course typically they're placed where they aren't visible to just anyone, but still, that's not the point."

"She doesn't want one now, but if she ever gets one, she'll be one of those people that get the itch and two years later don't have a visible patch of skin left," Winston jokes, taking a moment to readjust as I switch out colors and prepare to shade the wings.

"Yeah, that would never happen," Harlow quickly disagrees.

"Maybe two or three. I'd stop you after that," I tell her.

"You'd have to get me to agree to one first," she quips, the left side of her mouth twitching as she fights a smile.

If I didn't know any better, I'd say that not only is Harlow Cabell, or whatever the hell her name is now, buying into the act I'm selling, but she's enjoying the attention.

A slight twinge of guilt twists in my stomach, and I make a mental note to dial it back a bit. She isn't just any other woman, and I can't treat her as such. She's my best friend's little sister. My best friend's incredibly beautiful, recently separated from her husband, little sister.

I've dealt with enough women going through a break-up or divorce to know how unpredictable they can be. The last thing I want is to give her the wrong impression or lead her on in some way.

Hell, for all I know she could only be playing nice for her brother's sake. But I don't think that's it. We may not have gotten along in the past, but it was clear to me from the instant my eyes landed on her that she's not the same girl I knew all those years ago. Not that I expected she would be. Almost eleven years is a long ass time. I can't even begin to comprehend how much I've changed in that time.

I honestly never understood what her problem was with me. It was like one minute we were all friends and the next she hated my guts. I don't know if it's because we got older and started leaving her out or if she truly came to dislike me. Whatever it was, I don't sense anything like that coming from her now. Then again, this all very well could be an act.

Yeah, maybe she's just as good of an actor as I am. Not that I'm purposely acting where she's concerned. More like my entire fucking life is one big act. One I've gotten so good at putting on, some days I can't tell if I'm still acting or if this is who I am now.

"We'll get you there." Winston's response pulls me back to the subject at hand. "You should at least get something small," he continues. "Like a heart on your ankle or some shit like that. That way if you hate it, it's small enough that no one can see it."

"If I'm going to go through the pain of having a tattoo done, I sure as hell am *not* going to get a heart on my ankle." She shakes her head at her brother, that familiar Harlow sass making its first appearance of the night.

I was starting to think she'd lost it – that fiery part of who she used to be. Now, I'm wondering if it isn't just buried under whatever hell she's been through over the last decade.

"Is there something specific that you don't like about tattoos?" I ask, just out of curiosity.

"Alan," she starts, stumbling over her words for a moment. "My ex-husband. He hated tattoos. Considering he was the one who had to look at my body, I made the choice that they aren't for me."

"They aren't for you, or they aren't for him?" I challenge, never having pictured her as the type of girl that would let any man tell her what she can and can't do.

"For him I guess," she answers like she's embarrassed by this fact.

"Well fuck that." Winston jumps despite the needle pressed to his skin.

"Dude. Sit the fuck still," I warn, pulling the tattoo gun back.

"Sorry, man." He shifts, turning toward his sister. "What better way to show that mother fucker that he can't control you anymore?"

"You might be right." She shrugs. "But I'm still not convinced I want one regardless."

"Tell you what," I cut in. "You think about it, and if at any point you decide you want to get one, you come see me. I'll hook you up."

"Thank you. I appreciate that." She gives me a genuine smile, and it highlights just how fucking pretty she is.

"Now sit the fuck back." I turn my attention to Winston. "I don't know about you, but I'd like to be out of here before four a.m."

"Sorry, man." He laughs, readjusting so I can resume working on his piece.

We spend the next two hours talking about random shit. From things as simple as the weather to heavier topics like Winston's on again, off again, girlfriend that can't seem to commit.

I keep telling him that if she's still this back and forth after nearly two years, he needs to cut her loose, but for some reason, he can't seem to let her go. It seems ridiculous to me, but then again, I can't say I've ever cared for someone the way he cares about Stella, so what the hell do I know.

Harlow eventually moved to the tattoo chair at the next station so she could sit more comfortably. It was less than thirty minutes later that I looked over and she was out, curled into a ball with a mess of loose hair falling around her face as she slept. After that, I couldn't help but glance back at her every once in a while.

I finished Winston's tattoo just after three, slathering his new ink in Vaseline before slapping a piece of plastic wrap over the top of it for protection.

"You are all set, my friend," I tell him, standing to stretch out my back.

"I seriously can't thank you enough for this, man. It's incredible." Winston turns to look over his shoulder in the mirror on the wall.

"Glad you like it," I say, already starting to disassemble my station so I can head home for the night. Not that I'll get any real sleep once there, but for right now all I can think about is crawling into my bed and shutting my eyes for a few minutes. "Would you mind sticking that in the fridge in the back?" I ask, gesturing to the still nearly full case of beer he brought with him.

I won't have more than a couple when I'm working, and since Winston is driving, he only had one earlier in the night. I'll keep them here that way the guys or Delia can snag one if they feel like having a beer after their shift.

"Only if you handle that." Winston hitches his thumb toward his sister. "She's mean as shit when you wake her up." He chuckles, snagging the case of beer off the floor. "Or at least she used to be."

"All the more reason for you to do it," I holler after him, hearing him laugh in the distance.

"Sorry, too late," he calls from the back.

"Asshole," I grumble under my breath, shoving my tattoo gun onto the shelf before making my way toward Harlow.

I hear her soft intakes of air as she breathes, her body barely moving under the action. She looks so peaceful, and an instant wave of longing washes over me. Not for her specifically, but for the kind of peace, normal people find in sleep. Something I haven't known for years.

I imagine what it would be like to crawl into the chair behind her and pull her toward me. Feel her warmth against my skin and the steady thump of her heart against my chest. I wonder if it would rub off on me. I wish I could piggy back onto her dreams and for once be able to shut my mind off enough to find a moment of silence.

"Harlow." I reach out and run my hand gently down her forearm, trying not to startle her.

Her eyes immediately shoot open and a wave of confusion washes over her face.

"Winston's ready to go," I tell her, hoping that will remind her where she is.

"I fell asleep?" Her face calms and she sits up, stretching her arms over her head.

"About two hours ago," I confirm, taking a full step back.

"Sorry. I haven't been sleeping well recently," she says, sliding her legs over the side of the chair before pushing into a stand.

"No problem." I shrug, resisting the urge to tell her that I understand the feeling.

"Okay, beer is in the fridge, and I dropped some cash on your desk." Winston reappears from the hallway.

"Cash?" I question. "I thought beer was my payment."

"Yeah, like I'm not gonna give you one hell of a tip." He snorts.

"Man, how many times have I told you not to do that?" I scold.

"And yet I still do it every time." He smirks, turning his attention to his sister.

"You ready, sleepy head?"

"Yep," Harlow answers on a yawn.

"Thanks again for this." Winston gestures to his shoulder. "I really can't even begin to explain what it means that you thought of Mom."

"Don't even mention it. It's the least I can do."

"If you two are done bro-ing out, can we go?" Harlow cuts in, humor in her voice.

"Bro-ing out?" Winston laughs.

"Bro-ing out," she confirms, crinkling her nose at him.

"Yes, we're done." He chuckles, throwing a nod my way. "We'll talk soon," he says, leading his sister toward the front door.

"Sounds good. You guys be safe on your way home," I call after them, grabbing the sanitizer so I can clean my station.

"Hey, Miles." I look up to see Harlow in the doorway that separates the work area from the lobby. "It was really nice to see you again." She smiles, and the weirdest fucking sensation settles in my stomach. "I just might take you up on the tattoo," she adds.

"It was good to see you too, Harlow," I say, not sure how else to respond. "And I hope you do."

With that soft smile still on her lips, she gives me one last look and turns to disappear into the lobby, the front doorbell ringing seconds later.

I shake off the odd feeling still prominent in the air and refocus, almost thankful that I won't be able to sleep tonight. Because if I could sleep, if I could dream,

I have no doubt that Harlow Cabell would be the very thing I would see.

Chapter Six

Harlow

"What do you mean he refused to sign the papers?" I pace back and forth in my brother's living room, with my cell phone pressed to my ear. "Can he even do that?"

"Technically yes, but I can't see it lasting for long. He's just trying to test you," my lawyer, Regina, reassures me.

"Test me?" I stop mid-stride and look up, catching sight of a sleek black motorcycle circling into the parking lot through the open double windows of my brother's apartment.

"I've seen it a million times. He's trying to wait you out. He's hoping you'll change your mind."

"That will not happen," I grind out.

"We just need to be patient on this. We've got one hell of a case if he wants to try his luck. I can't see him pushing this to the point where it goes to court.

He'll settle eventually, and when he does, you can put this whole mess behind you."

"Eventually isn't now. I want this over with."

"I know you do. But sometimes things don't always go as smoothly as we'd like. Trust that I know what I'm doing. I'll get this closed for you as quickly and quietly as possible."

"I know." I blow out a breath, running a hand through my messy ponytail.

I've spent the entire morning scrubbing Winston's apartment from top to bottom and was heading toward the shower when Regina called with the update on my divorce. My brother isn't as bad as I'm sure some bachelors are, but he certainly isn't the cleanest person either. I swear I scrubbed two inches of toothpaste out of the bottom of his bathroom sink.

"I have a phone call scheduled with his attorney for Friday. Hopefully, by then Mr. Montel will have been able to talk some sense into his client."

"And what happens if he still doesn't sign?" I ask, my eyes still locked on the motorcycle as it pulls into a vacant spot before the driver quickly climbs off.

"Then it goes to court, and we air all his dirty laundry. Something tells me he won't let it get that far."

"I think you're right there," I agree, knowing Alan and how much importance he places in what others think of him. The last thing he'll want is his wife in a courtroom telling anyone and everyone that will listen about all his infidelities.

"Just work on getting yourself settled, and I'll take care of Alan Nagle."

"Thanks so much, Regina," I say, stepping closer to the window to get a better look at the motorcyclist right as he slides off his helmet and rests it on the seat of the bike.

"No problem. I'll touch base soon."

"Okay," I murmur, having stopped listening the moment I realized the man beneath the helmet is none other than Miles Hollins.

I haven't seen him since that night at the tattoo shop three weeks ago and even though I have no idea why he's been on my mind a lot more than I'd like to admit.

Regina says something else seconds before the call disconnects, yet several moments later I'm still standing with the phone pressed to my ear, watching Miles climb the outdoor stairwell toward the apartment.

The closer he gets, the harder my heart pounds in my chest and for the life of me, I can't understand my body's reaction.

I lose sight of him seconds before a hard knock sounds against the door.

Looking down, I'm painfully aware that I'm still dressed in my ratty plaid pajama shorts and gray tank. My hair is tied up from cleaning, and I don't have an ounce of makeup on.

Shit.

I freeze in the middle of the living room, not sure if I should answer the door and face Miles looking the way I do or if I should pretend that no one is home. I mean, it wouldn't be completely untrue. Winston stayed the night at Stella's and since I'm sure that's who he's here to see, not answering would be acceptable, right?

The second knock sounds and even though I've already talked myself into not answering, for some reason I cross the room toward the front door just the same.

Seconds later, I'm standing face to face with Miles, who in the late morning sunlight looks even more attractive than he did three weeks ago.

"Hey," I get out breathlessly, wedging my body in the open door frame.

"Hey." Miles slides his dark sunglasses off his face and gives me a quick once over, making me feel squeamish under his gaze. "Winston here?"

"No, he's at Stella's." I tuck a stray strand of hair that's fallen loose from my ponytail behind my ear, wishing I had at least looked in the mirror before making the impulsive decision to answer the door.

"I knew it wouldn't last long." He smiles to himself.

"What wouldn't?" I question, not hiding my confusion.

"The latest breakup."

"Breakup? Haven't they been together for a couple of years?"

"Yes, but they break up about once a month. It usually only lasts a day or two. This time I think they set a record though. Four whole days."

"They'd been broken up for four days?" I ask, more to myself than to Miles. I'm just trying to figure out how I missed that or why Winston never said anything.

"In case you're wondering why he didn't tell you, it happens so often he's gotten past the point of sharing the information. As I said, it never lasts."

"Then how is it *you* know they broke up?" I ask, crossing my arms in front of my chest, feeling next to naked in my thin tank top. Especially when his gaze dips downward, for a long moment.

"Because I'm the one he drags out for a drink after every one of their big blow-ups. He spends about two hours complaining about how impossible his girlfriend is, gets it out of his system, and then waits for her to call. They're beyond predictable at this point."

"Interesting." I clear my throat. "Well, as I said, he's not here. I can let him know you stopped by when he gets back."

"No need. I was just heading over to your dad's shop for a bit. Wanted to see if Winston wanted to come with."

"You're going to see my dad?"

"Yeah. I try to stop out at least one Saturday a month. Sometimes we just bullshit, sometimes he puts me to work." He shrugs, a smile playing on the corner of his mouth.

"I didn't know that," I admit, having realized over the last few weeks that there's a lot I don't know about where my family is concerned. "I was actually thinking about stopping by there later today."

"Oh yeah?" He rocks back on his heels, shoving his hands deep in the pockets of his dark jeans. "You wanna ride over with me?"

"Huh?" I stutter, caught off guard by the offer.

"To your dad's," he clarifies, clearly finding humor in my reaction. "If you're heading out that way, you can ride over with me if you want."

"Oh well, I can't right now."

"Why not? Too busy cleaning up after Winston's slob ass."

"How did you know I was cleaning?" I ask.

"Because I could smell the bleach and Lysol before I even knocked on the door."

"Oh." I laugh lightly. "Well, he certainly isn't the cleanest of people to live with."

"I'd guess not." He chuckles. "Are you almost done? I could wait. I really don't have anything going on this morning."

"You don't have to do that. I have to shower and get ready first."

"So go do it then." He steps forward causing me to instinctively step back, giving him room to enter the apartment.

His hard chest brushes past me as he steps inside and his incredible scent suddenly engulfs me. It takes me a good ten seconds to shake off the fog that settles over me.

"Please, come in," I grumble semi-playfully, closing the door behind him.

With Miles here, the apartment feels half the size, and I shrink under the incredible set of hazel eyes I find locked on my face when I turn back toward him.

"Place looks good." He smiles, looking around the room.

"Well, it better. I've been going at it for nearly two hours." I huff, blowing a strand of hair out of my face.

"It shows." His smile widens as his gaze comes back to me. "You gonna go get ready now or…" He lets the question hang.

"Um, yeah, okay. I guess," I stutter, shuffling both my feet without actually moving an inch forward. "You gonna just wait out here?"

"Pretty sure I know how to make myself at home." He chuckles, snagging the television remote off the coffee table before flopping down on the couch.

"Right. Okay. I won't be too long." I take off toward my room, not sure what the hell I just agreed to or if I actually agreed at all.

When I reenter the living room about a half an hour later, Miles is in the exact spot I left him in. He's flipping through channels but immediately stops when he senses my presence.

Powering off the television, he drops the remote back onto the table before looking in my direction.

"Feel better?" he asks, his eyes doing one long sweep down my body.

Even though I'm fully clothed in jean shorts and a dark blue shirt, that one motion makes me feel like I've been stripped bare in front of him.

"Much." I clear my throat and shuffle toward the kitchen.

Because I didn't want to keep Miles waiting too long, I decided to let my hair air dry, so I'd have time to apply a little bit of makeup to feel half human.

Since I moved back here almost a month ago, I swear I've spent more time in pajamas moping around than anything else. I finally decided that next week it's time to put myself back out there. I can only hide out in my brother's apartment for so long.

I need my own place. I need my own life. And to get that, I need a job. I may not have much work experience, but I still have a four-year degree. That has to get me somewhere. Or at least, I hope it will.

"You didn't have to wait for me, you know. I wasn't planning to go over until later anyway."

"I know. Maybe I just wanted a chance to spend a little time with you." His statement causes heat to flush my cheeks, but I hide it by ducking into the refrigerator to grab a bottle of water.

"And why on earth would you want to do that?" I regain my composure before turning to face him.

Lord help me, I don't know what it is about him that's caused me to become so flustered. Ten years ago I couldn't stand the sight of him. Fast forward to today, and the sight of him makes my knees go weak. Could he be any more attractive?

"Because your brother is my best friend and your family is like my family. Makes sense that we at least try to be friendly."

"You say that like it's such a chore." I pin my gaze on him as he stops on the opposite side of the island from me.

"Ten years ago it was a chore. If I remember correctly, I couldn't walk into a room without you staring evil daggers at me."

"I never did that," I object.

"You did," he cuts me off with a light chuckle. " We didn't much care for each other in the past. But I'm not the same person I was back then, and I'm willing to bet you aren't either. Who knows, maybe you'll actually like me if you take the time to get to know me."

"Not likely," I deadpan before a quick smile flashes across my face. "But I'll let you try to convince me otherwise. If nothing else it will be fun to watch."

"Alright, smartass, you ready?" Miles grins, pushing away from the kitchen island as I come around it, his gaze dipping to my feet. "Nope," he answers the question for himself. "You need to go change your shoes."

"What's wrong with my shoes?" I look down at my cute strappy sandals.

"I'm not putting you on my bike with those on. My luck you'd lose a toe, and then I'd really be on your shit list."

"We're taking your bike?" I blurt, for some reason not even thinking about the transportation part of this little field trip of ours.

"Yep. Now go put some real fucking shoes on, would ya?"

"I'm not getting on your bike," I interject, fear settling deep in the pit of my stomach.

"Why the hell not?" He cocks a brow. The humor is clear in his expression..

"Because I don't want to die," I say dramatically.

"Wow. Okay." He shakes his head and laughs. "For one, you aren't going to die. And for two, how do you know you won't enjoy it once you get on? Have you ever ridden before?"

"No," I stamp out like it's the most absurd thing I've ever heard.

"Then you don't know what you're missing. Now go. Change your shoes. I'd like to get there while there's still some daylight left," he jokes, considering it's only just after eleven in the morning.

"I'm not getting on your bike," I continue.

"What are you so afraid of?"

"I already told you. Dying," I half laugh. "I'll call an Uber and meet you over there."

"You're not calling a fucking Uber." He takes a commanding step toward me. "I don't know what happened to you in Arizona, but the Harlow I used to know wasn't afraid of anything."

I open my mouth to argue. To tell him he didn't know me well enough to know that about me, but I snap it back shut when I realize he's right. Ten years ago I would have jumped on that bike without a second thought.

In this realization, I give him the meanest look I can muster before spinning on my heel and stomping to my room to change my shoes.

Chapter Seven

Miles

I may have been able to convince her to get on the back of my motorcycle, but I didn't squash the fear she had about it. It's clear by the way she clings to my body like I'm the only thing keeping her from tumbling to her death. Which in a way I guess I am.

I can't help but smile every time her arms get a little tighter around my middle. Hell, I'd even go as far as to say I'm rather enjoying having her pressed against me, the rumble of the bike beneath us, the wind whipping around us.

It's very rare that I ride without a helmet, but considering I only have one, and there was no way I was putting her on the back of my bike without one, I had no choice but to go without. Luckily the ride over to her dad's auto shop is a short one. Though as we pull in, I find myself wishing it were a hell of a lot longer.

Pulling into one of the front spots that face the road, I quickly kill the bike, turning slightly to help Harlow slide off the back.

"Well?" I ask, kicking down the kickstand before climbing off.

"That was incredible." She smiles at me through the open visor of the helmet, and I swear it feels like someone punched me square in the gut.

"I knew you'd like it," I tell her, trying to shake off whatever the fuck is going on with me. "Come here." I step closer, unclasping the strap under her chin before gently sliding the helmet off her head.

Her damp hair is matted to her forehead and without really thinking, I take my hand and push it away, my fingers lingering at her hairline for a moment too long.

Pulling my hand away, I quickly straighten my shoulders and take a full step back. Setting the helmet on the seat of my motorcycle, I turn and head toward the two open garage doors that face out toward the street. The familiar sound of power tools and old country music blaring on the radio accosts me before I even make it inside.

There are two cars in the shop this morning. Sean and Dawson have an old Jeep up on the lift, removing the tires while Hatchet is under the hood of an old Chevy. None of them pay any attention to us as we step inside.

Harlow's behind me, but I make it a point not to turn around and look at her. It's fucking impossible to explain, but something about the way she looks at me makes me feel a certain way, and it's unsettling as hell. I felt it that night in the tattoo shop and again the instant she opened the door to her brother's apartment this morning.

And while I meant what I said to her earlier about getting to know her again, another part of me feels like I need to stay as far away from her as possible. Unfortunately, I'm not sure I could do that even if I wanted to.

The whole way over to Winston's I kept hoping she would be home. I've been looking for an excuse to go there for three weeks, yet have somehow managed to convince myself not to.

"There he is," Harold's booming voice hits my ears seconds before he pops out of his office and comes bounding down the metal staircase toward me.

"Hey, Harold." I smile, taking the hand he extends to me the instant he reaches me.

"I was wondering if you were going to make it over this weekend," he says, giving my hand a firm shake before releasing it.

"Hey, Daddy." Harlow steps up next to me.

"Well hell. Where did you come from?" He smiles, clearly not realizing she was behind me.

"I stopped by to see if Winston was heading over and found this one scrubbing his apartment," I tease, hitching my thumb in her direction. "Figured I'd drag her along."

"Well, I'm glad you did." Harold pulls his daughter into a quick, one-armed hug. "How are you, peanut?" he asks, releasing her.

"I'm good."

"Well, I'm glad you two are here. Jackie was just on her way over to take me to lunch. She'll be thrilled to have two to more join us."

"I've only got a couple of hours before I'll need to head back to the shop," I interject.

"No problem. We'll be done with plenty of time." He turns, heading back up the stairs. "Let me grab my things, and I'll meet you outside."

"So Harlow, Dad says you're going to start job hunting this coming week? Any ideas on what you're looking for?" Harold's wife, Jackie, shuffles her salad on the plate in front of her, her gaze locked on her stepdaughter.

"I'm not sure yet. I want something in finance. I know there are a lot of opportunities in the city, but I'm not sure how qualified I am."

"You went to school for accounting, right?" I interject, popping a fry into my mouth.

"Yes." Harlow nods, taking a small sip of her tea before setting the glass back down on the table.

"Why would you not be qualified?" I ask, trying to follow along.

"Alan preferred that I stayed home and let him earn the money," she says, looking down at her plate as if she's ashamed of this fact.

"I see." I nod, thinking this Alan character sounds more and more like a tool every time I hear something new about him.

"So while I do have a degree in finance, I've never actually worked in the field outside of the brief internship I did during my senior year of college," she continues. "Most companies will probably shy away from someone who's been out of the profession for over six years."

"I told you that you can always come work with me at the shop," Harold chimes in.

"I appreciate that, Dad. But there's no way you'd be able to give me the pay I need to make a decent living. Not unless you plan to fire Jackie." She grins across the table at her stepmom.

"You could work alongside Jackie. I'm sure she'd be glad for the help." He nudges his slender wife in the ribs.

"I would love that," Jackie agrees, nodding enthusiastically.

"I love you both for the offer, but no. I need to make money. Preferably without bankrupting your business because you're trying to take care of me. I'd like to not be living with my brother for the next year either if I can help it."

"I'm sure we could make something work," he insists.

"I'm sure you would, Dad, but it's time for me to make it on my own. Besides, you're retiring in a couple of years and you've already got Winston set up to takeover. There's no need to add more stress onto an already stressful situation. What you're doing is working. I don't want to come in and screw it all up. I'm a big girl. I'll figure something out."

"Come work for me," I blurt, the entire table going silent as I try to figure out where the fuck that came from.

"What?" Harlow's wide, green eyes land on me, a mixture of confusion and shock sweeping across her face.

"You heard me." I run with the offer, knowing now that I've said; it I can't very well take it back. Especially not with Harold and Jackie bearing witness to it. "I've been looking for someone to run my books for quite a while now," I tell her. Though I never in a million years expected to offer the job to Harlow of all people. Hell, up until about sixty seconds ago the thought had never even crossed my mind.

"You're serious?" Harlow continues to gawk at me from across the table.

"Delia's been helping me out for a while, but since the shop has really taken off, it's become harder for us to keep up with it. We need someone in there full time taking care of the business side of things. Neither of us is that great with the finance and bookkeeping aspect of the business, so you'll probably have your work cut out for you in the beginning. But yeah, why not? You need a job. I have a position open. It's full time. You could make your own hours, and we'll negotiate a fair salary. If nothing else you can use it as a stepping stone to put a little experience under your belt."

"I don't know what to say." Harlow looks around the table before her gaze lands back on me.

"Say yes," Harold chimes in, a wide smile firmly in place.

"It sounds like a perfect fit," Jackie agrees, jumping on the train as well.

"You're sure about this?" Harlow mouths to me, her voice never actually breaking the surface.

I want to say no. I'm not sure about anything I'm saying at this point, but instead, I smile and nod like I know exactly what I'm doing.

"Wow. Um, okay then." Harlow lets out a heavy sigh, her expression teetering between panic and relief.

"Perfect. You can start tonight," I tell her, watching her eyes once again go wide.

"Tonight?" she sputters.

"Got something better to do?" I challenge, pressing my back into the chair as I look across the table at her.

"Well, no."

"Then it's settled. You can come to the shop tonight. Observe the business and see how everything works. I can run over some of the book stuff with you between clients. If by the end of the night you still want the job then it's yours."

"Okay." She lets out another shaky breath, finally letting a smile stretch across her lips.

"Okay." I smile back, wondering what in the hell I just got myself into.

"Why did you do that?" Harlow waits until we're at my bike and out of the earshot of her parents before confronting me the way I'm sure she's wanted to since I brought up her coming to work for me nearly an hour ago.

"Do what?" I play stupid, snagging the helmet off the bike seat before turning toward her.

"Offer to let me come work for you."

"Because you need a job. I thought we already established this." I do my best to keep my voice even.

"But me? Really, Miles. Of all people, you think it's a good idea for *us* to work together?" She gestures between the two of us. "Last time I checked, you didn't like me, and honestly, I didn't like you either."

"Last time I checked that was a long time ago," I inform her, not able to hide the humor from my voice.

"I'm just saying, the last thing I want to do is cause issues."

I stare at her for a long moment, fighting the urge to reach out and brush her messy waves over her shoulder.

"Harlow, relax," I say, dropping the helmet onto her head. "You'll come work for me. If it works out then great; if it doesn't then it doesn't. I think we're old enough that we can be professional adults about it," I tell her, snapping the strap below her chin. "Besides, I think you're growing on me." I wink playfully.

I can tell by her expression that she's not sure how to respond, but after a few moments she asks, "You're not just doing this because I'm Winston's sister, are you?"

Her cheeks blush – the action clear even with the clunky helmet covering most of her face. I don't think I've ever been quite so attracted to someone as am I to her in this very moment.

It's the strangest feeling and yet oddly undeniable. Here I am, after knowing Harlow most of my life, wondering how it is I missed it for so long.

How did I not notice the way her green eyes seem to sparkle when the sun hits them just right? Or how the smallest dimple pops on her left cheek when she smiles? Or just how damn beautiful she is, especially when she is pink-cheeked and flustered?

I shake off the thought once again, frustrated with where my thoughts seem to continue to go.

"That's exactly why I'm doing it," I finally answer, chuckling lightly when her gaze darkens. "It's up to you to earn the right to keep the job," I snap down the helmet visor and turn, quickly climbing on the bike. "Now come on, we've got work to do."

"You're not going to take me home first?" she asks, settling on the bike behind me.

"Not unless you need me to."

"No, I guess not." She wraps her arms around my middle and fuck me if it doesn't feel even better than it did earlier today.

Letting out a deep exhale, I fire the bike to life, wishing like hell I could press reset on today. Lord knows I would do so many things differently. Or at least that's what I think until Harlow tightens her grip, her fingers flexing around my ab muscles as I veer onto the freeway toward downtown.

Chapter Eight

Harlow

"I don't understand how you've gotten by this long without a proper bookkeeper," I look up from the stack of papers littering the desk in front of me as Miles enters the office.

"We've managed," he shrugs, collapsing into one of the chairs that sits opposite the desk.

"No, you haven't," I shake my head. "You've got expenses from 2017 that haven't even been filed. You're lucky you haven't been audited. Trying to sort through this mess is going to be a nightmare."

"So you don't want the job then?" The corner of his mouth quirks up in a half smile.

"Well, no, of course, I do. I'm just saying…"

"Look, I get that it's a bit disorganized. Or rather organized chaos, as I like to call it, but I have every confidence that you'll get me in tip top shape in no time."

"I wouldn't say no time," I disagree, gesturing to the top of the desk that's piled with documents I've spent the last several hours trying to get into some semblance of order.

"Call it job security." He smirks, and my stomach instantly knots.

To say I've been on pins and needles all day would be one complete understatement. I've never felt so off-kilter in all my life. On one hand, I'm thrilled to have an actual job. On the other, I'm terrified to work with Miles, and I'm not sure I even fully understand why that is.

Since I moved home, he's been nothing if not nice to me. I've only been around him twice, but in that time, he's never made me feel unwelcome or like he didn't want me around. Hell, he even offered me a job. A job I'm clearly under qualified for and yet determined to prove I can handle just the same.

"Delia just took off for the night and Tubbs is almost finished with the tattoo he's working on. How about we call it a night and I drive you home?" Miles leans forward in the chair, resting his elbows on his knees.

"What time is it?" I glance at the clock above the door, instantly doing a double take when I see it's already after eleven. "Holy crap, is it really that late?"

"You've been hard at it." He nods. "I came back earlier, and you were so focused on what you were doing you didn't even notice me. I decided to leave you be. Got roped into doing a quick touch up; otherwise I would have offered to take you home a couple of hours ago."

"Yeah, I was in the zone there for a while. It feels good," I admit. "Having something to focus on other than my failed marriage and the fact that I have nothing going for me."

I wish I could take the statement back the second it leaves my lips. That may be exactly how I feel, but it certainly isn't something I should be sharing with Miles – my new boss.

"Don't say shit like that. You've got plenty going for you."

"Yeah. Okay." I lean back in the chair as I cross my arms in front of myself.

"God, you're so much like your brother sometimes." He grins, scratching the side of his beard.

"Well you love my brother, so I guess that's a good thing," I tease, butterflies erupting in my stomach when a full-blown smile stretches across his handsome face.

"Anyway, you about ready to head out?" Miles completely bypasses my statement as he stands, stretching his arms over his head causing his shirt to ride up.

My gaze locks onto the small sliver of naturally tan skin before eyeing a tattoo that looks to extend from his side to about the middle of his stomach, some of it still hidden by his shirt while the rest dips below the waistband of his jeans. I'm curious about what the tattoo is and just how far down it goes.

Heat creeps up my neck and spreads across my cheeks, and I quickly look down, pretending like I'm looking for something on the desk so that I don't have to meet his gaze.

"Yeah, give me just a minute," I finally answer his question, reshuffling a couple of the files in front of me.

"I'll meet you out front. Whenever you're ready." He drops his arms before turning toward the door.

"Okay, thanks." I barely look up as Miles exits the office.

"What the hell, Harlow?" I accost myself seconds after Miles disappears around the corner.

It's bad enough that I've spent most of the day fantasizing about my brother's best friend, but to ogle him in plain sight is taking it a bit far.

Don't get me wrong. I have no intentions of pursuing Miles Hollins. I'm not interested in any man at this point in my life, especially not one like him. But something is thrilling about the thought of it.

He's the exact opposite of Alan. Rough and rugged. The type of man you can look at once and know he's hiding a world of secrets behind his eyes.

Alan was always so proper. Khakis and polo shirts. Expensive cologne. Perfectly styled hair. I can't even remember a time in our entire relationship that he sported so much as a five o'clock shadow. He was so put together all the time that it had begun to bother me over time. At first, I loved that about him. Loved how he took care of himself and how much pride he took in his appearance. But then I started to realize that it was all a façade. A pretty picture to cover the snake within. God, what a joke.

But Miles…Miles is all man. Unapologetic. Sexy as sin without even trying. And while he seems comfortable and confident, I'd venture to say there's a lot more to Miles than he lets people see. There's something there. Something dark. Something I can't quite put my finger on. But instead of making me want to stay away, it's almost like it's drawing me in. I can't help but wonder if I peeled back the layers what I might find.

Letting out a slow breath, I try to refocus my thoughts on work. I quickly sort a few additional files off to one side because I'll need to work on them first. Since the shop is closed on Sunday I won't get to any of this until Monday.

I still can't wrap my head around how quickly all of this happened. This is the furthest from how I anticipated this day to go. I figured I'd clean the apartment, maybe visit Dad, then veg out on the couch for the rest of the day feeling sorry for myself and worrying the whole time about whether or not I'd be able to land a decent job anytime soon.

Now here I am, a full-time employee at Ink*ed*. Who would have thought after all these years that I'd end up working for Miles Hollins. Seems crazy to even think about.

And crazy is exactly how I felt when I accepted his offer to come work for him. But now I'm really glad I did. Not only does it give me the ability to start to rebuild a little, but it also gives me purpose. Something to focus on. Not to mention the pay is way more than I was anticipating.

I'm not sure if Miles was planning to pay whoever he hired this salary, but I certainly was not expecting what he offered. Maybe after I showed my worth a little, but not right off the bat. Hell, with what he's paying me, I'll be able to move out of Winston's within a few short weeks and not only make it on my own but do so comfortably.

A part of me worries that maybe he's doing this as a favor to Winston and he doesn't really want me here, but that thought only pushes me to be successful even more. No matter what his intentions, I'm determined to prove that he made the right choice in giving me this job.

Considering Miles is waiting to take me home, I quickly power off the computer to my right before standing, shoving my cell phone into my back pocket as I make my way out of the office.

The shop is pretty quiet compared to earlier. All but one of the artists have gone home for the night, and the only customer that remains is the one he's working on.

I didn't get a ton of time to spend with the guys that were working tonight, but they all seemed really nice. Tubbs, the guy that's still here, was even sweet enough to get me a sandwich from the sub shop next door without me asking for one.

While it's definitely a little outside of my usual surroundings, I can see myself fitting in here. It'll probably take me a little time, but with such a fun group I think us all being friends is inevitable. Well, considering they don't all hate me once they get to know me.

I hate that I even have to think that way. I know it stems from years of Alan convincing me I wasn't good enough, and it's not true. If only I could shut off that way of thinking.

But once something takes root it's a lot harder to shake than some might think, especially someone who's never dealt with such a manipulative and emotionally abusive person as Alan. Even all these weeks later, I'm still discovering damaged parts that I never knew existed until I was away from him.

"Bye, Tubbs," I call as I pass by his work area on my way toward the lobby.

He looks up and gives me a crooked smile.

While he's no Miles, Parson Tubbs is definitely good looking. I'd guess him maybe in his late twenties, around five-ten, with broad shoulders, and perhaps the thickest biceps I've ever seen. But it's his smile that really stands out. There's something so infectious about

86

it. Add in the dark eyes, two day-old-scruff, and one hell of a man bun, and Tubbs is one nice piece of eye candy.

"'Bout time boss man let you off. Slave driver I tell ya." He chuckles.

"He's the worst," I tease. "Have a good night." I throw him a quick wave.

"You too." He graces me with another smile before turning his attention back to the forearm tattoo he's working on.

"You better watch flirting with the guys like that." Miles' voice washes over me as I hit the lobby. I jump slightly and turn, having not realized he had come up behind me.

"Huh?" I start, pulling to a stop just inside the door.

"Tubbs. You give him an inch and he'll take a mile." He smiles, but the action doesn't quite reach his eyes.

"I'm not giving him anything," I insist, a little taken aback. "It's called being friendly," I inform him, gaining a little composure.

"If you say so." He shakes his head. "You 'bout ready?"

"Yeah. I've done all I can do for tonight. If it's okay, I'd like to come in early on Monday before the shop opens so I have some quiet time to strap down."

"Sure." He slips his hand into his pocket and pulls out a set of keys, fiddling with the ring for a long moment before finally freeing one of the keys. "Here."

He tosses it in my direction, and I quickly snatch it out of the air.

Opening my palm, I examine the silver key for a long moment.

"You're giving me a key to the shop?" I question, a little surprised that he trusts me so much. Then again, I guess we have technically known each other nearly our entire lives.

"Pretty sure you're not going to rob me. You're not, are you?" he adds on jokingly.

"Shut up." I laugh, shoving the key into my pocket.

"You're welcome to come and go as you please. I'll text you the alarm code so you don't set it off when you come in. The only thing I ask is that I know ahead of time what hours you'll be working each week."

"Okay." I nod. "I'll probably bounce around a little the first couple of weeks and see what works best. I want to make sure I'm here during business hours as much as I can be without getting in the way."

"You won't be in the way. The office is yours. Do with it what you want. Now that you're handling the books, I won't really need to be in there much. I'd much rather be out here." He gestures around the room.

"Okay. We'll figure it out."

"Well, I guess I should get you home." He takes off toward the front door, pushing it open seconds later. I quickly follow him out, thanking him for holding the door as I pass.

The night air is warm but void of the heavy humidity that was almost suffocating earlier this afternoon. I cross the sidewalk to where Miles' bike is parked on the curb, trying to contain the way my body trembles slightly when he settles the helmet on my head and clasps the strap under my chin.

"Here." He turns and lifts the bike seat, pulling out a sweatshirt before closing the seat. Turning back toward me, he drops the unzipped hoodie over my shoulders. "The breeze gets a bit chilly this late at night." He waits until I have both arms through the sleeves before zipping it up.

I look down, most of my view obstructed by the bulky helmet, before looking back up at Miles. I wish my heart didn't kick up at the sweet gesture, but I have about as much control over it as I do the weather – none.

"Aren't you going to need it?" I question, pushing up the sleeves that are nearly two times too long for my little arms.

"Nah. I'll be fine." He shrugs before climbing onto his bike. He reaches for me the moment he's on and helps me up. Instantly, I settle in behind him, wishing it didn't feel so good to wrap my arms around his middle and hold him tight, but at the same time loving that it does.

If I didn't know any better, I'd swear I was crushing on Miles Hollins. Correction – I *am totally* crushing on Miles Hollins. But that's normal, right? I mean, he's gorgeous. I'd have to be blind not to be a little smitten with him.

The bike purrs to life beneath us, breaking me from where my mind has drifted. Within seconds we're speeding down the road, the night air whipping around us.

The city is still bustling with activity as we make our way through traffic. I'd forgotten how alive this city is at night and for the first time in a very long time, I feel an odd sense of belonging.

Slowly, little by little, I start to remember all the things I loved about home. As well as finding new things to love. I know I didn't think so in the beginning, but I'm starting to see that coming home is the best thing I could have done.

I may not have it all figured out just yet, but for the first time in years, I feel like I'm exactly where I'm meant to be.

Chapter Nine

Miles

"You hired my sister?" Winston scratches the back of his head as he slides a beer into my hand.

I didn't intend to hang out but given that Winston pulled into the parking lot of his apartment building directly behind Harlow and me, I figured I should at least talk to him about what transpired today.

"I'm fucking confused," he continues since I'd yet to respond, dropping down onto the opposite end of the couch. "How the hell did that happen?"

"She needed a job. I had an opening." I give him the short version, glancing over my shoulder to ensure Harlow's bedroom door is closed so hopefully we're not overheard. Not that I have anything to hide, but I don't want to censor myself.

When we got up to the apartment, she made a beeline for her room and hasn't come out since. Either she really was as tired as she claimed or she's worried about her brother's reaction to seeing us on my bike and is hoping to avoid the conversation tonight. My guess is the latter.

"You really think Ink*ed* is the place for someone like Harlow? No offense, but have you looked at some of the dudes that come in that place?"

"What are you trying to say?" I shift to the side slightly so that I'm facing him.

"It's a tattoo shop, man. And Harlow, well she's Harlow. I don't want her getting fucked with."

"Do you really think I would let anyone fuck with your sister?" I give him a look that says he should know me better than that. "Look, I didn't plan to offer her the job. Hell, the thought had never even crossed my mind. But we were at lunch with your dad, and they were talking about her needing a job and what she went to school for. I kind of offered it without really thinking it through. But in truth, I think she'll be a great fit. She's already accomplished more tonight than Delia, and I have managed to do in six months. I need someone like her keeping my shit straight and she needs an income. If you ask me it's a win-win."

"You went to lunch together? How the hell did that happen?"

"I stopped by earlier this morning to see if you wanted to head over to your dad's shop with me. Harlow was here, and you weren't. She mentioned going to visit your dad, so I asked if she wanted to tag along with me."

"So, what? You guys are hanging out now?" If I didn't know any better, I'd say the thought bothers him. I'm not sure why it would though. I know he's pretty protective of Harlow, but he's never had to be with me. He's always known where I stand and that I would never fuck with her.

"I don't know that I would classify it as hanging out. We went to see your dad and had lunch. Something you and I have done a million times."

"Yeah, you and I, not you and Harlow. I don't know, man." He shakes his head, taking a long pull from his beer. "If you ask me it's kinda weird."

"What is?"

"You are hanging out with my sister. You two couldn't stand each other for years. Now all of a sudden you're buddy-buddy."

"For one, we're not hanging out. We did one thing together – once – because you weren't around. Two, I realize we didn't get along in the past, but people change. I would think you of all people would understand that. And three, I thought you'd be happy that I'm playing nice."

"Won't lie, I'm glad you two aren't ready to rip each other's heads off. But I gotta say, seeing my sister climb off the back of your bike at nearly midnight didn't make me all warm and fuzzy inside."

"Winston, we're talking about your little sister. Do you really think I would ever go there?" I shake my head like it's the most ridiculous thought in the world, when in actuality I've thought about it more times today than I care to admit.

"Nah, I guess not." He chuckles, taking another pull of beer.

"Your family is my family. It always has been. Even when I couldn't stand her, Harlow has always been included in that circle. You know that. And giving her a job is my way of helping my family."

"I appreciate that." Winston seems to relax, sinking further into the couch.

Guilt grips tightly in my chest but I push it down. I have nothing to feel guilty for. So I find Harlow attractive. What man wouldn't? She's not only beautiful, but I'm quickly learning she's also very sweet when she wants to be, and her funny and quick-witted banter is a lot cuter now than I remember it being when we were younger. But that's where it ends.

Or is it?

I shake off the thought, downing half my beer in one long gulp.

"I just hope you know what you're getting yourself into. You know how much Harlow has always loved busting your balls. Are you really prepared to deal with that on a daily basis?"

"Well I guess I don't have a choice now, do I? The job is already hers." I grin.

"You could always fire her," he jokes.

"Let's just see how this plays out first," I suggest, humor in my voice. "So what's up with you and Stella?

Harlow said you stayed at her place last night." I need to change the subject, knowing bringing up Stella will most definitely do the trick.

"Things are good. She finally forgave me."

"I didn't realize you did anything wrong." I tip the beer bottle to my mouth, a knowing smile playing on my lips.

"Neither did I." He chuckles. "When in doubt, always assume it was your fault."

"Now that's just sad." I shake my head. "I get that you care about the girl, Winst, but seriously, how long are you going to keep this up?"

"I don't know, dude. I'm not getting any fucking younger, and Stella is the whole package. I do want to get married and have kids, at least eventually. Fuck, I'll be thirty-five this year."

"And you think Stella is the woman to provide that for you?" I give him a doubtful look.

"I get that we're kind of all over the place."

"All over the place? You two are like a match and a stick of dynamite playing chicken."

"We're not that bad," he disagrees. "Okay, maybe it's not the healthiest relationship. But Stella's still young. She'll get there. And when she does, I'll be the guy who stood by her through all her crazy."

"She's twenty-seven. That's old enough for her to have figured her shit out."

"I just fucking love her." He blows out a hard breath. "I know we're toxic for each other, but I can't give her up. She's it for me. She's my person."

"Well, then what the hell are you waiting for?"

"Huh?" He seems confused by my question.

"You just sat here and said you love her. That one day you want to marry her and have kids. What are you waiting for? Maybe part of the reason things have been so up and down as of late is that she's growing restless."

"You think?" He scratches his chin like he's never actually considered this as a possibility. "I haven't really thought of that. You might be right. She has been dropping some serious hints over the past few months. I thought it was her just being a woman."

"You really are fucking clueless," I tell him, finishing off my beer before leaning forward and setting the empty bottle on the coffee table.

Winston opens his mouth to say something else, but snaps it shut when Harlow's bedroom door opens and light floods into the hallway.

She appears in the doorway seconds later, dressed in a thin tank top and solid blue pajama shorts, her long hair knotted on top of her head. Her steps falter when she looks up and meets my gaze, having not realized I was still here.

"Hey, sis," Winston calls, not missing a beat. "You wanna join your new boss and me for a beer?"

"I think I'm good." She forces a smile before taking off toward the kitchen.

"Well, would you at least mind grabbing us two more while you're in there?"

"Because cleaning your house wasn't enough, now I have to add servant to my ever growing job description," she says jokingly but with a hint of seriousness all the same.

"Thank you for that by the way," Winston says, giving his sister a wide smile when she strides out of the kitchen with a beer.

"Uh huh." She rolls her eyes, shoving the bottle into his hand.

"What? I don't get one?" I ask, holding up my empty hands.

"No." She shakes her head. "Unless you're planning to stay on the couch tonight, you can have this." She hands me a bottle of water.

"Damn, dude. You sure you want her working for you?" Winston laughs.

"Well, no one will be working for him if he drinks and then gets on that motorcycle and kills himself," Harlow interjects, giving her brother the stink eye.

"She has a point," I agree, taking the opportunity to call it a night. "I should get going anyway. I'm beat," I say, throwing in a forced yawn for good measure.

"Lame," Winston hollers as I cross around the couch.

"Yeah. Yeah." I snag my helmet off the breakfast bar before heading toward the door. "I'll talk to you later, man. And keep me posted on the Stella situation. I'm curious to know if I'm right."

"Right about what?" I turn around just in time to see Harlow cross her arms over her chest, her gaze coming to me before going back to her brother.

"Miles seems to think that Stella's behavior is her acting out because I haven't popped the question," Winston tells her, a grin on his face.

"Wait, what?" Harlow's eyes go wide as she starts to piece it together. "Are you going to ask her to marry you?" she half squeals.

"Maybe." He shrugs non-committal, twisting the cap off his fresh beer before taking a long swig.

"It's about time." She reaches over and playfully slaps him on the shoulder.

"I said maybe," he reiterates.

"He's going to," I interject, not able to hold in my smile when Harlow's eyes come to mine.

I swear I've smiled more today than I can remember smiling in years. Something tells me I know why that is and yet I refuse to acknowledge it. Even if I wanted to pursue Harlow, which I'm not saying I do, it would never work.

Even if you remove Winston from the equation, we'd never stand a chance. I can already see how it would play out. It would be fun in the beginning, but then she'd push for something serious. She'd become frustrated and hurt when I pulled back. And then eventually she'd end up hating me when I broke things off because I'm too closed off to let myself feel the things you need to feel to carry on with a real relationship.

I've accepted the fact that my life will be nothing more than a string of meaningless hookups, and honestly, I prefer it that way. But when I look at Harlow, when she smiles at me the way she's smiling at me right now, I forget why I can't have the real thing. At least for a moment.

But then reality starts to creep back in. I remember who I am and what I've done and why no one, especially not Harlow, deserves to take on the shit storm that is my life.

I'm better off alone. At least that way no one gets hurt.

"I'm glad you think you know me so well." Winston swivels his head in my direction, pulling me from my thoughts.

"I think we both know I do," I tell him, forcing an easy smile.

"I thought you were leaving." He turns back around, tipping his beer to his lips.

I laugh, shaking my head at him even though he's not looking at me. "I'll see you later, man," I tell him, throwing a small nod to Harlow before quickly slipping out into the darkness of the night.

I've barely made it a handful of steps when the door jerks open behind me. I turn right in time to see Harlow step out. She pulls the door closed behind her before quickly making her way toward me, stopping inches shy from where I'm standing next to the stairs.

"I don't know if I properly thanked you for today," she starts, shuffling her weight from one foot to the other.

"You don't need to thank me," I tell her before she has a chance to continue.

"But I do," she cuts me off. "Alan refused to let me work. He refused to let me have anything of my own. That's all I wanted, to do something for me. Today you made that dream a reality. You gave me an opportunity I'm not sure I would have found otherwise. A chance to build something for myself for the first time in my life. I need you to know how grateful I am for that." She pauses. "Anyway, I just wanted to tell you that. I promise I will not disappoint you," she adds when I remain silent.

"I'm glad I could help, Low." I don't know why, but I use the name her brother has called her for as long as I can remember. I don't even realize that *I've* never called her that before until I see the reaction it pulls from her.

Before I have a chance even to take a breath, her arms wrap around my middle, and she presses her cheek against my chest.

Without thinking, I instinctively pull her closer, dropping my face into her hair as I hug her back. It's only a brief moment before she pulls her head away and looks up at me, our eyes locking.

I don't know that I've ever seen her so open, so vulnerable, and it stirs something deep inside of me. The sudden urge to lean down and press my lips to hers comes on fast and strong, yet somehow I resist doing just that. It's like there's this magnetic force pulling me closer to her and yet an equally powerful one pulling me the other way.

I don't know how long we stand like that. Our faces inches apart gazes locked. A minute. Thirty seconds. Ten seconds. All I know is that when she pulls away it's like she takes a piece of me with her and all I want to do is bring her back, to feel her warmth for a second longer.

This realization is enough to rattle me to my fucking core.

"Thank you, Miles." She backs away slowly before turning and disappearing inside without another word.

Chapter Ten

Harlow

"Knock, knock." A light tap follows the deep voice from the hall.

I look up to see Miles standing in the doorway of the office, his toned body clad in faded jeans and an old Jack Daniels Whiskey shirt. It's such a casual everyday outfit yet based on the rush of want that runs through me you would think he was dressed to the nine.

"Hey." I clear my throat, sitting up straighter in my chair. "When did you get here?" I ask, having not heard him come in.

"Just now. You didn't hear the door chime?" He cocks his head slightly and gives me a puzzled look.

"No." I half laugh. "I must have been really focused."

"So, how's it going?" He enters the office, crossing around the desk to stand at my left.

"It's going." I tilt my face up to see him looking down at the paperwork in front of me. "I think it'll take another couple of days to get everything in order and then I should be able to start working on a system to streamline this whole process." I gesture to the receipts, payroll information, and invoices scattered on the desk.

"Awesome." He nods in approval. "Anything I can help with?"

"Actually, yes. I need all the guys, and Delia, to sign some paperwork. The employee files are a mess, and you're missing certain documents that are required to be on file. I printed everything out already," I say, reaching for the small stack of manila folders sitting on the filing cabinet and handing them to him. "I started new files for each person. I figure you'll likely see everyone sooner than I do, but if it's an issue I'm happy to make myself available to have them do it myself."

"No, that's not necessary. I'll get these taken care of in the next couple of days. I may have to stop by Jake's to have him do his because he's off for the next few days, but everyone else will be in sometime through the week, and I can get it taken care of."

"Perfect." I smile up at him.

"Anything else?"

"Nope. I think that's it for now, but I'll let you know if I think of anything else."

"Sounds good." He tucks the files under his arm and makes his way to the other side of the office, turning back toward me right as he reaches the door.

The second his hazel eyes land on mine a whoosh runs through my stomach. I grip the underneath of my chair to keep myself from physically reacting.

God, it's been so long since a man has made me feel so upside down. I truly don't know what to do with myself.

"I'll be out front if you need me. I've got someone coming in at noon but feel free to interrupt if you need to ask a question or something."

"Okay, will do." I smile, biting down on my bottom lip the moment he turns around and disappears around the corner.

It's nearly seven o'clock in the evening when I finally decide to call it a day. I've been so submerged in my work that I haven't eaten anything since breakfast except for a small pack of almonds I had in my purse. To say I'm hungry is putting it mildly.

After closing everything down and killing the office lights, I snag my purse off the chair and make my way toward the front of the shop to tell Miles that I'm heading out.

I've just reached the doorway that opens into the main part of the shop when a familiar voice hits me like a sledgehammer, halting my forward movement.

"I don't care who the hell you are. I demand that you let me see my wife."

I look up to see the one person I truly never expected to see again standing daringly close to Miles, his finger pointed upward into his face.

"Alan?" His name falls from my lips, and both he and Miles turn toward me. "What… what the hell are you doing here?"

I look to Miles, with what I'm sure reads as panic and confusion written all over my face and then back to Alan.

"My wife doesn't work here, huh?" Alan squares his shoulders.

"She doesn't." Miles catches him by the bicep and cuts off his path to get to me. "Because that's not your wife."

"Like hell, she isn't. Now take your hands off me." Alan's voice splinters through the shop. "Or would you rather spend the rest of the evening sitting in a jail cell?"

"By all means you can try. But if you don't get the fuck out of my shop, where I'm going to put you is going to be a hell of a lot worse than a cell," Miles threatens, his tone so menacing a chill runs straight up my spine.

Looking around the room, I'm suddenly aware of the various sets of eyes locked on the altercation between the two men. The shop is busy tonight, with all but two artists working and every single one with a client. Right now, is quite possibly the worst timing for something like this to happen.

105

"That's enough." I quickly close the distance between them and me. "Miles, thank you," I say, resting my hand on the arm that still has Alan restrained. "But I'll take it from here."

I can tell by the look in his eyes that the last thing he wants to do is let Alan walk away still standing, but after several seconds he nods and releases him with a stiff shove.

Alan stumbles back a couple of feet and immediately moves to fix his disheveled shirt. Heaven forbid anything prevents him from looking pressed and pristine – even in an altercation with a man twice his size that would likely kill him in a fight.

"I come to talk to you, and this is how I'm treated?" He looks down at me with disgust and judgment.

"Perhaps you should have called before coming all this way," I tell him, quickly turning on my heel and making a straight line to the front door.

I lead him outside and a few feet down the sidewalk before turning on him. By this point, my anger over seeing him here has reached a boiling point.

"What the hell are you doing here, Alan?" My harsh tone causes him to stop dead in his tracks.

"I needed to talk to you."

"About what? What could you possibly need to say to me that you couldn't have said through our attorneys?"

"I don't want to talk to you through someone else, Harlow."

"Well, that's too damn bad, Alan. You can't just show up here, at my place of employment no less, and start causing a scene. When are you going to get it through that thick head of yours? We are over."

"I refuse to believe that. You'll tire of this life, Harlow. You'll tire of places like that and people like him." He gestures back toward Ink*ed*. "And then you'll come crawling home. So why not save us both the trouble and come home with me now?"

"Are you delusional?" My voice shakes around the words, anger pooling out of me so rapidly that I can't control the physical reaction it's causing. "I'm never coming back to you, Alan. You are not my home. Arizona is not my home. You made sure of that when you chased me out of the state."

"Don't be ridiculous. I did not chase you out of the state."

"Yes, you did!" I explode. "By doing things like this. By showing up when you're not wanted. By trying to force yourself on me when the last thing I want is you. I don't want to be with you ever again. I don't love you. So leave me the hell alone!" I pull at the ends of my hair in frustration. "What more do I have to say or do to make you hear me?"

"You're being childish and unreasonable, Harlow."

107

"I'm being unreasonable?" I scream, my voice cutting through the air.

Alan straightens his posture and looks around, noticing that several people passing by have slowed to catch a glimpse of what's going on. Unlike Alan, I don't care who hears what I have to say.

"You are the one who showed up here uninvited. You are the one that walked into *my* place of employment and got into an altercation with *my* boss. You are the one who's refused to sign the divorce papers even though I've told you repeatedly that we are never getting back together."

"I just thought you needed time," he starts, his voice low.

"Time to what? To forget how you preferred the company of other women over that of your wife? To forget how miserable you made me? How unhappy I've been for years? I don't need time, Alan. In fact, I'm happier now than I've been in a very long time. You cheating on me is the best thing you could have done for me. Because now I'm free."

"You forget everything I've done for you." Anger teeters in his voice. "You, ungrateful bitch."

"Leave, Alan," I grind out, my patience long since vanished.

"I'm not leaving. I came all this way to talk and damn it, Harlow, you will talk to me. You're my wife."

"I am not your wife!" I scream. "The sooner you accept that, the better it's going to be for the both of us."

"Where do you think you're going?" Alan catches me by the forearm when I move to walk away.

"I refuse to let you do this to me, Alan. I may not be able to control you being here, but I can control whether or not I'm here," I grind out, our faces mere inches apart, his fingers biting into my skin. "Now let go of my arm, or we'll add assault to the long list of things my lawyer has to use against you."

"If I knew you'd turn out to be so petty and spiteful, I never would have married you." He tightens his grip on my arm.

"If I knew you'd turn out to be such a controlling, cheating psychopath, I never would have married you," I counter, my voice eerily calm.

"I'm not signing those papers. I will make sure to drag it out as long as possible, and when it's all said and done, you won't get a dime."

"Don't sign those papers and I will make sure every indiscretion of yours is made public. Everyone will know what a lying, cheating bastard you are. I don't want your money. In fact, I'm not asking for a dime from you." I try to pull my arm from his hold, but his grip is too tight for me to shake him. "Or didn't your attorney tell you that? All I want is to be free of you."

"You'll never be free of me." He presses his forehead into the side of my face, his breath hot on my cheek.

This seems to be my undoing, and every ounce of control I was struggling to keep in place falls away. I forcefully jerk backward, catching Alan off guard enough that I'm able to get my arm free. I turn, prepared to run when I hit a wall of hard chest and nearly go tumbling backward.

"I think it's time for you to leave," Miles says seconds after his arm snakes around me to keep me in place.

"I think you need to mind your own fucking business," Alan seethes. "This is between my wife and me."

"I'm not sure how much clearer she can be, so let me try. Harlow isn't your wife. She isn't anything to you anymore. Walk away before walking is no longer an option for you."

"Is that a threat?"

"It's a threat and a promise. You come back here again, and I will personally make sure you live to regret it for the rest of your life. Are we fucking clear?" The power in Miles' voice is enough to make me tremble against him.

"If I leave, I'm not coming back. Do you hear me, Harlow?" He raises his voice when I don't turn to face him. "Fine, if that's how you want to play it. In the end, you're the one that's losing. You're not fucking worth it anymore anyway." I hear his feet scuff the pavement as he turns and walks away.

I keep my face buried in Miles' chest, even after I'm fairly certain Alan is gone. I'm not sure if it's because it feels good to be here or that I'm too embarrassed by what happened to face Miles right now. Maybe it's a little of both.

"Hey." His soft voice filters around me seconds before his hands slide up my back to rest on my shoulders, gently guiding me back. "Are you okay?" He tips my chin up so that I'm forced to look at him.

The instant his hazel eyes find mine, tears begin to well. Anger, humiliation, and defeat all blend together and it takes only seconds before the tears spill down my cheeks.

"I'm so sorry," I croak, not sure what else to say. How does one apologize for their ex showing up and causing a scene in your place of employment? "I completely understand if you need to fire me."

"Harlow. Hey." Miles cups my cheeks, holding my face in his hands as he dips down to meet my gaze. "I'm not going to fire you. Are you kidding me? You have nothing to be sorry about . Do you hear me? Nothing. This isn't your fault."

"Yes, it is," I sob, my embarrassment growing with each second that passes.

"Stop," he says firmly, releasing my face to pull me into his arms. "You can't control what other people do. This isn't on you. Okay?"

I nod even though I don't feel like that's the case. It's only my first week on the job, and already I'm causing problems.

"But your clients…" I pull back enough to look up at him.

"Have seen a hell of a lot worse than that." He chuckles, tucking a stray strand of hair behind my ear. "What do you say we get out of here? Maybe grab a bite to eat. You must be starving. You didn't get lunch earlier."

"How do you know?" I ask, taking a full step back, missing the power of Miles' touch the instant it's gone.

"Because I pay attention." He gives me a small grin and a wink. "Come on. My treat." He drops his arm over my shoulder and tucks me into his side.

"Thank you for cutting in when you did, by the way," I say after several moments of silence, realizing I hadn't thanked him.

"You don't ever have to thank me for having your back. Just know I always will." His statement causes a wave of emotion to run over me and my tears start to well again.

I can't remember a time when someone has said that to me. And for him to say it – just when I needed to hear it – means more to me than he will ever know.

"Winston's lucky to have a friend like you."

"Then I guess you're lucky too." He bumps his hip playfully into mine. I'm sure trying to lighten the mood.

"Is that what we are now? Friends?"

"Aren't we?" He grins.

"Yeah, I guess we are," I agree, fighting a smile.

"Who would have guessed it? Miles and Harlow, friends." He chuckles.

"What is this world coming to?" I smart.

"My thoughts exactly." He smiles down at me and my stomach flips.

If this is what it means to be friends with Miles Hollins, then I might be in trouble…

Chapter Eleven

Miles

"So, does he do that often?" I ask Harlow who has barely touched the pasta on her plate. She's spent more time pushing it around with her fork than actually eating it.

I think she's still trying to process having her ex showing up here the way he did.

She gives me a weak smile and nods, finally deciding to abandon her food altogether. She drops her fork and leans back slightly in her chair, taking her glass of wine with her.

"I'm starting to understand why you left Arizona," I say, popping the end of a breadstick into my mouth.

"It was really bad," she agrees, tipping the wine glass to her lips before taking a long drink. "Though I have to say, I never thought he'd show up here."

"Crazy people do crazy things." I shrug.

"I guess." She blows out a slow breath, her eyes coming back to mine. "The sad thing is, if he put in even half of this effort into our relationship, maybe our marriage wouldn't have fallen apart."

"Do you still love him?" I don't know why I ask. It's none of my fucking business, but the question comes out just the same.

"That's a complicated question." She pauses. "I think a part of me will always love him in some way, but I fell out of love with him years ago. I just wouldn't let myself face it until the truth about his affairs came out."

I clamp down on my bottom lip to keep myself from saying what I really want to say. I can't look at the beautiful woman sitting across from me and fathom for even a second why any man would cheat on her. It makes my fucking blood boil just thinking about it.

"The truth is, I fell in love with one man and married a completely different one. When we first started dating it was so easy. He was smart and handsome and made me feel like a princess. I know it sounds cliché, but it's exactly how I felt when I was with him. I had never had a man make me feel so adored and so worthy. It was impossible not to fall for him. But then we got married, and it was like a light switch was flipped. He became jealous and controlling. He wouldn't let me work, insisting that he wanted to provide for me so that I could stay at home with the kids when we had them. But years passed and there were no children. Hell, he wouldn't even entertain the idea. Always making some excuse as to why we weren't ready. I had nothing for myself. That house had become my prison, and even though I knew it was happening, I refused to let myself see what my life had become. I'm sure that sounds crazy." She chuckles to herself before tipping the glass back to her lips, emptying the contents in one long drink.

"It doesn't sound crazy," I disagree. "Sometimes when you're standing too close, you don't see all the imperfections, but when you take a step back, everything becomes clearer."

"Spoken like a man who's been there before." She cocks a brow at me, setting her empty glass at the edge of the table.

"When I came back from my first tour overseas I met a girl. Rachel," I admit. "Though our time together was short, there were a lot of things I didn't realize until it ended."

"Like what?" Harlow leans forward, resting her elbows on the table. My gaze slides across the freckles that scatter over her nose and around her cheeks, and I wonder how I never noticed how fucking adorable they are.

"What?" I question, losing my train of thought.

"What kind of things didn't you realize?"

"Well, a lot of things. We went from zero to ten overnight. Typically when things happen that quickly, there are a lot of signs you miss. I was only home a couple of weeks before I had to report back to the base, but we agreed to keep seeing each other. We wrote letters, and I called when I could. It gave me someone to talk to. Someone to confide in. I don't know. I guess it just felt good knowing there was someone out there that gave a shit about me."

"A lot of people give a shit about you," Harlow interrupts.

"I know that. But there's something about having someone love you in that way."

"I get it." She pauses when the waiter appears. "Can I have another glass, please?" She gestures to her empty wine glass.

"Of course." He smiles at her a little too long, and I'm tempted to clear my throat to snap him out of it.

The funny thing is, I don't think Harlow has any idea that he's been giving her the *look* all night. The look that says I'd like to do more than just bring you wine all night. Kids got balls. I'll give him that. You would think with me sitting right here he wouldn't be so bold. Fucking college kids.

I can't help but wonder if Harlow's always been so oblivious to men openly ogling her. Tubbs has been stumbling over himself to talk to her at every turn, yet Harlow seems completely unphased. The only way a woman is that unaffected by the attention of a man is if she doesn't realize what kind of attention he's giving her.

I've seen girls practically melt at Tubbs' feet, but Harlow is an exception. A part of me is relieved. I don't know why, but the thought of her hooking up with Tubbs, or any guy for that matter, doesn't sit well with me.

She waits until the waiter leaves before turning her attention back to me.

"So what happened with this girl?"

"We did the long distance thing for a while. It wasn't ideal, but it was nice having someone to talk to. We stayed together through my second deployment, and she was here waiting for me when I was discharged. But by that point, my time away had such a monumental impact on my life. I didn't come back the same person. She realized pretty quick that who I was and who she wanted me to be were two completely different people. She ended things shortly after I returned home. I think she liked the idea of dating a military man. To have someone to use to garner sympathy from other people because I was fighting overseas and may never come home, but she didn't like the reality of what dating someone in my profession meant when it really boiled down to it. At the end of the day, I realized it was never about me. It was always about her and what she could get out of the relationship."

"Wow. I'm sorry to hear that." She nods to the waiter who reappears with her glass of wine but keeps her attention locked on me. This time he doesn't linger at the table. "How long were you two together exactly?"

She lifts her glass and takes a drink before setting it on the table in front of her.

"About two years. Though we only spent about two months of that time actually together."

"Did you love her?"

"I cared for her, but love, I can't say that I did. I thought I did for a while but after it was over, I realized what we had wasn't love." I shake my head. "That probably sounds bad."

"You can't help what you felt, or didn't feel for that matter." She shrugs, settling further back into her chair. "Do you still see her around?"

"From time to time. We're friendly, but that's about the extent of it."

"Do you think if you hadn't gone back overseas that maybe things would have worked out for you?"

"Hard to say." I blow out a breath. "But I doubt it."

"You said things happened over there that changed you." She leaves the statement open-ended and as much as I wish I could have this conversation with her, I can't.

I can't have her look at me the way I know she will. Not her. I don't know why, but not her.

Very few people know about what actually happened during my time overseas. As a matter of fact, other than the brothers I served with, only Winston and my mom know the truth. And that's the way it will stay if I have anything to say about it.

"I'm sorry. We don't have to talk about that," she adds after gauging my reaction.

"Sorry. It's not something I really like to discuss."

"I totally understand." She gives me an apologetic smile, and I feel guilty.

"It's just really difficult to talk about," I explain.

"Really, Miles, it's okay." She reaches for her wine. "So other than Rachel, have you had any serious relationships? If I remember right, you jumped around a lot in high school." She gives me a look that brings a smile to my face.

"You noticed that, huh?" I chuckle.

"I think the whole world noticed. It's not like you were discreet about it."

"I suppose not."

"So have you? Had any other serious relationships."

"Not really. There was one other girl I kind of dated for a while. We were stationed together in Hawaii before my first tour. She was a nice distraction but nothing that would have stuck long term."

"A nice distraction." Harlow rolls her eyes. "Sounds like that's what most of your relationships have been. If that's what you can even call them."

"You're not wrong there." I don't try to disagree. "I'm not proud of it," I admit. "If I could go back I would probably do a lot of things differently."

"You say that now, but somehow I find that hard to believe." Harlow gives me a doubtful look before tipping the wine glass to her lips.

"Maybe you're just jealous because I never tried to make a move on you." I fish for a reaction, not sure what type of response I'm hoping for.

"Ha. You wish." She sets her wine glass down and pins her green eyes on me. "Me, the girl who has never had a casual hookup in her life. Pretty sure I'm not your speed."

"Wait, what?" I choke out, my reaction confusing her.

"What?" She looks around the room like she's missing something.

"You've never had a casual hook up before?"

"Why are you looking at me like that's hard to believe?" I can tell she's not sure if she should be offended or not.

"Because it is," I tell her, watching her brows crease. "I mean, have you looked at yourself? You're gorgeous, Low." Her cheeks pink at my comment. "You mean to tell me that you walk around looking like that and you haven't had at least one guy talk you into his bed and it not amount to anything?"

"Um, pretty sure no one has ever tried," she says meekly, quickly retrieving her wine from the table.

"Not fucking possible," I disagree.

"It's true," she insists. "Not saying I would hook up with anyone but…"

"How many people have you slept with?" I ask, watching the blush on her face deepen further.

"You can't just ask me that." She shakes her head. "How many people have you slept with?" she fires back at me.

"I don't honestly know. Thirty. Forty, maybe."

"Forty?" She sputters on her wine, barely getting the drink down without choking. "Wait, you said maybe. How do you not know an exact number?"

"I haven't really been keeping track," I admit.

"Wow. You really are a whore. I always knew it but hearing it out loud." She shakes her head. "Forty," she says like she's still trying to process.

"Maybe thirty," I interject on a laugh.

"That's awful that you don't actually know the number."

"And I suppose you do," I challenge, hoping she'll give me a straight answer this time.

"It's not hard to keep track of." She holds up her hand, two fingers sticking straight up.

"Two?"

"I've been with Alan for almost ten years. Before him, there was only Tyson."

"Tyson Hames?"

"Yep." She nods.

"You lost your virginity to Tyson Hames?" I say, having never cared for the guy.

"Don't look at me like that. You don't even know how many women you've slept with." Her forehead creases as she stares back at me. "I bet you can't even remember your first."

"Bea Martin." I give her a shit-eating grin.

"As in Winston's ex, Bea Martin?" She cocks a brow.

"He dated her after."

"Ewwww." She crinkles her nose. "I knew you guys shared things, but that is taking it a bit far."

I clutch my stomach as laughter rumbles through me.

"We can change the subject now." She playfully narrows her gaze at me.

"Sure," I quickly agree, taking this opportunity to revert the conversation back to her. "So, Tyson Hames, huh? I know you all dated, but damn. You could have done way better."

"How do you even know him? We were five years below you."

"I was pretty close with his brother in high school. I went to their house quite a few times. Never cared for the kid."

"Last time I checked, you didn't care for many people back then. Unless they had a pussy between their legs."

Laughter erupts from my mouth for a second time, and Harlow's eyes go wide. It takes her a moment to realize why I'm laughing and once she does, a slow smile breaks across her face.

God, this girl. I don't know what she's doing to me. When I'm with her, I feel more like myself than I have in a very long time. I can't remember a moment in the last eight years where I've smiled so much or laughed so effortlessly. I don't know what it is about her – what makes me feel almost at peace.

Since she's been home, things have felt easier. I find myself thinking more about her than obsessing over the demons that haunt me daily. I find myself closing my eyes and seeing her face instead of his. I hear her voice instead of screams. And for a brief moment I forget.

Unfortunately, as soon as I fall asleep, it all comes back. I've accepted at this point that I will never know a good night's sleep again. I guess that's the price I'll pay for my sins. Not a high enough price if you ask me.

"I'm sorry. That word coming out of your mouth seems so out of place." I break out of my thoughts and refocus on Harlow who's smiling at me from across the table.

"You're as bad as Winston. I'm twenty-nine years old, Miles. I can say pussy." She tries to hold a straight face, but within seconds she dissolves into laughter. "You're right. It feels dirty," she admits, finishing off her fourth glass of wine.

"I think maybe I should cut you off." I gesture to the empty glass she sits on the table.

"I think maybe you're right. I really should have eaten more before swilling four glasses of wine."

"Probably would have been a good idea."

"I just, after Alan and everything, I didn't really have an appetite."

"I get it. We can get them to box that up for you. Maybe you'll feel up to eating later."

"Yeah, maybe," she agrees, falling silent for a long moment before turning her gaze back up to mine. "Thank you for this, Miles. I feel like all I've done recently is thank you."

"You don't need to thank me."

"But I do. First the job, then stepping in with Alan, and now taking me to dinner to try to get my mind off of it. If I didn't know any better, Miles Hollins, I'd say you're a closet sweetheart."

"I wouldn't get your hope up," I tell her on, smiling.

"Actions and words." She ticks her finger at me.

"Give it time. My true colors eventually show through." I try to be playful, but deep down I truly mean it. I always find a way to fuck things up.

"Guess we'll see." She shrugs.

"Guess we will," I agree. "You about ready to get out of here?"

"Yes and no." She chews on her bottom lip, the action drawing my gaze to her mouth.

"What does that mean?" I force my eyes back up, the action taking everything I have.

"It means yes, I'm ready to leave here. But no, because I need to sober up before I can go home."

"Not necessary considering you're crashing at my place tonight."

"I am not staying with you," she says, half panicked.

"Relax. I'm not taking you home to take advantage of you. I live a block from here, and you're in no condition to drive. You can take my bed. I'll take the couch."

"No funny business?" she teases, instantly relaxing.

"You have my word."

"Then fine. I'll go home with you tonight."

"Six words I never dreamed I'd hear you say," I smirk.

Chapter Twelve

Harlow

"It's too bright," I grumble, struggling to pull the covers over my face to shield myself from the light suddenly shining into the room.

"Maybe that should be your indication to wake up." Miles chuckles as the side of the bed dips. My eyes shoot open, but it takes a moment for my vision to clear before his face comes into view.

He looks so good. My stomach twists at the sight of him.

"Good morning." His smile widens.

"Morning," I grumble, keeping the blanket pulled up over half my face.

"I thought you might be hungry so I made some pancakes and sausage if you're feeling up to it."

The mere mention of food has my empty stomach letting out a loud growl.

"I'm starving," I admit.

"Good." Miles pats my hip before standing. "Your clothes are hanging in the bathroom, and I left a spare toothbrush in there for you to use. Come out when you're ready."

"Thank you." I stretch, waiting until he leaves the room before shooting up in bed.

I remember everything that happened last night. I wasn't nearly intoxicated enough not to, but it still feels almost shameful waking up in Miles' bed. Then again I have to admit it also feels exciting at the same time.

I take a deep inhale, loving the way his scent seems to be engulfing me from every angle.

I look around Miles' bedroom, from the long mahogany dresser to my left, to the massive walk-in closet on my right, to the two nightstands on either side of me, to the huge bed beneath me. While the furniture fits the room nicely, it still seems sparse. There are no pictures on the walls. No trinkets or decorations of any kind. It lacks anything personal connecting it to Miles other than the dog tags draped over one of the bedside lamps and a small framed picture of him and his mom when he was younger by the alarm clock.

My need for food pulls me out of bed quicker than I would typically move after just waking up. I tiptoe to the ensuite bathroom, tugging off the t-shirt Miles gave me to wear last night.

Slipping inside the bathroom, I lock the door before quickly changing back into the navy romper I wore yesterday. I make quick work of washing my face and brushing my teeth before deciding to tie my long hair up in a messy knot.

I take a long look at myself in the mirror, trying to steady the drum of excitement coursing through me.

I shouldn't be excited. Hell, I should be embarrassed that I drank too much to drive myself home and ended up sleeping at my boss' place. And while I do feel a little embarrassed by everything that took place yesterday, the giddy butterflies I feel around Miles overshadows everything else.

I know I'm being foolish, thinking about things I shouldn't be thinking about, hoping for something I shouldn't be hoping for, but I can't help it. The more time I spend with Miles, the more time I want. The more I learn about him, the more I want to know.

"Hey," Miles says with a light rap to the door. "Breakfast is ready."

"Coming," I call back, pinching my pale cheeks to try to give them a little color before reentering the bedroom.

I lay the shirt Miles gave me to sleep in at the edge of the bed and take one last look around the room, deep down hoping it's not the last time I step foot inside the space. It's crazy and stupid and reckless of me to think this way, but sometimes you can't help how someone makes you feel.

After years of feeling empty and alone with Alan, Miles brings a certain danger and excitement to my life that I've been desperate for. The way he looks at me sometimes makes my skin burn. Like his gaze alone has the power to bring every single nerve ending to life.

It's unnerving and unsettling and yet I don't ever want the feeling to end.

I've struggled for the last few days to admit to myself that what I have is a 'crush' on Miles. But after last night I've decided it's useless to deny it. Not that I ever plan to admit it out loud, but admitting it to myself has made me feel better.

I'm aware that nothing can or will happen between us. For one, he probably has no interest in me. If he did last night would have been the perfect time for him to make his move and yet he was a complete gentleman. Other than kissing me on the forehead after tucking me into his bed, he didn't touch me once.

Not to mention the fact that he's my boss and my brother's best friend. If something were to happen and then go south, it would have a ripple effect on the new life I'm trying to build. And after everything I've done to try to regain some sense of a life for myself, that's the last thing I need.

Taking a deep breath in, I let it out slowly before turning toward the door. I stop mid-motion when I catch sight of Miles leaning against the door frame watching me.

"Crap." I jump, my palm flattening against my chest. "You scared me. Why are you standing there like a creeper?"

"Just enjoying the view." He smirks, pushing away from the door before turning.

"Whatever," I force out, trying not to take it the way I really want to.

He's just messing with you, Harlow, I tell myself before quickly walking after him.

Miles' apartment is incredible. It's in the heart of downtown, a newer building with a balcony facing the Ohio River. The whole place is much like his bedroom – modern furnishings but lacking any personal touches.

Miles slides into one of the stools at the breakfast bar before turning, patting the seat next to him when our eyes meet.

"I didn't know you could cook," I say, sliding onto the stool as I look down at the large plate in front of me stacked with four large pancakes and a few pieces of sausage.

"There are a lot of things about me you don't know." He winks, before quickly adding, "My mom taught me the basics. Pancakes, eggs, grilled cheese, and I can even make a mean boxed mac and cheese." He chuckles.

"All the important things." I pick up my fork, unable to fight the smile on my face.

After pouring a healthy amount of syrup over my pancakes, I cut into them, shoveling a big bite into my mouth seconds later. The instant the fluffy goodness hits my taste buds I moan.

"I take it you approve?" Miles turns his face toward me.

"So good," I agree after swallowing. "You keep this up, and you might never get rid of me," I warn, wagging my fork at him.

"Maybe that's my master plan." He gives me a cheeky smile that makes me laugh.

"I'm serious. You gave me a job, saved me from my ex, gave me a place to crash when I had too much to drink, *and* you cooked me breakfast the next morning. I could really get used to this."

"Bet you wish you hadn't hated me so much when we were younger? Being my friend does have its perks."

"I'm starting to see that." My words catch in my throat when Miles reaches over and runs the pad of his thumb along my lower lip.

Our gazes lock, and for a brief moment, I get the ludicrous thought that he might kiss me. The air pings around us and everything seems to slow down. One second, two seconds, three.

"Sorry, you had some syrup on your lip." Miles breaks the connection, quickly turning back toward his plate.

"Thanks," I force out, filled with both disappointment and relief.

"I texted Winston last night and told him you were here," he says before taking a bite of his pancakes.

"Thank you. I didn't even think about that," I admit.

"Who could blame you? I'm sure after Alan showing up the way he did your mind was occupied by other things."

"Yeah, that it was." I blow out a breath, refraining from telling him that *he* was the other thing my mind was occupied by.

"You should take the day off." He reaches for the glass of milk sitting in front of him and takes a long drink before turning his head in my direction.

"That's okay. I'd rather work."

"You sure you don't want to go home and decompress? Work will be waiting for you tomorrow if you need some time."

"If I go home I'm just going to obsess. I'd rather stay busy."

"Okay." He nods before turning back to his plate.

"I do need to call my lawyer though. She's going to have a field day when she hears he showed up here. She's been trying to convince me to push for half of the house and alimony, but I don't want to. I don't want anything from him except for his signature."

"So you're not getting anything out of this divorce?" Miles asks, swiveling his stool in my direction.

"Nope. I don't want it either. My lawyer thinks I'm crazy. And based on how you're looking at me you think I'm crazy too."

"Not crazy. It's just rare."

"What is?"

"For someone in your situation to not want to get everything you can out of him."

"I'm not a vengeful person."

"I don't think it's vengeful to take what you deserve for being married to him for so long, but at the same time, I get where you're coming from. Sometimes it's easier to wash your hands of someone completely and move on."

"Exactly."

"So how long until this whole thing is final?" he asks, swiveling back toward the bar.

"Hard to say." I shrug, shoveling another large bite of pancake into my mouth. "Alan has been dragging his feet. Even though I'm asking for nothing, he still won't sign the papers. My lawyer is pressing him, though. Threatening to take him to court where he'll be forced to have his dirty laundry aired. He'll never let it get that far. He holds his reputation higher than anything else. Probably why he's refusing to sign."

"So you think he wants you back because…"

"He's worried about what other people will think," I finish his sentence. "That's exactly what I think."

"Wow. He's a real fucking piece of work." Miles shakes his head.

"You have no idea," I murmur under my breath but loud enough that Miles hears me.

"How did you put up with him for so long?"

"I don't know," I admit. "I guess I got comfortable, complacent, and it was easier to accept what was, than fight for what could be. I knew I wasn't happy, but like I said last night, I don't think I realized just how unhappy I was until it was over."

"So how long do you expect him to drag this out for?"

"As long as possible. My attorney is only giving him two more weeks and then we'll take it to court. Unfortunately, if it does go that far, it could be months. But if he signs it will be over in just a few short weeks." I take a drink of milk before wiping my mouth with the napkin Miles set next to my plate. "Bet your glad you've never been dumb enough to marry someone," I tease.

"I don't think it's dumb to marry someone. At least not if you really love them. But it's definitely not for me," he quickly adds.

"No?" I question, keeping my focus on my plate.

"I would never be selfish enough to bring someone into this fucking mess I call a life."

"I don't know what mess you're talking about, but you seem to have your stuff together. You own a tattoo shop, which clearly makes you good money, you have an awesome apartment. You're kind and funny, and very attractive. I think you have a lot to offer someone."

"Did I hear that right? Did Harlow Cabell just call *me* attractive?" he teases, nudging my shoulder with his.

"Oh shut up. You know you're hot." I roll my eyes, shoving another bite of pancake in my mouth. "All I'm saying." I swallow my food before continuing, "Is that you have the tools to make someone very happy."

"I'm glad you think so. But unfortunately, I think you're giving me too much credit."

"And why do you think that?" I flip my gaze to him to find his eyes locked on me.

"Because things aren't always as they seem. You, Harlow, should understand that better than most considering what you're dealing with right now."

"Is that your way of saying you don't let the world see the real you?"

"Something like that." He gives me a sad smile before standing. Crossing around the counter, he drops his half-full plate in the sink, keeping his back to me while he rinses the food off into the garbage disposal. "Finish up, and I'll walk over to the shop with you to get your car." He turns and exits the kitchen.

"You don't have to do that. I can walk myself," I call after him as he disappears into the bedroom.

"Not a chance in hell. I'm walking you," he tells me, walking into the living room seconds later with his boots in his hand.

"Has anyone ever told you you're bossy?" I tease, trying to lighten the heavy mood that seems to have settled over him.

136

"Only every day for my entire life." He looks up at me and grins. "Now finish your damn pancakes."

"Yes, sir," I say dramatically, rolling my eyes as I turn back to my plate and do exactly as he says. Not that it's a difficult task considering they are probably some of the best pancakes I've ever tasted.

Chapter Thirteen

Miles

"What the hell is up with you today?" I look up to find Delia standing in the doorway of the private tattoo room I've spent most of the day in. I've been working on a back piece for the last four hours and am finally getting a chance to clean up and take a much-needed break.

"Huh?" I question, not really sure what she means.

"Don't huh me." She walks straight into the room and flops down in the chair in the center of the space. "You've barely said two words to anyone today."

"In case you haven't noticed, I've been stuck in here since four."

"Yeah, but I can always tell when something is off with you, and something is definitely off."

"Nothing is off. I just had a long night."

"Is that code for you spent the night fucking some random bimbo you picked up at a bar and didn't get any sleep?"

"Fuck you," I spit playfully.

"Nah, if you were getting a piece you'd be in a better mood," she teases.

"I'm in a fine mood," I argue.

"If you say so, boss man." She rolls her eyes.

"Is there a reason you're in here busting my balls?" I gesture for her to get up so I can sanitize the chair.

"There is actually. I thought you'd like to know that your girl is out there discussing ink options with Tubbs." She hops up from the chair.

"My girl?" I give her a confused look.

"Harlow."

"Not my girl." I shake my head, extending the spray bottle and proceeding to thoroughly sanitize the entire surface of the chair.

"Okay." She gives me a look that doesn't quite sit well with me.

"And what do you mean she's discussing ink options with Tubbs?"

"Apparently, she's decided to get a tattoo and Tubbs volunteered to be the one to do it for her. He even offered to do it for free. We both know what that means. He's hoping his generosity will land him a place in the new girl's pants."

"That won't fucking happen," I say confidently.

"Perhaps not, but he's sure as shit giving it his all."

"Why are you telling me this?" I tap my foot on the ground impatiently.

"Just thought you'd like a heads up. Figured if anyone were gonna ink her for the first time you'd want it to be you."

"And why the fuck would you think that?" I clip, trying to make it clear that whatever she thinks is going on with Harlow and me is inaccurate. Even if my gut instinct is to run out there and stake some kind of claim, I'd never admit that to Delia.

"Um, because she's Winston's sister. Remember, your best friend, Winston?"

"And?"

"And aren't you supposed to be looking out for her? Think maybe that includes not letting her get a tattoo from a guy who's only doing it to try to get into her pants."

"Fuck," I grind out, rubbing the back of my neck.

The truth is she's right. If anyone is going to give Harlow a tattoo in this shop, it's going to be me. I justify this by agreeing with Delia. I am supposed to be watching out for Harlow. But in reality, it's because I can't stand the thought of anyone but me permanently inking her body. One, because I don't trust anyone else to do it to my standard, and two, because at this point I'll use any excuse I can to be able to touch her.

It's fucked up, I know. But I haven't been able to stop thinking about running my hands along her smooth skin since I walked into the bedroom last night to see her sprawled out, asleep in my bed, way too much of her perfect body visible. The t-shirt I'd given her to sleep in had ridden up, putting her slender stomach and barely there panties on full fucking display. It took everything in me not to crawl into that bed and take her right then and there.

It's been the only thing I've been able to see since last night. It's like the image is burned into the back of my retinas and everything I look at is overcast by her almost nakedness.

"Go. I'll finish up here." Delia gives me a knowing smirk.

I open my mouth to argue but end up snapping it closed without saying a word. Nodding only once, I hand Delia the sanitizer and head out into the main area of the shop.

Chuck is prepping one of his regulars for an addition to his sleeve, but there's no sign of Tubbs or Harlow.

"Hey, Chuck, have you seen Tubbs?"

"Yeah, I think he's in Room C," he says, referring to one of the four private rooms.

I nod and spin around, heading back in the direction I came. When I reach Room C, I push my way inside without knocking.

"What the fuck do you think you're doing?" My gaze goes directly to Harlow who's laying on the tattoo chair in shorts and a pale pink bra.

"Tubbs is going to give me a tattoo." She smiles excitedly, but it quickly falls when she registers my reaction.

"Like fuck, he is," I growl, spinning my gaze to Tubbs who's standing next to the supply counter, a transfer paper in his hands. "You, out." I jerk my head toward the door.

"Miles," he starts, but I quickly cut him off.

"No one in this shop touches her, you hear me? Spread it around. If I find out anyone of you inks or pierces her without going through me, you'll be finding yourself a new job. We clear?"

"Understood." He nods once, hands the transfer paper to me, and quickly exits the room.

When my gaze goes back to Harlow, she's looking at me like I have five heads and I swear every ounce of color has drained from her face.

"What the hell were you thinking going to Tubbs for a tattoo?" I bite out harshly.

"What does it matter who I go to? I've been off the clock for the last hour," she stumbles out, apparently confused by my reaction.

"It's not about you being on the clock or not, Harlow. Why would you not come to me?"

"Because you were busy and it was kind of a spur of the moment thing," she explains. "Tubbs was in the back on break, and we got to talking about tattoos. He said he was free for the next few hours and offered to do one for me. I didn't really think it through. I just kind of accepted. I thought you'd be happy I was getting one."

"It's not about the tattoo, Harlow. It's about who does it. Tubbs is good, don't get me wrong. But I'm better. And if you're going to get one done, I'm going to do it. Besides, I'm pretty sure your brother would be pissed if I let anyone else ink you."

"So this is about Winston?" She gives me a doubtful look.

"And it's about you. A tattoo is forever, Harlow. At least if I do it, I know that it will be perfect."

"Um, confident much?" She crosses her arms over her chest.

"There's nothing wrong with being confident when you know you're that good," I smirk, holding up the transfer paper to get a look at what she chose. "Inhale the future, exhale the past," I read the scripted font out loud, my eyes scanning along the three small birds that extend out from the last word.

"I thought it was fitting. A reminder to look forward." She smiles softly.

If only she had any idea just how hard I've tried to do just that. To let go of my past. To forgive myself. But sometimes we aren't meant to move on. Sometimes we don't deserve to. Of course, I don't say any of this to her.

"Where are we doing it?" I ask, stepping toward the chair.

"Wait, you're going to do it?" she asks, her eyebrows knitting together.

"I thought we already established this." I let out a breath.

"Well yeah, but you don't have to do it right now," she objects. "I was going to let Tubbs do it because he was free."

"Well, lucky for you, so am I." I hold up the transfer paper.

"Are you sure? We really don't have to do this right now. You've been working all day."

"Harlow," I interrupt. "Will you shut the hell up and tell me where we're putting this?" I grin.

She studies me for a long moment before a small smile graces her lips.

"Right here." She leans back and traces her finger directly below her left collarbone.

"Okay then. You're sure about this?"

"I'm sure." She smiles nervously.

"You'll need to pull your bra strap down." When she does, I swallow hard, the swell of her breast making it difficult for me to focus on what the fuck I'm supposed to be doing.

Trying to keep my eyes on her collarbone, I press the transfer paper down on the spot she indicated, holding it there for a few long moments. I can feel her eyes on me, but I don't look at her. I'm afraid if I do I'll end up doing something I'll regret.

It's one thing sitting across a table from her. It's quite another to be this close to her when she's half-naked and breathing heavily in anticipation.

Once I feel confident that the design has fully transferred onto her skin, I peel back the paper and discard it in the trash can next to the workstation.

Luckily Tubbs has already prepped everything, so all I have to do is pull the tray next to the chair and sit down. Once I have myself settled, I slowly recline the tattoo chair, so Harlow is lying flat on her back before inching my stool closer, the tattoo gun in my hand.

"Last chance to back out," I tell her, dipping the gun in ink before holding it centimeters from her skin.

"Do it." She glances at me and our eyes meet.

"Okay." I nod, "Here goes nothing." The gun buzzes to life and Harlow flinches the instant the needle hits her skin.

"You okay?" I ask, chuckling at the grimace on her face.

"Yeah, it stings a little more than I anticipated."

"Well, it's only going to get worse so be prepared."

"I can handle it," she assures me. "I'll take this kind of pain over emotional pain any day."

I'm tempted to agree with her but decide against it, not wanting it to spark a conversation that may lead to yet another thing I'm unwilling to talk about.

Instead, I focus on my work, stopping a few minutes in to turn some music on before continuing. Harlow stays completely still, but I feel her heart beating rapidly against my hand that's pressed to her shoulder holding her in place.

Normally when I'm tattooing, I lose myself in the art. I forget about who I'm working on or where I even am. All I see is the art. But with Harlow, that's not the case. I'm hyper-aware of every move she makes, every sound, every little gasp she makes when I hit a sensitive area.

Her body is the perfect canvas, and I'm enjoying inking her more than I realized I would. I lie to myself and say it's because I get a rush being someone's first, but in reality, I'm enjoying having an excuse to touch her. To have my hands on her body and no one, including her, having any reason to question my intention.

I take extra care with Harlow. Paying close attention to the curve of the letters. Making sure each and every swipe of my gun leaves a perfect mark.

Because of the simplicity of the tattoo, it only takes me about forty-five minutes from start to finish. By the time I finish, her pale skin is raised and red around the tattoo but otherwise looks incredible.

I wipe away the excess ink on her skin and smile down at the finished product.

"All done," I announce, turning to grab a handheld mirror off the workstation before handing it to her so she can get a look.

She angles the mirror so she can see, her hand reaching up to trace beneath the ink as she stares at the reflection in the mirror.

"It's perfect." She smiles, turning her gaze to me.

"You're perfect," I say, wishing I could take it back the moment it leaves my lips.

I watch her expression shift, something dark stirring in her eyes. And try as I might, I can't stop myself from wrapping my hand around the back of her neck and pulling her face to mine. It's less than a second before my mouth crashes to hers, but the instant it does my entire body ignites.

Harlow opens up to me effortlessly, allowing my tongue to slide into her mouth and taste her. I hadn't realized until now just how badly I had been craving to do exactly that.

She moans into my mouth when I deepen the kiss and her reaction only spurs me on more. With one hand still around the back of her neck, the other slides along her bare stomach and across her back. With one swift jerk, I pull her out of the chair, her feet barely hitting the floor before my mouth is on hers again.

There is no gentleness to the kiss. I'm not soft or sweet, but rough and punishing instead. I've wanted to do this so badly that now that I am I can't control myself. I want to kiss her so hard that she'll still be able to feel me on her lips hours from now.

I don't think. I do. All I can see is her. All I can taste is her. All I can feel is her. All I want is her. And just when I feel like I've lost all control, a firm knock sounds against the door causing us to jump apart.

Harlow stumbles back into the chair, her fingers going up to trace her lips while I try to catch my breath and figure out what the fuck I just did. It's like all reasonable thought went out the fucking door, and now I'm standing here trying to figure out how it happened.

The knock sounds again, reminding me of what broke us apart, to begin with. I clear my throat and straighten my shirt, meeting Harlow's gaze for a brief moment before turning back toward my workstation.

"Yeah," I holler over the music.

The door swings open and Winston steps inside, catching sight of his sister laying in the tattoo chair topless.

"For fuck's sake, Harlow, put some clothes on." He quickly slides his gaze to me. "What the hell are you two doing in here? And why is my sister half naked?"

"I'll let her show you," I say, giving him a casual smile. As long as I don't act like he just interrupted me about to fuck his sister, he'll never know. Fucked up logic, I know, but right now it's all I got.

"You can turn around now," Harlow calls, and we both turn to see her sitting up, her legs draped over the side of the chair. "Look." She pulls down the front of her shirt just enough that her brother can see the fresh ink below her collarbone.

"Shut the fuck up." He smiles, taking a step closer to get a better look. "I can't believe you finally talked her stuck up ass into some ink." He looks back at me impressed.

"It was all her idea." I shrug.

"Damn, it looks good too." He nods.

"What are you doing here anyway?" Harlow asks, her gaze bouncing to me and then back to her brother.

While she definitely seems a little flustered, I don't think it's enough to give Winston the impression that anything was going on in here other than me giving her a tattoo. I'm not even sure he'd give a shit that I was kissing her. He'd probably just tell me not to fucking hurt her, and move on because that's Winston's style.

No, this is more about me than Winston. If Winston accepts that I'm into his sister, then nothing is stopping me from being with her. And being with her means hurting her and that's the last thing I want to do.

"I'm meeting Stella at Nicholson's. Wanted to see if either of you wanted to join," he says, looking to me and then back to Harlow.

"I love Nicholson's." Harlow smiles.

"I know you do. Hence why I'm here."

"What do you say, boss man? Can I steal her away?"

"Her shift has been over for quite some time. She's good to go." I turn, trying to keep myself busy by cleaning up the station.

"What about you?" He turns toward me. "You in?"

"I probably shouldn't. I've got a ton of shit to finish up here." It's a lie. But the last thing I need right now is to spend another night staring across a table at Harlow. I nearly slipped and lost all control tonight. I can't let that happen again.

I need to put some distance between me and this girl, and I need to do it now.

"You work too hard," Winston tells me, clapping me on the shoulder.

"So I've been told," I smirk.

"Alright then. If you're sure." He gives me one more chance before turning back to his sister. "Okay, looks like it's a party of three."

"Let me grab my purse from the back." Harlow slides out of the tattoo chair and quickly exits the room.

"She seems to be doing good," Winston says out loud, but the statement feels more like he's talking to himself.

"Well she's doing one hell of a job, I can tell you that." I slide my tray to the side before turning to face him.

"Thanks again for giving her this job. I know I wasn't thrilled about it in the beginning, but I think this is exactly what she needed. To put herself out in the world."

"Of course, man. It was my pleasure. Like I said, she's doing amazing."

"Okay, I'm ready." Harlow reappears before Winston can say anything else.

"Right. Okay." Winston heads toward the door. "We'll talk later. Maybe catch a beer later this week?" he asks, pausing in the doorway.

"Yeah, sounds good." I nod.

"See ya," he calls, slipping into the hallway.

"Later," I call back.

Harlow hesitates on the other side of the doorway. She looks up and meets my gaze, a million things running behind those big green eyes of hers, but she doesn't voice a single one. Instead, she gives me a small, hesitant smile and turns on her heel, following her brother out of the shop.

Chapter Fourteen

Harlow

"Good morning." I look up from the register and smile when Miles walks into the shop.

It's been two days since I've seen him. Two days since our unexpected and yet very welcome kiss. Two days and I swear my lips still tingle every time I think of him. Which is a lot. As in all the time. As in nearly every second of the last two days.

"Morning," he grumbles, barely meeting my gaze as he slides past the counter and heads toward the back.

An instant knot forms in the pit of my stomach.

I gather all the receipts from yesterday's transactions and quickly follow after him, wanting to talk to him about a program I read about that will make tracking purchases a lot easier than the one he uses now. It's mainly for my benefit, but it will make keeping track of tips simpler for the artists as well.

When I enter the back room, he's in the office, his back to me as he shuffles through one of the filing cabinets.

"Something I can help you find?" I ask, hesitantly entering the office.

"Chuck needs a copy of his W2 form from last year," he says, his back to me.

"Here." I dip into the office and kneel down in front of the small locked cabinet next to the desk. Grabbing the key out of the top drawer of the desk, I quickly unlock it and retrieve Chuck's file. I rummage through it for a quick moment, locating the form pretty quickly given how organized the files are now. Everything is in order with a small table of contents posted on the inside of the folder so anyone can locate what they need in an instant.

"2017, correct?" I look up to find Miles standing next to me.

"Yeah." He nods.

"Let me make you a copy." I quickly stand and cross to the printer on the far side of the room.

"Thanks." I hear Miles shuffle his feet, but I don't turn around to verify that's what he's doing.

There's this weird energy in the air. An awkwardness that up to this point hasn't existed between us. It's more than enough to put me on edge, especially after what happened the last time we were together.

Once the copy prints, I take it and the original and head back toward the desk, stopping next to Miles.

"Here ya go." I extend the copy to him. "When you have time I really should go through all this with you," I advise, kneeling back down to replace Chuck's file in its original order before closing the cabinet and locking it. "That way if I'm not here and you need anything you won't have to rummage the entire office to find it."

"Yeah, that's probably a good idea," he says, once again barely meeting my gaze when I stand and face him.

"Is everything okay?" I ask, not able to ignore how off he seems this morning.

"Yeah, everything's fine. Just have a lot on my plate today. Need to get some shit done before my one o'clock appointment gets here."

Sensing that's not entirely the truth, I bite back the urge to question the real reason he's acting strangely. Now is not the time or the place to have this conversation. Then again, it wasn't really the time or place for him to kiss me when he did, but that sure as hell didn't stop him. Not that I'm complaining. That kiss will go down as the hottest I've ever experienced in my life.

I've never had someone kiss me like that. It was like he was suffocating and my mouth was his oxygen. There was so much need. An almost desperation between us. It did something to me that even now I'm not sure I fully understand.

"You sure that's it?" I ask hesitantly, wanting him to know he can tell me, no matter what it is.

"What else would it be?" he clips, his words slicing through me.

I take a step back, trying my damnedest to hide the hurt on my face.

"Okay, well I won't keep you then." I nod once before quickly exiting the office.

After how closed off Miles was this morning, I made a point to avoid him as much as I could throughout the day.

He left for a little while, showing back up about twenty minutes before his first appointment. Again, he barely looked at me, and by that point, I knew something was up. And not just because he was busy or whatever lame excuse he gave me. No, something was up.

By the end of my shift, I have zero doubt that Miles' behavior toward me is because of the kiss. It *has* to be. I spent all day trying to convince myself otherwise, but at this point, there's really no sense in denying it any longer. We've spent nearly every day of the last couple of weeks together, and he's never once treated me this way. It's like he's put up a wall between us. A wall so tall I can't even attempt to look over it.

"Hey, freckles." I look up to see Tubbs just as he enters the office.

"Freckles?" I question, hoisting my purse over my shoulder as I prepare to leave for the day.

"It's my new nickname for you," he informs me, a smile playing on his lips.

"And why is that?"

"Because you have the cutest fucking freckles," he says, quickly closing the distance between us. "Here." He gently traces his finger down my nose. "And here." His finger slides to where my freckles extend to my cheeks.

"I can't believe you noticed." I hold my hand to my chest, my tone full of sarcasm. My freckles are pretty easy to spot, even if you're not paying attention.

"You don't have to be an asshole about it." He laughs, pulling his hand away.

"Telling a girl she has cute freckles is like telling her she has pretty eyes. Unoriginal and overplayed." I tap his chest, smiling widely as I slide past him and out of the office.

"You wound me, freckles," he calls after me, laughter in his voice.

"And you insult me," I call back, turning just enough to offer him a small wave before heading out into the main area of the shop.

"Hey, where do you think you're going?" It's only seconds before Tubbs catches up to me, following me toward the lobby.

I completely ignore him, though it does little to deter him.

"See ya, Bryan." I wave to the only other artist I pass on my way out.

"Have a good night, Harlow."

"You too."

"Hey, hold up." Tubbs' hand lands on my shoulder right as I reach the front door.

"Can I help you?" I play annoyed as I spin to face him.

"What's your hurry?" he asks, his dark eyes locked on mine.

"It's been a long day," I say truthfully. "I'm ready for a glass of wine and a hot bubble bath."

"You know, I have a huge bathtub in my apartment." His grin widens and try as I may I can't help myself from smiling in return.

"That's awesome. Take a lot of bubble baths, do you?" I tease.

"I'm just saying if you ever want to come over and use it…" He rocks back on his heels.

"Wow." I laugh, shaking my head at him. "Does that actually work on women?" I ask, calling out his game, or lack thereof.

"I don't know. I've never used that one before." He chuckles.

"And yet somehow I find that hard to believe." I reach out and pat his chest. "Goodnight, Tubbs."

"How about a drink then?"

"Going home now," I say as if I'm announcing it to a room rather than speaking directly to him.

"That's okay. I'm a patient man." He laughs. "If that's how you want to play it."

"I'm not playing anything," I tell him. "And technically I'm still married, so maybe you shouldn't exhaust your efforts on someone who's unavailable."

This seems to be a theme with Tubbs that's formed over the last couple of weeks. He flirts, tries to convince me to go out with him, and I blow him off with some excuse as to why I can't. It's always been in a joking manner, but as of recently, I'm starting to think maybe he really is interested.

I could totally see myself being into someone like him. He's funny, attractive, wildly talented, and makes me laugh, which to me is more important than anything else. Unfortunately, I can't seem to shake the thought of Miles long enough to entertain the idea really. Not that I'm anywhere close to ready to jump back into a relationship.

I think that now, but deep down I know that if Miles came to me tomorrow and said he wanted to see where this crazy chemistry of ours will go, I'd jump at the chance.

"Ouch. You're really killing my self-esteem here, freckles." Tubbs' comment cuts into my thoughts, pulling me back to the conversation.

"I think your self-esteem is doing just fine." I shove playfully at his arm.

"Good to see you two are cozying up to one another." My stomach instantly drops at the sound of Miles' voice.

Tubbs and I turn our heads in unison to find him standing in the doorway of the lobby watching us, his expression hard.

"I'm trying." Tubbs laughs. "She's not making it easy."

"Don't you have fucking work to do?" Miles clips, completely shifting the mood in the room.

"My next appointment doesn't come in for another thirty," he explains. "What the fuck has crawled up your ass today?"

I turn wide eyes on Tubbs who seems completely at ease as if talking to your boss in such a way is an everyday occurrence.

"Maybe I'm sick of seeing you try to tag the new girl. Need I remind you that Harlow is off limits." He takes a commanding step toward us.

"Harlow is off limits when she says she is," Tubbs counters, throwing me a wink.

The entire interaction completely dumfounds me, and yet, , like a train wreck, I can't seem to look away.

"You really don't value your job much, do you?" Miles taps his booted foot against the floor.

"Shut up. You're not going to fire me."

"You sure about that?" Miles challenges. "Perhaps you want to keep it up and find out. I promised her brother I'd look out for her." He gestures to me without once looking in my direction. "That includes keeping asshats like you from trying to get her into bed."

"Good to know you think so little of me." For the first time Tubbs shows signs of irritation. "For the record, you're worse than all of us. So remember that next time you try to play the knight in shining armor," he bites before turning his gaze to me, his expression instantly softening. "I'll see you later, freckles." He winks and quickly takes off through the lobby, jamming his shoulder into Miles' as he passes him.

"Would you care to explain to me what the hell that was?" I ask as soon as Tubbs is out of earshot.

"Tubbs is a whore. Trust me. I did you a favor." He crosses his arms in front of his chest.

"Newsflash, I'm a big girl. I don't need you doing me any favors. I can take care of myself."

"Clearly." He rolls his eyes and anger instantly boils inside of me.

"What the hell is your problem today?" I throw my hands up in frustration.

"I don't have a problem."

"Really? Is that why you kissed me two days ago, but now you can barely look at me? I hate to tell you, but you clearly have a problem, and whatever it is, you can leave me the hell out of it." With that, I spin on my heel and shove through the front door, the warm evening air doing nothing to clear my clouded brain.

"Harlow, wait." Miles follows me outside, grabbing my forearm to stop me from walking any further.

"Get off of me." I quickly jerk out of his hold and pivot to face him.

"I'm sorry." He takes a step back and holds both hands up.

"Sorry for what? For embarrassing me in front of my co-worker? For treating me like a child? Or are you sorry for something else, Miles?" Angry tears sting the back of my eyes.

"Harlow." My name comes out on a slow breath, and his shoulders instantly sag.

"What, Miles? What is it? What did I do?"

"You didn't do anything. It isn't you."

"Oh god, here we go. It's not you; it's me. Is that it?" An angry laugh bubbles in my chest.

"It *is* me," he insists, his voice going soft.

"We kissed, Miles. That's it. It doesn't have to mean anything. All you had to say was it was a mistake and move on. Instead, you've spent the entire day avoiding me."

"It *was* a mistake." I pull back like he's just smacked me right across the face. Sensing my reaction he quickly moves to explain. "I mean, it was, but it wasn't. I don't regret kissing you. I haven't been able to think about anything but kissing you again since it happened. But I'm not good for you, Harlow. Hell, I'm not good for anyone. I refuse to make you believe I can give you something that I can't. I think it'd be better if we keep things professional going forward."

"Professional?" I bark out a laugh. "For the record, I get to decide what's good for me and what's not. Not you. I've spent the last ten years allowing a man to dictate my life. I won't do that again."

"I'm not trying to dictate your life."

"It sure as hell seems like it from where I stand."

"Harlow."

"Don't." I hold up my hand when he moves to take a step toward me. "You say you want to keep things professional, then fine. That's exactly what we'll do. I'll see you tomorrow, Mr. Hollins."

I move to turn but freeze mid-motion when he lets out a frustrated growl and looks up to the sky, his fingers threading through his messy locks. It's like he's fighting an internal battle and I'm here, bearing witness to the whole thing.

"I can't fucking do this," he says more to himself than to me.

"Can't do what?" I ask, his gaze moving back to me.

"I can't fucking look at you, and not want to kiss you. I can't be around you and not think about touching you. I can't stand here with you without wanting to drag you back to my apartment and bury myself deep inside you."

"Then why don't you?"

"Because you're Harlow."

"And?"

"You're Winston's sister. He'd never forgive me for hurting you."

"Why are you so convinced you're going to hurt me?"

"Because I will," he tells me, his gaze locked on mine.

"Well, that's a chance I'm willing to take." Without a thought, I take one step toward Miles, wrap my hand around the back of his neck, and pull his face down to mine.

He doesn't fight me, doesn't for one-second attempt to stop me. Our lips meet and in an instant everything else fades away.

Chapter Fifteen

Miles

"Don't stop," Harlow pants beneath me, thrusting her hips upward to match my relentless pace.

She's getting close. After our second round, I began to learn her little tells. Hell, I've learned more about Harlow Cabell in the last three hours than I ever dreamed I would know about her.

Like how fucking sexy she looks sprawled out on my bed, completely bared to me. Or how unexpectedly wild she is, not afraid to beg and plead for what she wants, or take for that matter.

When I slid inside of her for the first time, and she whispered, *"Your cock feels so good inside of me,"* I nearly lost it right there on the spot.

This isn't what I planned. After kissing her, I spent the next two days hating myself for it. I know what fucked up looks like. I'm up close and personal with it daily. The last thing I wanted to do was bring

Harlow into my mess of a life, especially after everything she's been through these past few months.

I thought I could explain to her that *us* together in any capacity beyond friends is not a good idea, but then she looked at me with tears in her eyes and every ounce of nerve in me disappeared in a flash.

It just goes to show how weak I really am when it comes to this woman. One look and she completely flips me upside down. I don't understand it. I've never met someone who can melt my resolve quite the way she does.

After she kissed me on the sidewalk, I couldn't get her back to my apartment fast enough. We had half of our clothes already off as we stumbled into my living room. That's as far as we made it.

After fucking her hard and fast against the front door, I spent the next hour and a half learning her body. I studied her curves, pressed kisses to every inch of her perfect skin, and tasted her in a way I've wanted to taste her since that first day she walked into Ink*ed* with her brother.

After that, she climbed on top of me and took me so deep into her throat that I think for a moment my heart stopped beating. She worked me to the tipping point before sliding up, mounting me, and taking me inside her. I lasted less than two minutes, and I'm not even a little ashamed to admit it.

"Harder, Miles." Harlow's nails dig deeper into my back as her thighs tighten around my hips. "Harder."

Even though I'm convinced I have to be hurting her, I do as she asks and pound into her with so much force her head nearly slams into the headboard.

"Put your hands up, baby," I tell her, sucking her bottom lip into my mouth.

Once I'm sure her hands are secure against the headboard, I rear back and slam into her again, her cries of pleasure ringing out into the room around us.

Warmth starts to spread through me and I know I'm getting close. Repeating the action, I pick up speed, not sure how the fuck I'm even still going at this point. Sweat beads at my forehead while little droplets slide down my back. My body feels fucking exhausted in the best possible way. And while my muscles are begging for me to stop, Harlow feels too fucking good around me to even consider it.

"Miles." Harlow arches her back as her orgasm rips through her. She moans deep in her chest, and it instantly sends me over the edge.

Pleasure burns through my entire body, singeing a path from the top of my head all the way down to the tips of my toes. All of me trembles under the intensity.

Once the fog of my release starts to lift, I slow to a stop, dropping my weight down onto Harlow seconds before burying my face in the side of her neck.

"You are something else, Harlow Cabell." I press my lips against her raging pulse and lay a kiss to the soft skin there.

"I could say the same for you." She pants, still trying to catch her breath. "I thought the first two times were good, but that was…" She lets out a loud exhale without finishing her sentence.

"Yeah," I agree, finally rolling off of her before sitting up to deposit the condom into the small trash can next to the nightstand.

"I guess I should head home soon," she says moments before I feel her bare chest against my back followed by her lips pressing to the side of my neck. She peppers kisses up to my ear and then settles her chin on my shoulder.

"You're leaving?" I question, having not really considered that she would.

"I'm sure you're ready for me to get out of your hair and let you get some sleep." She starts to move, but I quickly turn, rolling my arm around her waist as I guide her back onto the bed.

"Stay," I whisper, my face hovering just inches above hers.

"Are you sure?" She looks up at me with those big green eyes, and I feel like all the fucking air leaves my body.

"I'm sure."

I roll over top of her and latch my arm around her from behind before tugging her into me, cocooning her body with mine.

"I didn't take you for the sleepover and snuggle kind of guy," she murmurs as she relaxes back into me.

"I'm not." I kiss her shoulder.

"Miles." She pauses.

"Yeah?"

"Can we do this again?" she asks, instantly bringing a smile to my lips.

"You can count on it," I promise, resisting the urge to grind into her backside. The last thing I need is to get either of us worked up again. I'm not sure either of our bodies could handle another round this soon. "Now go to sleep," I tell her after a long moment.

"Okay." She yawns around the word.

It's clear that she's just as exhausted as I am. The only real difference is that she'll probably be able to sleep a while whereas I'll likely be up in a couple of hours, if I can sleep at all.

"Goodnight, Miles," she whispers.

"Goodnight, Harlow." I flatten my hand on her stomach and focus on the rise and fall as she breathes.

I open my eyes to feel the warm sun on my face. Stretching my arms above my head, I freeze when I glance at the bedside table, and my gaze lands on the clock.

Shooting up, I look around the room, confusion the most prominent thing I feel. Certainly, my clock must have lost power through the night. There's no way it's eleven thirty.

I snag my cell phone off the charger and tap the screen, confirming that it is, in fact, that late.

How the hell did I sleep nearly nine hours? I can't remember the last time I slept that long. If I'm being truthful, I don't think I have since returning home from my second tour in Iraq.

Rubbing my eyes with the back of my hands, it takes my brain a full minute to catch up to last night's events.

Harlow...

I look around the room, but there's no sign of her or any of her belongings.

I throw back the covers and quickly climb out of bed, not the least bit concerned with clothing as I exit my bedroom and head down the hallway toward the living room and kitchen.

The apartment is quiet. The blinds are drawn, and there are no lights on. It's clear that Harlow must have left sometime while I slept.

Still feeling a bit disoriented, I return to bed, sinking deep into the mattress before tugging the blanket up to my waist.

My mind flashes back to last night.

Strawberry blonde hair splayed out on my pillow. Big green eyes staring up at me. Perfect porcelain skin soft beneath my fingertips.

I remember losing myself in her. Wishing I could bury myself inside of her, and never leave. And then I remember holding her. Counting each time her stomach rose and fell as she breathed. The calm that washed over me as I did.

I don't know at what point I dozed off. The last time I looked at the clock, it was nearly two thirty in the morning. The next thing I know I'm waking up nine hours later, wondering if everything I think I remember from last night was a dream – a much-needed break from the constant nightmares that usually plague my sleep.

But I know that's not true either. I can still smell Harlow all around me like her smell has imprinted itself all over my bed, and perhaps all over me as well.

"You're up." Harlow's voice startles me out of my thoughts, and I glance toward the doorway where she's standing holding two cups of coffee and a bag from Broad Street Bakery.

"I thought you left," I tell her, sitting up as she reaches the bed.

"I was going to, but then I thought maybe you'd be hungry. I bought danishes." She shakes the bag in her hand.

"Well, I'm glad you came back," I tell her truthfully, wondering how the hell I didn't hear her come in the front door. I must be more out of it than I realized.

She smiles, taking a seat on the edge of the bed before pressing a cup of coffee into my hand. "Black, two sugars."

"You know how I take my coffee?" I question, not able to stop the slow smile that pulls at my lips.

"Delia told me." She shrugs. "Guess she thought it was useful information for me to know. It turns out she was right." She sips from the cup in her hand before extending the small brown bag toward me. "Now, she didn't tell me what kind of pastry you like, so I got cream cheese, strawberry, and apple."

"I'm not picky." I drop the bag on the bed in front of me and open it with my free hand, pulling out the top Danish which appears to be apple.

"I prefer the cream cheese myself," she tells me, sipping her coffee again.

"Aren't you going to have one?" I ask, eating half of the pastry in one big bite.

"I had one on the walk back." She grins. "I was starving." Her cheeks turn the palest shade of pink when she meets my gaze, and I know she's thinking about last night.

Hell, right now I'm thinking about last night too, especially every time I look at her mouth.

I shove the remainder of the pastry into my mouth and immediately go in for another, afraid that if I don't, I'll have her pinned beneath me in a matter of seconds. Although if last night was any indication, I don't think she'd object.

But things feel different in the light of day. Last night I let my desire rule my decision and not my brain. Today, I need to proceed cautiously; at least until I figure out what the hell we're doing here. This is a delicate situation. Not only is Harlow my best friend's sister, but she also works for me.

"I also swung by the little boutique on the corner and got me a new outfit and some makeup. If it's okay, I thought I'd shower here and then head to work." She pauses. "If it's a problem I can always run home and do it."

"You can get ready here," I quickly interject, sensing her unease. It's clear she's not quite sure how to act around me, and I'd be lying if I said I wasn't getting some satisfaction knowing she's squirming a bit, no doubt wondering what happens next. I've got a few ideas of what I'd like to happen next, my earlier thoughts of proceeding cautiously exiting almost as quickly as they had entered. "There's no sense in you going all the way home to turn around and come back," I tell her, considering my apartment is only a block from Ink*ed*.

"Okay." She lets out a slow breath and tips her coffee to her lips, taking a small sip before resting the cup just above her knee.

"Under one condition." I wait until her gaze comes to me before continuing, "I get to shower with you." The color in her cheeks grow deeper.

"I thought after last night you would have had your fill," she says, a small smile playing on the corner of her mouth.

Grabbing the coffee from her hand, I lean forward and set both cups on the nightstand before swinging my

172

legs over the side of the bed and standing, the blanket falling away as I do.

I don't try to hide my obvious arousal or how pleased it makes me to see the way she reacts to me standing naked in front of her.

"It's going to take a hell of a lot more than one night to get my fill of you, Harlow Cabell." Leaning down, I scoop her into my arms. "We'll start with the shower, and then we can go from there."

Chapter Sixteen

Harlow

"It looks like it's healing nicely." Miles trails his finger along the border of my tattoo, careful to avoid touching it directly. "Does it itch much?"

"Not really." I smile up at him from my place on the tattoo chair.

He just finished up with a client, and I came in to see him, using the excuse I wanted him to check on my ink and make sure it was healing okay. In reality, I just wanted a few minutes alone with him.

"That's good." He pushes up, his hands pressing into the chair on either side of my hips as he leans into me. "I can't stop thinking about last night." He kisses me gently. "Or this morning." He trails his tongue along my bottom lip, and my hands instantly go into his hair.

"Me too." I practically moan at the thought, melting into him when he deepens the kiss, his tongue sliding expertly against mine.

I swear I don't know how it happened. How we went from barely tolerating each other to not being able to keep our hands off each other. It seems surreal.

"Maybe I should fuck you right here," he whispers against my lips, his hand sliding up my bare leg before dipping between my thighs.

I wish I could say I picked this skirt because it's cute and not because I was hoping it would drive Miles crazy, but that simply wouldn't be true. Lucky for me it seems to be working so I can't be too mad at myself for it.

The moment his fingers brush against my panties my whole body tenses, instantly craving the feeling of him inside of me.

This feeling is foreign to me. I've never been an overly sexual person. I honestly never understood what the big deal was. It was something I always did with Alan out of obligation, never because I really wanted it. But last night Miles opened my eyes to an entirely different world. He showed me so much pleasure and took my body places even I didn't know it could go.

I wanted to taste him, touch him, and feel him everywhere. And it's safe to say those feelings have only intensified over the last eighteen hours.

"Well, what are you waiting for then?" I finally respond, having been rendered speechless for a long moment as his thick fingers slid inside me.

"You're so greedy," he grinds against me as I move my hips in time with his fingers, causing waves of pleasure to course through my body.

"Fuck me, Miles," I practically beg, already feeling an orgasm coming on even though he's been touching me for less than two minutes.

"Shhh," he whispers against my lips before kissing me good and hard.

"Miles," I whimper, feeling the deep build start to work its way up.

"Come for me, baby." His lips are against my mouth, swallowing up my cries of pleasure when I explode around his fingers seconds later. "Good girl," he rasps, slowly pulling his hand away after the last waves of my orgasm have passed.

I reach for the buckle of his pants, nowhere near finished, when a hard knock sounds on the door.

"Miles, your seven o'clock is here," Chuck calls from the hallway.

"I'll be right there," Miles calls back, his eyes locked on mine.

As if suddenly remembering where I am and what the hell I'm doing, I quickly jump down from the chair and head for the door, feeling embarrassed by my actions.

"Where do you think you're going?" Miles cuts me off, spinning me around seconds before pressing my back to the door.

"I don't know what I was thinking." I shake my head, looking anywhere but at his face. "We're at work," I whisper yell.

"Harlow, look at me." He forces my gaze to him before continuing, "This is my business, and as long as I own it, I will touch you and fuck you anywhere and anytime I want. Are we clear?"

"Yes," I pant, his assertiveness super sexy.

"Good." He kisses the tip of my nose in an unexpectedly sweet gesture. "Now get your ass back to work. We'll finish this later," he tells me, promise in his eyes.

"Okay." I don't try to hide my smile as I snake my hand around his neck and pull his mouth down to mine.

"I was beginning to think you forgot where you lived," Winston says seconds after I step inside his apartment.

"Sorry. I had a few drinks last night. Crashed at Delia's," I lie, instantly feeling guilty for doing so.

The sad thing is, Winston would probably love Miles and me together. He loves Miles like family. But I'm not ready to share with him that I'm falling hard and fast for his best friend. Mainly because beyond the incredible sex, I don't know what, if anything, Miles wants out of this. Better to keep it between us for now.

"And you couldn't have called?" he questions, flipping off the television before giving me his full attention.

"It was late. I figured you were asleep. Besides, since when are you, my father?" I quickly add.

"I'm your brother. That's the next in line." He smirks, crossing his arms in front of his chest as he lounges on the couch.

"Uh huh." I shake my head at him before taking off toward my bedroom.

"Hey, you want to do Chinese food and a movie tonight? That new movie about the creepy porcelain doll just came out," he calls after me.

"Um, I'll pass." I stop at the base of the hallway and turn back toward him. "You know I hate movies like that. Besides, it's getting late, and I'm exhausted."

"Pussy."

"Really?" I cock my head. "Says the guy who slept on my floor for two days after watching IT for the first time."

"I was like twelve at the time." He throws his hands up in the air.

"Yeah, a twelve-year-old sleeping on his seven-year-old sister's floor." I laugh.

"You're never going to let me live that down, are you?"

"Never." My smile widens as I spin and disappear inside my room, closing the door behind me.

I collapse on my bed the instant I reach it, feeling both mentally and physically exhausted. Miles had asked me to come back to his apartment with him again tonight. While I really wanted to, after last night and then what transpired today at work, I felt like I needed some time to let my brain catch up with everything that's happened over the last couple of days.

I know it's silly, but I feel a little guilty about sleeping with Miles. Alan and I are divorced in every way that really matters, but the fact that it's not final on paper yet bothers me probably more than it should.

It's not about Alan. He slept with plenty of women during the span of our marriage. No, this is more about me and the person I thought I was. For years I had perfection drilled into my head. I felt like I had to be on point twenty-four hours a day and do everything a certain way. I guess it's hard for me to shut that part of myself off and realize that I don't have to be perfect because life isn't perfect.

Being with Miles isn't cheating on Alan. Being with Miles has nothing to do with Alan.

I let out a loud sigh, wishing I could purge my mind of Alan Nagel and never think of him again. Unfortunately, you don't spend nearly ten years with someone, six of those years married, and then walk away thinking you can erase them from your life.

I still hear him in the back of my head. The doubts he used to plant inside me boil to the surface. It's been months since I left and I still can't escape it.

Except last night I did. Last night I didn't hear his voice. I didn't think or fear or question. I acted on feeling alone, and to be honest, it was probably the first time in my life I've honestly felt free.

Miles Hollins has been a surprise and one I certainly never saw coming, but something deep down I know I've needed for a very long time.

It's hard not to overthink it – not to get inside my head and run through all the doubts and questions still swirling there. I've always been an all or nothing kind of person. I don't do well in limbo which is why I ended up with Alan. I rushed into the first thing that came my way because I was desperate for the security that relationships offer.

I won't do that with Miles. I won't make demands, and I won't push for more than he's ready to give. Hell, I'm still technically married, still fresh out of that relationship. I don't need to hop out of a ten-year relationship and into another one within a couple of months' time. I promised myself last night that I would let this unfold naturally, even if it goes against every fiber of my being.

I have to stamp down my urge to put an instant label on us and accept that things will work out the way they're meant to. Maybe it will just be sex for a while. Maybe it will blossom into something more. Maybe it will end in a fiery crash, and we'll both go up in flames. I guess at the end of the day only time will tell.

My cell phone chimes in my purse and without sitting up, I reach for where I dropped it behind me. Finally snagging the strap, I pull the small bag toward me and dig out my cell phone.

My heart instantly picks up speed when I see Miles' name dancing across the screen. I debate whether or not I should answer it for less than half a second before I've got the device pressed to my ear.

"Hello."

"What are you doing this weekend?" he says without as much as a greeting.

"I was planning on looking at a few apartments on Saturday, but other than that I don't have anything planned. Why?"

"Apartments can wait. I've arranged for Delia to take my two clients on Saturday so I'm free for an entire weekend for the first time in maybe ever."

"I wish I could, but I really have to start trying to find a place," I object. I'd much rather spend the time with Miles, but I really need to get this ball rolling. The sooner I'm out of my brother's apartment, the better.

"Too bad. You're mine Friday night through Sunday."

"Have I told you lately how bossy you are?" I smile into the phone, butterflies flapping around wildly in my stomach.

"Only like every five minutes." He chuckles. "I'll give you a couple of days off next week for apartment hunting. This weekend it's just you and me. I'm going to lock you in this apartment and not let you out for two days straight."

"Is that so?"

"Do you have a problem with that?" he questions, his tone giving away that he already knows I don't.

"I suppose I could make that work." I sigh playfully.

"Wear a skirt to work again tomorrow. I like the easy access." I can hear the smile in his voice seconds before the line goes dead.

I pull the phone away from my ear and stare at it for a long moment.

How the hell did we go from barely friends two weeks ago to ripping each other's clothes off in a matter of days? It's like we were two people yesterday and today we are two completely different people.

I drop my phone on the bed next to me and stare up at my ceiling, fighting the sudden urge I have to scream and dance around my room like a teenage girl.

Chapter Seventeen

Miles

"I think maybe we should eat, but I'm too damn comfortable to move." I kiss the top of Harlow's head that's perched on my chest.

"Five more minutes." She nuzzles deeper into my embrace, her hand sliding across my stomach.

It's Saturday afternoon, and we've yet to leave this room today. Part of that is because we slept late, having stayed up into the wee hours of the morning. The other part goes without saying.

Like the first night, Harlow stayed, sleep came easier and more peaceful than it normally does. I thought the first time was a fluke, but then after last night, I know without a doubt that it's because she's here. She calms my mind and makes me feel oddly at peace in a way I haven't felt in a very, very long time.

I've slept with more than my fair share of women over the years and not one has made me feel the way

Harlow does. She doesn't have to say anything. Just being near her makes me feel better. I can't quite explain why because I don't fully understand it myself.

"Tell me about this tattoo." Harlow interrupts my thoughts, running her fingers lazily along my stomach where a large tattoo stretches down one side and across part of my abdomen.

I look down at the large piece Dexter did for me not long after I started working for him. It's of three silhouetted soldiers huddled together in a field of poppies – helmets on their heads and guns in their hands. I had it done just a few months after I had left the military. To say I was struggling to adapt to being back on U.S. soil would be a complete understatement.

Those first couple of years were the hardest. Coming home when so many of my brothers never did left me with more guilt than I knew how to process. Hell, even now, eight years later, I still haven't been able to fully deal with everything that happened during my time overseas.

"Dexter did it for me," I say, clearing the knot out of my throat.

"The guy who used to own Inked?"

"Yeah." I nod even though her eyes are turned down toward the tattoo.

"Three soldiers," she says, tracing each one lightly with the tip of her finger. "Does it mean something specific?"

"Patterson, Rodgers, and Perez." It's the first time I've said their names out loud in years.

"They served with you?"

"Yep."

"Why poppies?" She moves her finger down, tracing around one of the flowers.

"Poppies are a symbol of remembrance," I inform her as I stare up at the ceiling, trying to push down the instant tightness that forms in my chest.

"What happened to them?"

"They were killed on a mission."

"Were you with them?" She continues to trace the tattoo with her finger, her touch keeping me grounded in some weird way.

"Yes." I barely get the word out. I haven't spoken about this in years, and it feels almost harder to talk about now than it did back when it happened. "There were four of us that got pinned down inside the building we were searching. One made it out. Three didn't."

"You were the only survivor."

"I was."

"I'm so sorry, Miles," she whispers against my skin as she turns her face into my chest to lay a gentle kiss against the top of my ribs. "I can't imagine what that must have been like for you."

"It was a long time ago." I try to sweep it under the rug in hopes that the conversation will end here. Only two people know what happened after my brothers were killed and I have no intention of adding her to that list.

As if sensing that I'm done talking about it, Harlow sits up and turns her face toward me, offering me a soft smile. "I think I'm ready for that food now." I know her change of subject is for my benefit and I appreciate it more than she knows.

"Oh yeah?" I grin, reaching out to tuck a chunk of hair behind her ear, my hand lingering on the side of her face for a few additional seconds. "What are you in the mood for?"

"I really want Sotto." She crinkles her nose at me. "But that means we will have to shower and get dressed."

"I don't know. I like having you here all to myself," I counter.

"Well, when you put it like that." She grins, tapping her chin as she thinks. "Oh, I know. Let's order pizza." She claps excitedly. "It's been probably two years since I've had a slice of pizza."

"What?" I laugh.

"I'm serious. Alan was always really particular about what we ate. Clean eating was my life. I think the last time I had pizza was when Alan was out of town on business and my friend, Andrea, came over with a loaded pizza and a big bottle of wine. Those nights didn't happen often, but when they did, I took full advantage."

"Pizza it is then." I grin as I sit up, grasping her chin between my thumb and index finger before laying a light kiss on her lips. "Anywhere, in particular, you want it from?" I ask, sliding my legs over the side of the bed. I snag my boxers off the floor and stand, quickly pulling them on before turning back toward Harlow.

"I don't even remember what they have around here. What do you suggest?"

"Goodfellas is the best. They don't deliver, but I could run over and pick it up."

"Are you sure? We can order from somewhere that delivers."

"You just told me you haven't had pizza in two years. This calls for Goodfellas. Trust me. You won't be disappointed." I extend my hand to her, helping her out of bed the moment she takes it. "Why don't you throw on something comfortable?" I pause, looking down at her bare body, my eyes dipping to her perfect curves. "Or not. I quite prefer you this way." I wink.

"You can't keep me naked all the time." She swats playfully at my chest.

"Pretty sure I can try." I grin, not able to resist the urge to lean forward and press my lips to hers.

"Food," she groans against my mouth just as the kiss starts to heat up.

"Fuck food." I sweep my tongue against hers, pulling her bare chest flush with mine.

"Miles." She half moans, half whines.

"Okay. Okay." I pull back, dropping my forehead against hers. "But after I feed you, I'm finishing what I just started."

"I think I can live with that." She smiles up at me, and I swear the fucking ground beneath my feet sways.

"Okay, you were right." Harlow leans back against the couch; her hands splayed across her stomach. "Best pizza ever."

"I told you." I grin, taking a swig of my beer.

"I'm so full I think I might bust," She sighs loudly.

"Well, hopefully, you saved room for dessert." I wink at her and the cutest fucking giggle bubbles in her throat. "You're adorable. You know that?" I can't help but say.

"Shut up." She shakes her head, turning her gaze toward the television which is quietly playing some property show in the background.

"And you're shit at taking compliments," I say, pulling her attention back to me.

"I am not," she argues.

"Really?" I give her a knowing look. "This from the girl who can't even look me in the eye when I tell her how beautiful I think she is."

"I'm looking you in the eyes right now," she says matter of fact.

"You're beautiful, Harlow," I say, watching her gaze instantly dart away. "Ha! There, see I told you."

"Whatever." She huffs, giving me an evil glare. "Maybe I just think you're full of crap is all."

"Or maybe you don't know how to take a compliment," I reiterate my previous statement.

She opens her mouth to respond but closes it when a soft knock sounds against the front door. She looks at me and then toward the door, her eyes going wide.

"Relax," I tell her, pushing to my feet. "It's probably just the neighbor needing to borrow something." I cross to the front door and look out the peephole just as the second knock sounds.

The instant I catch sight of red hair I freeze, glancing back at Harlow who's watching me curiously. I make the decision not to answer it seconds before the unwelcome visitor says, "I know you're in there, Miles. Your bike is out front, and your car is behind the building." She knocks again. "Answer the door."

"Shit," I grumble.

"A friend of yours?" Harlow shifts sideways on the couch, pulling her knees to her chest

"Hardly." I snort.

"Miles, open the door," Wendy speaks loudly enough that her voice filters into the room.

"Sounds like you should answer it," Harlow says, her expression flat.

The last thing I want to do is open the door and make Harlow face one of my more recent hookups. We certainly weren't dating so I'm not sure how else to refer to her.

"She'll go away." I shrug, walking back toward the living room.

"One of your girlfriends, I presume?"

I can tell she's trying to seem unaffected that another woman is currently standing outside my front door, but she's not doing a very good job of it.

"We were seeing each other for a while, but I haven't spoken to her in over a month."

"Seeing each other," Harlow repeats with an eye roll. "You mean sleeping with each other."

"If you want to get technical, yes," I say, knowing there's no reason in hiding it from her. Wendy was before Harlow even came back to town.

"Are you done sleeping with her?" she asks, looking toward the door when Wendy knocks again.

"Are you seriously asking me that right now?"

"Answer the question, Miles." She holds my gaze intently.

"I'm here with you, Harlow. I think there's your answer."

"So you're not planning on sleeping with anyone else?"

"Not so long as we're doing whatever it is that we're doing here. Are you?" I ask, snagging my beer off the coffee table and taking a long pull.

"I think you already know the answer to that." She stands and walks toward the door.

"What are you doing?" I ask, my eyes following her every move.

"You'll see." She grins over her shoulder seconds before unlocking the door and pulling it open.

"Who are you?" Wendy sneers the instant her eyes land on Harlow.

I make it a point to step out of her line of sight but stay close enough that I can easily hear what they're saying.

"You're Wendy, right?" Harlow's voice is sickeningly sweet, and I instantly bite back a laugh.

"Yeah, and you are?"

"I'm Harlow, Miles' girlfriend. I know you two were sleeping together for a while, but that's officially over. So if you don't mind, I'd appreciate it if you didn't show up here again."

I swear to god my jaw is on the floor by the time she's done. To be honest, I didn't think she had it in her to be so assertive.

"I, uh…" Wendy stutters.

"Have a great day, Wendy." Harlow switches back to her sweet voice seconds before the door slams closed.

"My girlfriend, huh?" I smirk when she turns back to face me.

"Well, what else would you have had me tell her? She needs to know you're off limits."

"Staking your claim." I nod. "I like it."

"Oh shut it." She grins. "And you're welcome. It didn't sound like she was going away anytime soon." She stomps back toward the couch.

"Yeah, she is a little stalkerish at times." I laugh, stepping in front of her before she has a chance to sit down.

"Seeing you put her in her place was hot as fuck." I smile at her.

"You have a foul mouth. Has anyone ever told you that?" She chews on her bottom lip to keep her own smile at bay.

"You love my mouth." I lean down, trailing my tongue from the base of her neck all the way to her ear in one long swipe.

"Seriously though, are there any other Wendy's I should be aware of?" She pulls back, narrowing her gaze.

"Um…" I tap my chin like I'm really thinking.

"Miles!" She shoves my shoulder and tries to step away, but I'm too fast. I snag my arm around her waist and secure her firmly against my chest.

"I'm not going to lie and say there haven't been other women in the last few months, but Wendy was the only repeat. All the others were just one time things."

"And that's supposed to make me feel better," she crinkles her forehead as she looks up at me.

"It should. I haven't been totally exclusive with someone since Rachel, but I want to be with you. I don't want to touch another woman or kiss another woman or even look at another woman. Right now you're all I want, Harlow."

"Right now." She calls me out on my choice of words, doubt swimming behind those beautiful eyes of hers.

"Hey." I tip her chin up when she tries to look away. "I can't predict the future. All I know is how I feel right now, and right now you're all I can see. When I'm not with you, I'm thinking about you. When I am with you, all I want to do is kiss you and touch you and hear you laugh. Can't that be enough for now?"

She stares back at me for a long moment before answering, "It's enough," she whispers.

"Now, what do you say we take this conversation back to the bedroom? Or better yet, how about we don't talk at all." I raise my eyebrows up and down suggestively.

"You're insatiable." She drops her head back and laughs.

"For you, baby, hell yes I am." I hoist her into my arms, loving that she instantly wraps her legs around my waist before her mouth comes down on mine.

Chapter Eighteen

Harlow

"This is really nice." Jackie pops her head out of the bathroom of the apartment we're currently looking at.

I decided this morning that I wanted someone to go look at apartments with me and give me a second opinion. While Miles was my first choice, he wasn't really an option after taking the whole weekend off work. So I called Jackie, knowing she'd drop everything to go with me because that's just who she is.

"I love the high ceilings and the open floor plan. It's small, but what more do you really need? For the price, I think it's the best we've looked at so far."

"Yeah, I agree." I smile, looking around the open space.

It's a loft style apartment about six blocks from Miles' building in downtown Cincinnati. It's close to Ink*ed* which means I could walk to work and return the car my father has been letting me drive since I came home.

While the building itself is not as new as the one Miles lives in, the apartment is really modern and well kept. It's one large room, set up like a studio apartment, and there's a small staircase in the corner that leads up to the loft bedroom. It only has a half wall and is open to the downstairs, but considering I'll be living alone, privacy isn't really an issue.

"I think this is it," I say, looking back to Jackie.

"I agree." She bounces on the balls of her feet. "Let's head back down to the leasing office and see about getting a deposit put down. You don't want to wait and risk losing this place."

"You're absolutely right," I agree, nervousness forming in the pit of my belly.

I knew moving out on my own would be different at first – a little exciting, a lot scary – but that eventually, I would settle into it just like I have all the other changes that I've gone through in the past couple of months.

My mind instantly moves to Miles, and I can't help the smile that forms on my lips. Out of all the changes, he's by far the best. Words can't describe how quickly my feelings have developed for him.

We've been 'sleeping' together for a week, and already I feel on the verge of professing my love to him.

I've always been someone that falls too hard, and too fast and once I do, I have a hard time letting go. I think that somehow stems back to my childhood and losing my mom. I know what it's like to have everything ripped away, so instead of being scared, I dive in head first and hold on with everything I have. Sometimes it's a good thing, sometimes not so much.

I have yet to decide if this is one of those times or not.

"You ready?" Jackie cuts into my thoughts, and I look up to see her watching me curiously.

"Yeah." I smile, taking one last look around the apartment. "Let's go."

After filling out the application for the apartment, Jackie insisted we go out to lunch. The apartment manager said he could have an answer for me in as little as an hour or two, so we decided to stay in the city a while longer in hopes that I can head over and sign the lease today if I'm approved.

"So." Jackie waits until our waiter delivers our drinks and walks away before leaning back in her chair and pinning her gaze on me. "You going to tell me who's responsible for the smile you've been wearing all day today or are you going to make me guess?"

"What?" I nearly choke on my sweet tea, picking the exact wrong time to take a big gulp.

"Oh, don't look at me like that." She leans forward, placing her elbows on the table. "I know that look, Harlow."

"What look?" I play dumb.

"The look that says you're falling in love. Or maybe you're already in love. Whatever it is, a mother can always tell."

My gut instinct is to correct her and remind her that she isn't my mother, but I immediately shove that away. Jackie has been more of a mom to me than she ever needed to be and for that, I will always be grateful. But I've always struggled a little with the guilt that carries. Sometimes it feels like my mom left and Jackie stepped in and replaced her, and that's that. I feel this need to keep my mom here, as my mom, even though she's been gone for years. As such I don't give Jackie as much credit as I should most days.

"I think maybe you forgot to take your meds this morning," I tease, casually taking another sip of tea.

"Is it someone you work with? I've always found guys with tattoos very attractive." Her grin widens.

"We are not talking about this right now."

"So there is someone." She lightly smacks the table.

"No, there isn't." I realize my mistake and move to cover my tracks. "I'm still married, remember? I'm in no place to start up a new relationship."

My phone chooses that moment to buzz to life on the table, and Jackie's eyes instantly go to the screen.

"It's Miles," she says, my stomach completely bottoming out the instant it leaves her lips.

"What… No. No, it's not," I stutter out, tripping over my words.

Her eyes widen in surprise, a slow grin spreading across her mouth.

"I meant, Miles is calling you," she says, gesturing to my phone just as I silence the ringer.

"Oh, yeah. I knew that."

"So, Miles, huh?" She nods slowly.

"Definitely not," I say, feeling heat spread across my cheeks. "Miles is my boss."

I've never been a very good liar which is why I typically don't even attempt it, but that doesn't mean I'm ready to admit that she's caught me red-handed either.

"Uh huh." She gives me a knowing look.

"Honestly, Jackie," I try again but stop when I clearly see it's getting me nowhere.

"How does Winston feel about this?" she asks, sliding the paper off her straw before dropping it into her ice water.

"He doesn't know," I say without thinking it through.

"So it really is true. You and Miles?" She practically bounces out of her seat in excitement.

"It's not what you're thinking. We're just keeping things casual," I say.

"Honey, I know casual, and what you're doing isn't that. You're walking around with stars in your eyes and that, my darling, is not just a casual relationship. It never is once your heart gets involved."

"Well, as far as he's concerned it is," I tell her, really not sure how he actually feels.

He said we're exclusive and that he only wants to see me, but that's all we've established. Not that I expect anything more from him at this point in our relationship. It's way too early, and honestly, I feel like I'm ten steps ahead of where he is emotionally.

"He's a guy. It always takes them longer to catch up," she says as if she knows exactly what I was just thinking. "For what it's worth, I approve." She smiles widely. "Miles is such a good guy. And he's pretty easy on the eyes too." She winks.

"Jackie!" I openly gawk at her.

"What? Just because I'm old enough to be his mother doesn't mean I can't appreciate that he's one fine piece of eye candy."

"He is pretty gorgeous," I agree, smiling.

"That he is." She nods enthusiastically. "But not only that, he's got a good heart. And lord knows after everything he's been through he deserves to find someone who makes him happy."

"Everything he's been through?" I question, assuming she's talking about his time away overseas but wanting to clarify.

"You weren't here when he came home. I've never seen a man more broken in my entire life. It took a long time for him to pick himself back up. Even when he finally did he wasn't quite the same."

"What was he like? After he came back." I can't help but want to know. Miles talks so vaguely about his time in the military even though I know it shaped who he is today.

It's obvious he still carries a lot of weight from that time in his life. Maybe one day he'll trust me enough to open up to me completely.

"Quiet. Withdrawn. We had him over for dinner a couple weeks after he came home. He was staying with Winston because his mom had just moved to Florida to take care of her own mother. He has no other family in the area." She pauses when the waiter reappears with our salads, waiting until he places them on the table and walks away before continuing, "He barely spoke the entire dinner. Your father and I kept trying to start conversations with him, but he kept his eyes down on his plate, shuffling the food around with his fork. I'm pretty sure he didn't take a single bite during that entire meal."

"Wow," I say, finding it hard to picture Miles like that.

"He had a hard time adjusting. He was in and out of support groups, but nothing stuck. But then he found Dexter, and I swear, that man saved his life. He didn't just give that boy a job; he gave him a sense of purpose."

"It's hard to imagine Miles like that. He always seems so strong."

"We are all weak at times. Even the strongest of us."

"Yeah, I guess you're right." I pick up my fork and push my salad around the plate, suddenly not feeling very hungry.

"But that's all in the past." Jackie claps her hands together. "Now look at him. And look at you. Sometimes God pushes us down, so we're able to find where we're meant to be once we get back up."

I nod, really considering what she's saying. Maybe she's right. Maybe everything happens for a reason and Miles, and I were meant to find each other. Not ten years ago when neither of us had any idea what we wanted, but now. I think it's true what they say. Timing is everything.

"Don't say anything to Dad, okay?" I request after a long moment.

"I promise it will stay between you and me until you're ready for other people to know. Until then, know I'm here for you if you ever need to talk."

"Thank you, Jackie," I say, realizing just how lucky I am to have someone like her in my life.

"That's what moms are for." She grins, shoveling a big bite of salad into her mouth moments later.

"Hey, sorry I missed your call. I was at lunch with Jackie," I say seconds after Miles' voice comes across the line.

"No problem. I was just calling to let you know that Caster Point called me to confirm your income," he says, referring to the apartment complex where I submitted my application earlier.

"Well, that has to be a good sign. If they weren't considering me they wouldn't be going through all the trouble, right?"

"I'd think not. Plus, I gave you a glowing review. Said you were the most reliable and hardworking employee that I have."

"No, you didn't." I laugh.

"Actually, I did. Figured if I could help in any way it wouldn't hurt to try."

"You can be incredibly sweet when you want to be. Has anyone ever told you that?"

"Shhh. Let's not be announcing that. I have a reputation to uphold."

"Is that so?" I giggle into the phone.

"So how was lunch? Did you and Jackie have a good time?"

"We did, actually. "She just headed back home. I'm headed your way now."

"You're coming to the shop?"

"Yeah, if that's okay. I know you said I could have the whole day off, but right now I'm kind of playing a waiting game and it would be nice to have something to do to pass the time."

"I can think of a few ways to pass some time." I hear his smile in his voice.

"I bet you could." I laugh. "But I really do have work I need to get done. This guy I'm kind of seeing is very distracting and making me slack on my duties."

"Well, we can't have that. Someone might complain to your boss."

"And then my boss might fire me," I counter.

"Not likely." He chuckles. "How long 'til you get here?"

"I don't know, maybe ten minutes."

"You coming home with me tonight?" His voice lowers.

"I would, but I think my brother might start to get a little suspicious if I keep *not* coming home."

"Well soon enough you'll have your own place, and it won't matter."

"Thank goodness."

"Well if you're not coming home with me, then I guess I'll just have to take you in the storage room and get my fix before you leave."

"So romantic." I sigh dramatically.

"You weren't complaining last time," he reminds me.

"I'm not complaining this time," I tell him.

"There's my girl." He laughs. "See you in a few."

"See you then." I shake my head before quickly ending the call.

Chapter Nineteen

Miles

"You going to get that?" I ask Harlow as her phone buzzes on the desk next to her.

"Yeah, I just have to enter this one thing." She types something out on the computer and punches the enter key. "There, all done." She lets out a sigh of relief.

I've been sitting here watching her work for the last hour, my sketch pad in my lap. I'm supposed to be working on a design for one of my clients, but instead, I've been sketching Harlow's face. I can't help it; she's just so damn beautiful. How could I not want to put that down on paper?

Harlow's entire demeanor shifts when she turns her attention to her phone. She hesitates for less than a second before picking it up and answering.

I watch ten different emotions pass over her face before a slow smile forms on her lips.

"Are you serious?" she practically squeals into the phone. "Oh my god, Monica. I can't thank you enough for this."

She pauses, presumably listening to whatever the other person is saying.

"Uh huh. Yep. I got it." Another pause. "Okay. I will. Thank you so much." She ends the call and breaks into a loud squeal seconds before jumping to her feet. "He signed!" she announces excitedly.

"Huh?" I question, having yet to catch up.

"Alan. He signed the papers!"

"That's amazing!" I stand just in time for her to propel herself into my arms.

"I can't believe it." She squeezes me tightly, her face going into the crook of my neck as I lift her from the ground.

I hold her for a long moment before slowly lowering her back to her feet.

"So what happens now?" I ask, keeping my hands on her shoulders.

"Monica will file the paperwork with the courts, and it should be final within the next month or so." She bounces up and down on the balls of her feet.

"Wow. That's fast."

"Since I didn't ask for anything, all we had to do was sign paperwork saying we agreed on everything. The only real problem was getting him to sign. But now that he has it should be smooth sailing," she rattles off, a little out of breath. "I can't believe I'm finally going to be free."

"We should celebrate," I offer, feeling about as relieved as she looks. I knew how heavy this was weighing on her and I'm glad that fucktard of an ex-husband wised up and signed. Otherwise, I may have had to pay him a little visit in Arizona – something I've considered more than once.

"Not yet." She steps back. "I don't want to jinx it."

"When it's final then?"

"When it's final," she agrees, her smile wider than I think I've ever seen it.

"It's a date," I tell her, pulling her back into my arms. "Are you sure I can't convince you to come home with me tonight?" I try again, hoping to capitalize on her good news.

"I really shouldn't." She looks up at me, laughing when I pout out my lower lip.

"Please," I playfully beg.

"You're awful." She shakes her head, her gaze going behind me seconds before she jumps out of my embrace. "Hey, what are you doing here?" I turn just in time to see Winston slide into the office.

"I have an appointment." His gaze slides to me.

"Fuck, is it six o'clock already?" I glance down at my watch, not sure how the hell time got so far away from me.

He nods. "What's going on in here?" he asks, his gaze jumping between his sister and me.

"Alan signed the papers," she squeals.

"Holy shit. That's amazing, Low!" Winston instantly pulls his sister into a hug.

"Thank you." She pulls back, her earlier smile returning. "So what are you having done today?"

"Not me. Stella."

"Stella's getting a tattoo?" Harlow seems a little surprised.

"She has four already," he tells her, chuckling softly.

"She does?"

"Yep, and this guy has done every single one of them." He hitches his thumb toward me. "Unlike me, she actually makes an appointment and waits months to get in."

"She does it the right way," I take a playful shot at Winston.

"I take it these tattoos aren't visible?" Harlow interjects. "There's no way I didn't notice she has tattoos."

"Shoulder, hip, lower back, and the inside of her ankle. All the places you wouldn't really notice unless she was in a bathing suit or something," I explain.

"Where is she getting this one?"

"On her foot," Winston answers Harlow's question.

"Oh, that's awesome. I was thinking about doing my foot next."

"You were?" I ask. "You know the foot is one of the most painful places to get ink, right?"

"So? I think I can take it." She squares her shoulders, her hands going to her hips.

"I tell you what. You hang around, and when I'm finished with Stella, I'll tat your foot."

"Seriously?" She arches a brow.

"Seriously." I grin.

"This is fucking weird," Winston grumbles pulling both of our gazes back to him.

"What is?" Harlow asks first.

"This." He gestures between the two of us. "Seeing you two all buddy-buddy. I'm used to playing the middleman to keep you guys from killing each other. It's just weird."

"Would you like us to go back to hating each other?" I ask jokingly.

"Nah, I'm not saying it's a bad thing. Just different is all."

"Come on, man." I clasp him on the shoulder. "Let's get this woman of yours inked."

"You coming, Harlow? I'm sure Stella would much rather gossip with you than have to listen to Miles and me." Winston turns toward his sister.

"I don't gossip." She crosses her arms in front of her chest dramatically.

"Yeah. Okay." He chuckles. "You coming or what?"

"I've got a few things to finish here first. I'll pop in when I'm done," she tells Winston before her eyes come to me. "What room are you going to be in?"

"Probably B. I'm pretty certain that one's open for the night."

"Okay." She nods, quickly turning and walking around the office desk.

I throw her one last glance before following Winston out of the office.

"How bad is it?" Harlow leans forward, watching me fill in the green vine that extends down Stella's foot.

I glance in her direction and for a moment lose my breath. That's what Harlow does to me. She takes my fucking breath away.

I've always thought Stella was attractive. The perfect match for Winston. Tall and slender with long blonde hair and sky blue eyes. But next to Harlow she blends into the background. Harlow is like the sun. When you look directly at her, you are blind from seeing anything else when you look away.

I expected for her to join us an hour ago, but clearly she was trying to make herself sparse. Don't get me wrong. I get it. Neither of us are ready for Winston to find out about us. At least not until we know where this is going.

I keep telling myself this is just another hookup and the fewer people that know, the better. But deep down even I know that's not the case. I think maybe I'm just not quite ready to announce that to the world yet.

"It's pretty bad." Stella cringes, pressing her head back into the chair.

"It looks awesome though." Harlow smiles.

"It better for how painful it is."

"Maybe I should reconsider." She looks down at me and then back up to Stella.

"No, you'll be fine. I'm just a huge baby." Stella swipes her hand through the air.

"It's true," I agree. "She's complained this way with every tattoo I've done. You handled yours like a champ."

"Thanks, I think." She switches her weight from one foot to the next. "Where's my brother anyway?" She looks around the room, clearly just noticing he's not here.

"I made him go out and get me an iced caramel latte," Stella informs her. "I'm in need of calories. All the calories."

"Women." I chuckle to myself.

"Hey, I heard that." I can feel Stella's glare on the side of my face, but I keep my eyes focused on what I'm doing.

211

Over the last couple of years I have gotten to know Stella pretty well, and while she can be a bit over the top at times, I love her for Winston. But I think I love fucking with her even more. She's really easy to rile up and poke fun at.

"Good. I meant for you too." I grin, dabbing the needle in more ink.

The buzz of my gun once again fills the room and the conversation lulls for a long moment. Harlow takes a seat on the opposite side of Stella and watches me from a distance.

Even though she's too far away to reach out and touch, it's the only thing I can think about doing. I can't wait to get Stella done so I can move onto Harlow. There's something about pressing the needle into her perfect skin that does something to me. With everyone else, it's just part of my job, but with Harlow, I'm leaving my mark, permanently etching myself into her body. It's a part of me she'll never be able to get rid of, and I like knowing I'll always be with her in that way.

"Did you hear anything from the apartment complex?" I finally ask, glancing up at Harlow as I dab the needle in more ink.

"No." She frowns. "The guy did say that it would depend on how quickly my background check came back. He said sometimes it could be within an hour or two while others can take up to three days."

"You applied for an apartment?" Stella joins in on the conversation.

"I did. Just a few blocks from here." Harlow crosses one leg over the other as she gets comfortable. "I love my brother, but I'm dying to have my own place. Besides, maybe once I'm gone you can finally move in there."

"That would require your brother asking me to move in with him." Stella rolls her eyes and huffs. "Besides, I think it would be him moving in with me. My apartment is way nicer." She grins. "Don't tell him I said that."

"Your secret is safe with me." Harlow pats her forearm. "Maybe you should ask him to move in with you."

"I've thought about it, but I'm kinda old fashioned in that way. I think he needs to be the one to ask."

"I get that. But then again you know Winst, it takes him longer than most to catch up."

"Well, he better hurry up. Otherwise, I'm going to find someone who's ready for the kind of commitment I'm looking for."

"I don't think you'll be waiting for that much longer," Harlow reassures her. "I'll be happy to give him an elbow to the ribs if you think he needs a nudge." She grins.

Harlow knows what I know, that Winston is planning on proposing to Stella. Or at least that's the last I heard, but it's not like either of us can say that to her.

"Who needs a nudge?" Winston steps in the room, clearly catching the last part of the conversation.

"Give me. Give me." Stella reaches out for her cup, ignoring his question.

"Give me a second, woman. I gotta figure out which one is yours." He turns, setting the drink carrier on the counter that lines the back wall.

I sit up, stretching out my back for a moment allowing Stella to move around for a second.

"Here." Winston steps up next to the chair and slides her cup into her hand before dropping a quick kiss to the top of her head. "Got you a regular coffee, man. Figured you could use the caffeine," he says, turning toward me.

"I appreciate that." I nod, taking a quick drink of the hot liquid as soon as it's in my hand.

"And for you." He turns back and grabs another cup out of the carrier before pivoting toward Harlow. "I wasn't sure what you drink these days, but I know this used to be your favorite."

"A non-fat vanilla latte with extra foam?" She grins up at her brother.

"That's what you like?" He looks momentarily confused. "Well hell, I thought you were the one who liked the Macchiato things."

"I'm just messing with you." Harlow laughs, taking the cup from her brother.

"Lord, you're as bad as Stella." He shakes his head. "These women, dude." He looks at me and grumbles.

"I'm going to pretend you didn't say that," Stella interjects, biting on the straw sticking out of her whipped cream covered drink.

"Say what, dear?" Winston looks back at her and bats his eyelashes.

"Pretty sure that only works for women," Harlow teases her brother.

"Bull shit. Why can't men bat their lashes and get away with shit too?"

"Because men don't have vaginas," Stella says loudly causing Harlow to nearly choke on her drink.

"On that note." Harlow stands. "I think I'm going to leave you three to it."

"I thought I was going to tattoo you next." I stop just as I'm about to press the needle to Stella's foot and look up at Harlow.

"I'm actually kind of tired. Rain check?"

"What she means is she has watched you torture me long enough and has decided she wants no part of it." Stella laughs.

"That might also be true," Harlow agrees as she turns, offering her stool to Winston. "Will you be home after this?"

"Probably not. I think I'm staying at Stella's tonight."

"Okay, well I guess I'll see you all later. Stella, make sure you send me pictures of the finished product."

"You know I will."

"If the guy from the apartment calls I might be in a little later than normal tomorrow," she tells me.

"No problem. Just shoot me a text and let me know what time you'll be in," I respond, wishing I could say a hell of a lot more.

"Will do." She nods before heading toward the door.

Chapter Twenty

Harlow

"Hey." I smile into the phone the moment Angela's voice comes on the line. I meant to call her weeks ago, but things have been so crazy, I haven't found the time.

"It's about time you called me." She sighs playfully. "I was thinking I was going to have to board a plane and fly to Kentucky to make sure you were still alive. You realize I've called you like twenty times, right?"

"I know. I'm sorry. Things have been insane. Catch me up. How is everything?"

"Really good." I can hear the smile in her voice. "Tom and I just found out yesterday." She pauses for a long moment, no doubt for dramatic effect because that's how Angela is. "We're expecting!" she squeals. "I'm going to have a baby!"

A combination of emotions hit me one after the other. Happiness. Jealousy. Anger. Sadness. Love.

"Oh my god, that's so amazing." I blink away the tears that sting the back of my eyes.

Don't get me wrong. I'm thrilled for my friend. But hearing this news, hearing how happy she is, reminds me of all the things I've wanted for so long that I'm not sure I'll ever have at this point.

"Thank you. I think we're both still kind of in shock. You know we've been trying for nearly a year. I was starting to think it was never going to happen."

"Well, at least it was a fun year," I tease.

"I wish it was. When you're having sex on a schedule, it becomes more of a chore. It definitely takes some of the sparks out of it."

"I guess I could see that," I say, having a hard time picturing sex with Miles being anything short of incredible. Regardless of how or why we were doing it. Now with Alan, that was a completely different story. It always felt like a chore no matter what.

"So what's new with you? Tell me everything. I feel like I haven't talked to you in forever."

"I don't even know where to begin," I admit, letting my mind drift back to just how much has happened since I returned home.

"Let's start with the most pressing matter. How's everything with Alan? Have you spoken to him since you've been home?"

"Actually, he showed up here a couple of weeks ago."

"Shut up!"

"Oh yeah. Decided to come to my new job and make a scene. Thank god my boss is my brother's best friend otherwise he might have cost me my job."

"Oh lord. The nerve of that man."

"Tell me about it. Just when I thought things were starting to quiet down, there he is. But, on the plus side, Monica called me a couple of days ago. Alan finally signed the paperwork."

"That's amazing news, Harlow. Did she say how long before it will be final?"

"A month. Maybe longer. Either way, we're in the home stretch."

"I can only imagine how relieved you must feel to almost have this behind you."

"That's for sure." I let out a slow breath.

"So you said he showed up at your new job? Where are you working?"

"I'm working at Ink*ed*. It's a tattoo shop my brother's friend, Miles, owns. I mainly manage the files, do payroll, state forms, and make sure everything is in compliance."

"So you're pretty much running the business."

"The back side of it, yes."

"That's awesome. It looks like you can actually put that degree to use after all."

"Yeah. I was definitely worried that I wouldn't be able to find something, but then Miles stepped in and saved the day." I look up at the apartment building in front of me.

I left work an hour ago, telling Miles I was heading home, which I was planning to do. But then instead of merging onto the freeway as I should have, I found myself turning in the opposite direction. Now here I sit, in the parking lot of his complex, anxiousness swimming in my stomach at the thought of him coming home and finding me here.

I haven't stayed with him for the last three nights, despite his efforts to get me to do just that. I had needed a moment to clear my head a little. It feels like everything is moving so quickly, and honestly, I'm afraid of how fast I've fallen for him. And no matter how badly I want this to work out, there's this little voice in the back of my head telling me to enjoy it while it lasts because it won't last forever.

I'm trying to balance myself so that when this ends, I've established some semblance of a life outside of Miles. But tonight, I don't know. The urge to be with him was just too overwhelming to resist.

We've found time to *be* together, but sex in the office or locked in one of the tattoo rooms isn't the same as being able to take our time without worrying about someone hearing us. Plus there's the whole falling asleep in each other's arms afterward, which is by far my favorite part.

"Is that a smile I hear?" Angela pulls me back to the conversation, and it takes me a second to remember what we were talking about.

"What?"

"Who is this Miles person again?"

"He's been Winston's friend since they were little," I say, not mentioning that I used to hate him and now I'm pretty certain I'm in love with him.

Pretty certain? I chuckle internally. More like one hundred percent certain. The way I feel about Miles is unlike the way I've ever felt about another person before, and that includes when Alan and I were just dating, and things were really good between us. There's something different there with Miles.

"And my new boss," I tack on even though I already said that part.

"Is that all?" she questions.

"What else would there be?"

"I don't know. You just sound funny all of a sudden."

"I do?"

"Now you sound guilty." She laughs.

I swear this girl knows me better than anyone. Then again, we did live together for four years during college and remained very close after Alan, and I married, despite his efforts to keep us apart.

Alan hated that I had anyone in my life that I cared about outside of him. He thought he should be my one and only focus. Because of it, I pulled back a lot from Angela over the years while I was married, but she never let me slip too far away. She clearly saw what was happening and, like a true friend, she stuck by me even when I didn't really deserve her.

"He may also be the guy I'm sleeping with," I admit after a long pause, a wide smile sliding across my face.

"Shut up!" She squeals in my ear. "I knew it! The instant you mentioned his name something changed in your voice."

"You know me so well it's scary." I laugh.

"Tell me everything. I want every single detail."

I spend the next twenty minutes filling Angela in on everything that's transpired over the last few weeks. From the kiss in the tattoo room to the next day when he was cold and distant, to that night when he kissed me outside and we couldn't get back to his apartment fast enough.

About how happy he makes me. How alive I feel when I'm with him. And like she always does, Angela just listens. She doesn't judge or give me a hard time for sleeping with someone while I'm still married. In fact, based on her reaction I'd say she's pretty proud of me for putting myself back out there.

I'm so lost in my conversation with Angela that I don't notice Miles arriving home until I look up to find him watching me through the windshield of my car, a wide smile on his handsome face.

"Angela, I have to go," I blurt, cutting her off mid-sentence.

"He's there?" she guesses, considering I told her a few minutes ago that I was at his place waiting for him to get home.

"Yep." I smile, my gaze locked on him as he stalks around the car and jerks the door open.

"Okay, you two have fun. And call me sooner next time, yeah?"

"I will, I promise. Love you, Ang."

"Love you too."

My finger lands on the end call button seconds before Miles hoists me out of the car. He slams the door shut and instantly backs me against it.

"I thought you were going home tonight." He grins, his face dipping down until it's an inch away from mine.

"I changed my mind." I shrug like it's no big deal. "You got a problem with that?"

"What do you think?" He speaks against my lips before his mouth closes down around mine.

He kisses me so slow and deep that by the time he pulls away, I'm questioning how in the hell my legs are still supporting my weight.

"I think you're happy to see me?" I phrase it like a question.

"You think right." He chuckles, stepping back before taking my hand and pulling me toward his apartment building.

Like most times when Miles and I are together, there's not a ton of lead up. It's like the second we kiss we can't keep our hands off each other.

We no more than step in the front door before he has me pressed against it, his mouth devouring mine.

"Fuck I've missed you," he groans against my mouth.

"You just saw me an hour ago," I remind him, grabbing the hem of his shirt before pulling upward. He ducks down slightly to make it easier for me to pull the material over his head.

I take a long moment to appreciate the sight in front of me. Miles' body is what fantasies are made of. Broad shoulders, lean muscle, toned six-pack, dark hair peppering his chest and abdomen, and various pops of color everywhere from his tattoos. He's so perfect. Sometimes it's hard to believe he's real.

I run my hand down his chest and across the ripple of his muscles, biting my bottom lip to hold in the groan building in my throat. I never knew it was possible to be this turned on by only looking at someone.

"An hour is too long." Miles meets my gaze, a knowing smirk on his face. "Like what you see?"

"You know I do," I say, my hands going to the buckle of his jeans.

He looks down and watches me with hooded eyes as I pop open the button and slowly slide the zipper down before pushing the material open.

Sliding my hands to either side of his waistband, I grab the fabric and tug down. Miles pushes his weight to one side, kicking off his shoe before stepping out of his pant leg. Repeating the same to the other side, he abandons his jeans on the floor as he steps forward, taking me with him as he guides us toward the couch.

The instant the backs of my knees hit the leather sofa, I collapse onto my back. Miles hovers over me, stripping me bare, layer by layer until every inch of my body is exposed. Normally I would feel self-conscious having someone look at me so openly, but Miles has a way of making me feel sexy.

"Do you know how badly I've missed being able to see you like this?" His eyes trace across my bare chest and down my stomach.

"Pretty sure you saw me like this earlier today."

"Not like this. Not when I could stand and appreciate how incredibly beautiful you are."

His words send a flutter through my chest, and I instinctively reach for him.

Grabbing his hand I pull, and without hesitation, he lowers himself down, giving me exactly what I want. To feel his weight on top of me.

"I don't have a condom." He moves to get back up, but I stop him.

"You don't need one. I'm on birth control, and I trust you."

"You're sure?"

"I'm sure." I lean up and press my lips to his.

"Tell me what you want, Harlow." He sucks my bottom lip into his mouth.

"You." I moan when I feel the heaviness of his arousal at my entrance.

"You want me, or you want this?" He inches forward, pressing into me slowly.

"All of you." I arch my back as he fills me completely in one fluid movement.

"I want all of you," he whispers against my mouth, pulling out and pushing back in so slowly it's like some sweet form of torture. "Not just this." He slides deep and then retreats. "But this too." He drops his face and kisses right above my heart.

I swear to god it feels like the floor is crumbling beneath me and suddenly I'm free falling. Down, down I go with no hopes of ever finding the ground again.

"Miles," I whimper, his emotional and physical assault making me feel way too many things all at the same time.

"I want this, Low. All of it." He starts to speed up, pressing me deeper into the couch. I slide my legs up and lock them around his waist.

"Me too." I meet his gaze, my hands going to either side of his face. "Me too," I repeat.

"God." He groans openly. "You feel so fucking good." He leans forward and kisses me, his tongue sliding against mine in a way that makes my toes curl. "I'm not going to last, baby." He strains out the words, sending my already building orgasm barreling out of control.

I cry out as my body explodes around him. Waves of pleasure assault every single one of my senses and the feeling is only intensified when I feel Miles' release spill inside of me. Warming me from the inside out.

"What are you doing to me, woman?" He drops his face into the crook of my neck as he tries to catch his breath.

"I could ask you the same question." I smile, running my hand lazily through his hair.

He pulls back and looks down at me, a sudden seriousness on his face.

"I meant what I said. I want this, with you." He reaches out and pushes my hair away from my face.

"Me too," I agree without a moment of hesitation.

"I mean for real, Harlow. As in, I want to tell Winston."

"What?" I stare up at him in shock.

"I don't want to keep us a secret. I want to take you out on dates and kiss you whenever the hell I want without worrying who might see us."

"I want that too, but…"

"No buts. Do you want to be with me?"

"You know I do."

"Then it's time we go public."

"You're sure about this?" I smile up at him, my heart beating so hard, it's a wonder it's not pounding out of my chest.

"A million percent."

"But I'm still married."

"Only on paper and not for much longer. Your legal marital status holds no weight in this decision."

"Do you think he's going to freak out?" I ask, suddenly incredibly nervous.

"Who, Winston?" He cocks a brow, waiting until I nod before answering. "Nah, I think he'll be cool with it. I'm more worried about your dad." He chuckles, dropping a kiss to my nose.

He slides out of me and sits up, grabbing my hand to pull me up with him.

"Really?" I laugh. "I think Winston is scarier than my dad."

"Not when it comes to you," he disagrees.

"Well if it helps, Jackie already knows," I tell him, kneading my lower lip nervously.

"She does?"

"She guessed when we were at lunch the other day. I tried to deny it but…"

"You're an awful liar," he says on a laugh. "And how did she take the news?"

"Really well actually."

"Well, there's one less person we have to tell." He grins, pulling me closer before laying a kiss to my temple.

"Aren't you worried?" I voice my concern.

"Why would I be worried?" He entwines his fingers with mine before resting our adjoined hands on his stomach.

"I don't know. I mean, if things between us don't work out…" I trail off.

"The way I see it, we're already past the point of no return. Telling people doesn't change that. Besides," he pauses, releasing my hand to hoist me into his lap. I go willingly, settling my knees on either side of him. "I can't see myself wanting to let this go anytime soon." He grins, gently trailing his hands down my sides, goose bumps peppering my skin.

"So you're just with me for my body," I joke, looping my hands around the back of his neck.

"Among other things." He nudges upward, making me aware of his growing erection.

"Already?" I smile, lowering my face to his.

"What can I say, he likes you." He chuckles against my lips.

"Well he's lucky because I like him too," I murmur, reaching down to grasp his length in my hand. Pressing up slightly, I slowly lower myself down onto him, inch by painfully slow inch until he's buried deep inside of me.

Chapter Twenty-one

Miles

"Hey." I step into the doorway of Harold's office and lightly rap on the open door.

"Hey." He smiles, closing the laptop in front of him. "I didn't know you were stopping in today." He gestures for me to come inside.

"Actually, I was looking for Winston," I say, sliding down into one of the hard metal chairs that sit opposite the desk.

"You just missed him. He went to lunch with Stella but should be back in about an hour. Anything I can help you with?"

"Well," I clear my throat. "Actually there is. I was going to have this conversation with Winston first, but I guess it can wait until he's back."

"Well, what is it, son? Everything okay with you?" Harold leans back in his chair, crossing his arms in front of his chest.

The sounds of the car shop filter in through the open door and for a moment I consider closing it to give us a little more privacy. Then I decide it might be better to keep it open in case he reacts badly to what I'm about to say.

"Yeah, everything is fine. It's just…" I take a deep inhale and blow it out slowly. "I just wanted to come here and let you know that I like your daughter. More than like, actually. I'm falling pretty hard for her. And I want to let everyone know that we have decided to officially be together," I force the words out so quickly they all end up running together.

I brace myself for whatever reaction he might throw my way, mentally trying to prepare myself for any outcome.

When a slow smile moves across his mouth, I'm not sure what to make of it. But then he tilts his head back and lets out a full belly laugh – one that bounces off the walls around us.

"Well hot damn." He smacks the desk in front of him excitedly. "That's the best news I've heard in some time."

"It is?" I openly gawk at him. Sure he must be losing his damn mind.

"Of course it is."

"Sir, I…"

"Let me guess. You thought I'd be upset?"

"Truthfully, yeah. I guess I did." I let my shoulders sag forward.

"And why would you think that, Miles? Why would you ever think I'd be anything short of ecstatic?"

"Well, honestly, because I think she can do better, and I think you know she can too."

"Son, they don't get much better than you."

"I'm going to have to disagree with you there, Harold." I shake my head, knowing he would disagree too if he truly knew the person I am.

Harold knew me as a child, and even though I came back from the military a much different person, I allowed him to believe I was still the guy his son grew up with. Obviously, he could see some of the changes in me, everyone could. There were simply some things I could not cover up. But eventually I got better at hiding those parts of me, and now it's almost like second nature. Like hiding behind this fake façade *is* who I am now.

Except with Harlow. She's the only one that makes me feel real. The only one that makes me feel safe. The only one I don't try to hide from. Then again, that's not entirely true either. Because I'm still hiding one of the most significant parts of myself – even from her.

I keep saying I'll tell her eventually and I will, but the truth is, Harlow and I are still so new and laying something like that on her right out of the gate is a sure fire way to ensure this relationship goes nowhere. And I want it to go somewhere. As shocked as I am to admit that to myself, I really do.

In just a few short weeks' time, Harlow has changed my entire life. I went from barely existing, having to force myself through every second, to looking forward to what the day will bring, and the next day, and the day after that.

The future.

It's something I haven't really thought about in years.

"You just told me that a man I love and respect is going to be taking care of my little girl." Harold's response breaks into my thoughts, as he leans forward to place his elbows on the desk in front of him. "Why would I be anything but over the moon right now?"

"So you're okay with this?" I question again, needing additional confirmation even though he's done nothing but give me just that since I told him about my feelings for Harlow.

"I'm more than okay with it." He smiles. "You know you're like a son to me, Miles. And I know how hard of a time you've had these past few years. You deserve to be happy, and so does Harlow. If you two can find that together, then even better."

"Thanks, Harold." I let out a breath and release some of the tension in my back by resting it against the back of the chair.

"Now let's hope Winston will be as accepting as you are." I look up and meet his gaze.

"He's Winston." He swipes his hand through the air. "Even if he doesn't like it at first he'll get over it."

"Get over what?" Winston suddenly appears in the doorway, his gaze bouncing from his father, to me, and then back to his father.

"I thought you were at lunch." Harold looks at his son.

"Left my wallet." He shrugs, crossing toward the large filing cabinet at the back of the office. Pulling open the top drawer, he reaches inside, retrieves his wallet, and shoves it in his back pocket before turning back toward me. "What's up? Why are you here?"

"Miles just came by to talk," Harold says, standing from his chair. "I'm going to go check on the boys. See if anyone needs anything." He gives me a wink and quickly slides out of the office without another word.

"What the hell was that about?" Winston gestures toward the door of the office. "Is it just me or is he acting kind of weird?"

"I don't think he's acting weird," I disagree. "Is Stella downstairs waiting on you or do you have a minute to talk?" I ask, feeling my earlier tension and nerves as they return in full force.

"She's waiting, but I can give you a minute." He snags the chair next to me, angling it in my direction before taking a seat. "What's up?"

"Okay, so before I say anything, I need you to know that you're like a brother to me and I would never do anything to jeopardize that."

"Shit. This must be bad. What the fuck did you do?" He sighs, adjusting the ball cap on his head.

"You're probably going to be pissed." I try my best to prepare him.

"Dude, spit it out already. The way you're acting I'm gonna start thinking the worst. Like you're fucking my sister or something," he blurts. The smile that appears on his face instantly falls when he catches my expression. "No?" He sits up straighter. "No fucking way." He shakes his head slowly from side to side.

"I think I'm in love with her, man," I admit, watching his eyes widen even further.

"What the fuck?" He looks at me like he has no idea who I am, but oddly enough there's not a hint of anger in his voice. Confusion, definitely, but no anger. "Is that what you were in here talking to Dad about? Did you tell him too?"

I nod slowly. "I did."

"And what did he have to say?"

"He's happy for us."

"Happy for you." Winston snorts. "Of course he's happy for you. Because if Harlow's with you then he doesn't have to worry about her leaving home again."

I try not to take offense to his statement, knowing I've really caught him off guard.

"Look, I didn't plan for this. I was just trying to help her out by giving her a job. I didn't know working with her every day would lead to this. It just happened."

"How long?" he cuts me off.

"Around a month."

"A month?" He stands, shoving the chair backward. "And you just conveniently forgot to tell me? Like that's not information, I need to know?" Hurt masked as anger covers his face and I quickly move to explain.

"I didn't know it would turn into this. I didn't want to make a big deal out of it by telling everyone until I knew for sure."

"Knew what?"

"That I wanted to be with her."

"So you fucked her but didn't know if you wanted to be with her, but now you do know so you're coming clean to something you should have told me a month ago."

"It wasn't like that, Winst. I swear. Man, it just happened so fucking fast, and I was trying to process it all. You know how I am." I push to a stand, turning to face him head-on.

"Yeah, you're right. I do know how you are. Meaning, I know how quickly you move through women."

"Harlow isn't like any of those other women, Winston. The fact that I'm telling you I'm in love with her should speak for itself. When have I ever said that to you about someone?"

"Does she know?" His voice levels out.

"Know what?"

"That you're in love with her?"

"Not yet." I shake my head.

"And why is that?"

"Because I don't think she's ready to hear it."

"You don't think she's ready to hear it or you're not ready to say it?" he questions.

"Maybe a little bit of both," I admit truthfully. "But it doesn't make it any less true."

"I should have known something was up. That day when I walked into your office, and she was with you. I should have seen it right then. I guess maybe I didn't want to see it. I didn't want to believe my best friend and my sister would be stupid enough to get involved with each other." He lets out a loud breath. "I don't know, man. I just don't know." He shifts his weight from side to side. "Does she know about what happened overseas? Does she have any clue what she's actually signing up for with you?"

I draw back slightly, a little caught off guard that he would throw my past up at me like that.

"She knows some things."

"Some, but not all," he says condescendingly.

Anger boils in my chest, and I have to fight the urge to lash back at him. Pulling in a deep breath through my nose, I let it out slowly before allowing myself to reply.

"I know what you're thinking, Winst. But I'm telling you, it's different with Harlow. I'm different. She makes me want to be better. She makes me want more for myself. She makes me forget…" I leave the statement hanging.

"Fuck," he grumbles, shoving his hands into the front pockets of his jeans. "She needs to know everything, Miles."

"She will. It's just going to take me a while to work my way up to that."

He nods. "And what about Alan?"

"What about Alan?"

"You realize she's still married, right?"

"I'm not a fucking idiot," I grind out. "I realize that she is *technically* still married, but we both know that won't be the case in a couple of weeks." I pause, trying to calm my voice. "I know your real issue here is that I didn't tell you sooner, and I'm really sorry about that. I guess I just didn't know how. If I could go back, I'd do it differently."

After a long pause, he says, "You're going to hurt her." It's not even a question.

"I won't," I insist.

"You will. And when you do, and I'm forced to choose between the two of you, I'll choose her."

"I wouldn't expect anything less."

"I don't like it." Winston's gaze finally comes back to mine. "I don't like it even a little bit. But on the off chance that you can make each other happy, I won't stand in your way either."

"I appreciate that," I tell him, not really sure what else to say.

"I gotta get back to Stella." He turns and starts for the door.

"Hey, Winston," I call, waiting until he turns back toward me before continuing, "Are we good?"

"I guess." He shrugs unconvincingly.

"For what it's worth, I really do love her," I tell him in a last ditch effort to try and make him understand.

"Let's hope for all our sakes that ends up being enough." With that, he turns and disappears from the office.

"Hey." The moment Harlow's voice comes on the line I instantly relax. It's crazy how just hearing her say something as simple as "hello" brings a smile to my face despite the day I've had.

"Hey," I return. "What are you doing right now?" I ask.

"As in right this second?"

"As in right this second."

"I'm actually just getting ready to leave the shop. Why what's up?"

"Stay put. I'm coming to get you," I say, sliding onto my motorcycle.

"And where are you taking me once you get me?" I can hear the smile in her voice.

"I haven't decided yet. I'm in the mood for a ride."

"Everything okay?" Her voice dips.

"Yeah, it will be." I let out a slow breath.

"I don't know that I like the sound of that." I hear her shuffling papers in the background. "What's going on?"

"I'm leaving your Dad's shop."

"Why are you at Dad's shop?" she asks

"I did it."

"You did it," she echoes. "As in you told them?"

"I did. I talked to both your father and Winston."

"Oh god. Do I even want to know how it went?" she asks nervously.

"Your dad was surprisingly very supportive. Winston on the other hand…"

"Is he mad?"

"I don't know if I'd say mad. I think he's a little hurt that we kept it from him. And he's worried about you."

"Worried about *me*? Why?"

"I'll tell you everything when I pick you up."

"Okay." She lets out a slow breath. "I guess it's a good thing I have actual shoes on today," she says, knowing I won't put her on my bike in those damn strappy things she wears all the time.

"I guess so." I fire my bike up, feeling the rumble beneath me. "I'll be there in about fifteen."

"I'll be ready."

Chapter Twenty-two

Harlow

I tighten my grip around Miles' waist as he guides the motorcycle from side to side down a narrow and curvy road.

I have no idea where he's taking us. If I had to guess I'd say we've been driving for at least an hour. I stopped recognizing my surroundings when he exited the freeway quite some time ago.

All I know is we're somewhere north of Cincinnati in a very rural area. And while I'm still getting used to being on the back of a motorcycle, I'm rather enjoying the peaceful ride. Something tells me Miles really needed it.

He was quiet when he picked me up. He smiled and kissed me and tried to seem normal, but I could tell that whatever Winston said to him struck him hard. Even though I wanted to demand that he tell me everything the moment he picked me up, I knew he probably needed some time to digest everything.

Knowing my brother, he didn't make it easy on Miles. The last thing I want to do is add to that. I want to be the person that makes him feel better – not worse.

Miles turns down a side street and takes us through a heavily wooded area. After a few moments, the trees open up to a reveal a beautiful lake stretched out in front of us. Pulling the bike into a near-vacant lot nestled between two large patches of trees, he snags the far left spot and kills the engine.

I slide off the back, using his shoulders to leverage myself up and over before quickly removing the helmet Miles purchased for me last week.

"Where are we?" I ask as Miles takes off his own helmet.

"Cowan Lake." He drops the kickstand before climbing off the motorcycle.

"I know this place," I say, the name a familiar one from my childhood. "We used to camp here when we were kids," I say, looking out over the water.

"Yep," he confirms, setting his helmet on top of the seat before taking mine and resting it next to his.

"I haven't been here in years." I pause, turning my gaze to the side when he steps up next to me and looks out over the water. "Is there a reason you brought us all the way out here?"

He shrugs. "I thought it would be nice to get away from the city for a while."

"I wish I would have known this was where we were coming. I would have brought a swimsuit."

"For what I've got planned, you won't need one. Come on." He grabs my hand and pulls me toward the concrete walkway that leads down to the water.

There are several boats already out and one that's backed into the boat ramp being loaded into the water as we approach the dock.

"Hey, Preach." Miles greets the guy currently unstrapping the boat from the trailer. He's a middle-aged man, maybe late thirties, with thick dark hair and wire-rimmed glasses.

"Miles Hollins." He grins wide, taking the hand that Miles extends. "I gotta say I was surprised as hell to get your call. It's been what, two years?"

"Probably close to that," Miles agrees. "I appreciate you hooking me up on such short notice."

"Anything for one of my brothers."

"You two served together?" I interrupt, bringing both sets of eyes to me.

"We were stationed together in Hawaii for our first assignment," Miles tells me, squeezing my hand.

"Charles Wilson, but all the guys like to call me Preach."

"He liked to give little sermons every Sunday morning. Hence the name Preach," Miles informs me.

"My dad is a preacher. What can I say? It runs in my blood."

"Well, it's nice to meet you, Preach. I'm Harlow." I smile with a nod.

"She's a pretty one," he tells Miles, throwing me a side wink.

"That she is," Miles agrees, bumping his shoulder gently against mine. "Is she about ready?" he asks, turning his gaze to the small white boat with a thick blue stripe down the side.

"All gassed and ready to go."

"How much do I owe you?" Miles asks, reaching for his wallet. Preach holds his hands up to stop him.

"Not a chance, man," he says, shaking his head.

"At least let me pay you for the gas," Miles insists.

"Nope." He smiles.

"I don't feel right not giving you anything." Miles pulls out his wallet despite his friend's insistence.

"Tell you what, if I ever get my ass to Cincy, you can hook me up with a tattoo."

"You've got yourself a deal." Miles chuckles, shoving his wallet back into the rear pocket of his dark blue jeans.

"Wish I could stay and chat, but I gotta be home to get the kiddos off the bus. I'll be back after dinner to load her up. Just have her back here around six thirty?"

"I can do that." Miles reaches out and shakes Preach's hand for the second time.

"It was nice to meet you, Harlow." His gaze slides to me.

244

"Nice to meet you as well."

With that, Preach climbs into the truck and fires it to life. "You two kids have fun." He throws a wave out the window as he drives away, the boat trailer sliding out of the water behind him, leaving the boat bobbing next to the dock.

"Shall we?" Miles smiles down at me before pulling me toward the dock.

"We're going out on a boat?" I say excitedly.

"Looks that way, doesn't it?" he teases.

"When did you have time to arrange this?"

"I made a quick phone call after we got off the phone," he tells me, releasing my hand to climb onto the boat before turning around to help me on board. "It was a spur of the moment thing."

"Have you taken this boat out before?" I ask, watching him untie the ropes that Preach had placed on the dock to keep the boat in place.

"A couple of times. It's been a while. Since I bought the shop from Dexter, I haven't had that much free time."

"And yet you keep finding ways to make time for me." Knowing he's rearranged his very tight schedule on more than one occasion so that we could do something together.

"What can I say? I like being around you." He winks, tossing the last rope toward the dock.

"Hmmm. Well, I guess I like being around you too," I say sheepishly.

"Well good, because I don't plan on going anywhere." He smiles, taking a seat behind the steering wheel before patting the seat next to him.

The boat is small. Other than the two seats in the center of the deck, there is only a small three-person bench along the back, about three feet separating it from the captain area. There's also a small stretch of deck in front of us with metal stairs on either side, no doubt for entering and exiting the water.

"What kind of boat is this anyway?" I ask, watching him flip a switch as the boat comes to life.

"A bowrider, I believe. I have to admit. I'm not really an expert on boats." He grins, slowly guiding the boat out of the docking area. "Preach uses it mainly for tubing and stuff with the kids. Today, we're just going to enjoy being out on the water."

"That sounds perfect to me." I relax back into the comfortable bucket seat, enjoying the breeze whipping through my hair as the boat approaches the open water and we begin to gain speed.

We drive several miles away from shore before Miles slows and kills the engine.

"You hungry or thirsty?" he asks, turning toward me. "Preach packed us some waters and a couple of snacks. He said it was all he had in his fridge, so lord only knows what he stuck us with." He chuckles, climbing out of his seat.

I smile, turning to watch him pull a small cooler out from underneath the bench seating behind me before popping it open.

He looks inside the cooler for a long moment and laughs, dropping down to sit on the floor. "Well, we have Lunchables." He holds one of them up, shaking his head. "And some water." He riffles through the cooler. "Oh and lookie here!" He grins, holding up a couple Gogurts. "Bonus."

"Lunchables and Gogurt." I drop my head back and laugh. "How romantic." I bite my bottom lip to contain my grin.

"If this wasn't so last minute, I swear I would have had something better to give you."

"Oh shut up and give me one of those." I push out of my chair and stalk toward him. "I love Gogurts and Lunchables," I tell him, pulling one of the tubed yogurts out of his hand before sliding down to sit next to him on the floor.

"This is what I get for asking Preach to pack us snacks. I should have known the only food he'd have in his fridge would be the shit he packs for his kids' lunches." He chuckles.

"Hey, I happen to think he did pretty good." I rip the top off of the Gogurt tube and slide some of the strawberry sweetness onto my tongue. "Mmm." I wiggle my eyebrows up and down playfully.

"You are something else. You know that?" Miles drops his head as another wave of laughter rolls through him.

"Here, you try it," I say, holding my tube of yogurt in front of his face.

"I am not eating that." He curls his nose and shakes his head.

"Oh come on," I insist, using my thumb and index finger to squeeze some of the yogurt to the surface. "You know you want to."

"Oh hell." He chuckles, snatching the Gogurt out of my hand before placing the plastic tube between his lips.

"Well?"

"Okay, so it's not horrible," he says, looking at the tube for a long moment before going in for a second taste. "Actually, it's pretty damn good."

"Right!" I reach for the Gogurt, laughing when he pulls it out of my reach.

"Heck no. This is mine. Get your own," he jokes, handing it back to me.

Seconds later, he tosses a pepperoni and cheese Lunchable in my lap before pulling one out for himself, sitting it on the ground next to him.

I can't help but giggle when he pulls out the second Gogurt and rips the top off, sucking back half of the tube in one swipe.

"What?" He gives me a funny look when I laugh harder.

"It's just funny," I say, covering my mouth to try to keep it in.

"What is?" He looks down and all around like he's trying to figure out what I find so humorous.

"You."

"What? Do I have yogurt in my beard or something?" he asks, running his hand down the front of his beard.

"No, it's not that." I shake my head. "It's just funny seeing a man that looks like you, sitting Indian style on the floor, eating a Lunchable and a Gogurt. I feel like I need to capture this moment or no one will ever believe it's true," I say, reaching for my phone in my back pocket.

"Don't you dare," Miles playfully warns, trying to snag my phone the instant he sees it.

"Oh stop it and let me take a picture." I swat at him, quickly pulling up the camera app. "My big, bad, tattooed, motorcycle riding military man." I smile, pouting out my bottom lip when he refuses to look at the camera. "Please," I whine.

He lets out a loud sigh and shakes his head before looking toward the camera.

"Now smile," I tell him, making sure I can get his food in the picture as well.

"Oh hell, woman." He rolls his eyes before plastering on a wide, cheesy smile.

I snap three pictures back to back, then decide I've probably tortured him enough. Lowering my phone,

I'm just about to shove it back in my pocket when Miles snags it out of my hand.

"My turn." He smirks, turning the camera on me. He snaps several pictures, most of them of me trying to block my face, before he tugs me next to him and reverses the camera to get both of us in the shot.

"I didn't take you for the selfie type," I tease, running my nose gently across his jaw.

"Are you going to keep busting my balls or are you going to take a damn picture with me?" He groans.

"Okay, okay." I lean further into him and look up at the phone.

"One, two, three." I smile, and he snaps the picture, pulling the phone toward him to look it over. "Not too bad." He nods, handing the phone to me.

"I beg to differ. I look awful," I inform him, holding the phone at an angle so I can see it better. With the sun shining down on it, putting a glare on the screen it makes it hard to get a good look.

"That's not possible," Miles tells me, taking the phone from my hand. He locks the screen and sets the device on the bench seat next to him. "You always look incredible."

"You're funny." I crinkle my nose at him.

"And you're beautiful," he counters, causing an instant whoosh to run through my stomach.

"Come here." I lean in and lay a light kiss to his lips before settling back into my previous position. "You know, you're not anything like I thought you were," I tell him, peeling the top off of my Lunchable package.

"How so?" he asks, doing the same thing to his.

"I don't know. You always seemed like such an arrogant asshole, but now that I know you better, I realize you're not that at all."

"Oh yeah?" He grins, popping a cracker into his mouth. "How am I then?" he asks, his mouth full.

"You're funny and witty. Sweet and caring. And you're so gentle with me sometimes I think you're afraid I'm made of glass. It's like the complete opposite of what you portray on the outside."

"I'm only that way with you," he tells me. "It's like you've cast some witchy spell on me and I can't help but be a total pussy around you." He laughs.

"Me and my witchy magic." After a beat, I ask, "So, are you going to tell me what happened with Winston today?"

He goes silent for a full thirty seconds, staring down at the food in his lap.

"He's convinced I'll hurt you," he finally says.

"And what do you think?" I ask, setting my Lunchable off to the side before climbing to my knees in front of him.

"I think he might be right." He lets out a slow sigh.

"Hey." I take his Lunchable and set it next to mine before forcing his gaze up. "You won't hurt me," I reassure him. "Or did you miss the part where I said you treat me like I'm made of glass?"

"He seemed pretty sure."

"Winston seems pretty sure of everything and is rarely ever right about anything." I smile, straddling his legs before settling down in his lap. Wrapping my hands around the back of his neck, I lean in closer. "Obviously, he didn't have too big of an issue otherwise he would have made a bigger fuss about it."

"I think it's because he knows how much I care about you." He leans forward and rests his forehead against mine.

"And how would he know that?" I run a hand into his hair.

"Maybe because I told him." He smiles, snaking his arms around my waist and pulling me tighter against him.

"And what exactly did you tell him?" I ask.

"That I'm falling in love with you." The moment the statement leaves his lips, all the air rushes from my body, and a tingle starts in my head, working its way through every extremity. "Did you hear what I said, Low?" he whispers, waiting for some kind of reaction from me.

"Yeah," I croak out, completely caught off guard by his admission.

"And what do you think of that?" He pulls back slightly to meet my gaze.

"I…" I stutter, trying to calm my raging heart that feels like it might beat out of my chest at any moment. "I feel the same way," I admit, watching the instant relief flood his face.

"Yeah?" His smile is so full it warms me from the inside out.

"Yeah," I admit, never actually getting a chance to say the words because within seconds Miles has his lips on mine, and I know that the time for talking is over.

"Hello?" I press the phone to my ear, the warm sun blaring down on my naked body as I lay in the boat, nestled in Miles' arms.

"Ms. Cabell?" A male voice comes on the line.

"This is she," I say, only half paying attention. Hell, the only reason I even answered was because the number called twice in a row and I was worried it could be important.

"This is Clark from Towne Properties. I was calling about the loft apartment you filled out an application for." This gets my attention, and I quickly sit up.

"Yes. Hi, how are you?"

"I'm well, thank you. I am calling to let you know that your application was approved. I apologize for the delay, but there was a system issue with the company who does our background checks, and it took a lot longer than it normally does to get everything back."

"So, I got it?" I practically squeal into the phone, feeling Miles shift beside me.

"If you still want it, the apartment is yours. You can move in the first of the month."

"As in next week?" I question.

"Yes, ma'am. If that works for you."

"Yes. Thank you so much." I look over to Miles as he sits up next to me.

"We will need you to stop into the leasing office in the next day or two to sign the lease and pay your deposit and the first month's rent."

"I can come by tomorrow morning if that works." I smack Miles' leg excitedly, holding my finger up when he asks what's going on.

"Perfect. I'll be in the office from eight to five tomorrow."

"Then I will see you in the morning."

"I look forward to it, Ms. Cabell."

"Thank you again." My hands are shaking by the time I hang up the phone. As if this day couldn't get any better – learning that I landed the apartment I wanted is the cherry on top of this perfect day. "I got the apartment," I announce excitedly, turning to wrap my arms around Miles' shoulders.

"Congratulations." He pulls me closer and squeezes tighter. "That's amazing news."

"He said I could move in on the first. I have to go in tomorrow morning to pay the deposit and the first month's rent."

"I'm really happy for you, Harlow. I know how badly you've wanted this," he says, reaching up to secure my chin between his thumb and finger.

"Thank you. It's crazy how everything seems to be falling into place."

"You deserve this. You deserve to be happy." He leans forward and kisses the side of my mouth.

"You make me happy."

"You make me happy," he repeats, smiling as he presses his lips directly onto mine this time. "And as much as I hate to say it, I think we should probably head back." He groans, releasing my chin.

"Is it that time already?" I pout, not ready to call an end to our time away.

This has been one of the best days of my life. From laughing and joking with Miles, to hearing him say he's falling in love with me, to making love as the boat bounced in the water below us, there is not one thing about this day that hasn't been absolute perfection.

"I know," he agrees, reaching for his jeans next to him. "But Preach might kill me if I keep him waiting. Or rather, his old lady will." He chuckles, tugging his jeans up his legs before standing and securing them around his waist.

"Well we don't want that," I agree, quickly strapping on my bra before sliding my shirt over my head.

Helping me to my feet, Miles pulls me to his chest without giving me a chance to zip up my jean shorts.

"Thank you for today," he says, kissing the tip of my nose.

"I think it's me who should be thanking you." I smile up at him.

"I don't know what it is that you're doing to me, Harlow Cabell, but whatever it is, don't stop doing it."

"I think I can manage that." Linking my hand around the back of his neck, I pull his face down to mine.

Chapter Twenty-three

Miles

"Is this seriously all you have?" I look around Harlow's bare apartment.

Other than the bed Winston gave her from his spare room which we placed up in the loft. She has zero furniture.

"I told you I was starting from scratch." She huffs, both of her hands going to her hips as she stands in the center of the empty living space.

"Yeah, but I didn't realize you meant this," I tell her, shaking my head.

"Don't worry. I should have enough money to get a couch in the next couple of weeks."

"In the next couple of weeks? Where do you plan to sit until then? You don't even have a place to eat."

"Jackie and Dad are giving me their old table. Jackie decided on Friday that she wanted a new one. I think she just wanted to make sure I had a table and chairs but knew I would never agree to let them buy me one."

"And where do you plan to sit and relax? Those hardwood chairs are hardly comfortable."

"The floor works just fine."

"As if that's any better," I counter.

"It's only temporary. I'll take a little out of each paycheck and buy things as the weeks progress. It's not like I have to have every single thing right now. I can manage."

"There are certain things you need in your home. One of the most important things being furniture," I tell her, snagging her purse off the kitchen counter. "Come on, we're going shopping," I say, extending the bag to her.

"What?" She looks from me to the purse and then back again.

"Shopping," I say, shoving the bag into her hand. "You and me. Let's go."

"Miles," she starts, but I immediately cut her off.

"We're doing this," I tell her sternly.

"I don't have the money right now," she objects. "I spent most of what I had saved on the deposit, first month's rent, and having all the utilities turned on. Did you know that if you've never had electric or water in your name they make you pay deposits? I've never heard of such a thing." She sighs.

"You don't need money. This is on me."

"Like hell it is." She crosses her arms in front of herself, her purse dangling from her hand. "You are not buying me anything."

"Yes, I am."

"No, you're not." The frustration in her voice is undeniable. "I've never done anything on my own. Alan always handled the money. He decided what to buy and when. I was just along for the ride. It's important to me that I do this for myself. So thank you, but no thank you."

"I'll tell you what." I try another angle, clearly seeing how important this is to her. "Come with me to the furniture store, pick out a couch, and I will pay for it." I hold up my finger when she begins to open her mouth, surely to object. "And then you can pay me back."

"No." She shakes her head.

"Okay, what if we set up a paycheck deduction?" I suggest. "I'll buy you a new couch. And a T.V.," I say, looking around the empty space. "And we can agree upon an amount that will be deducted from your paycheck each week to pay me back."

"Now I need a T.V. too?" She taps her foot.

"I saw you looking at some online the other day. Don't act like you don't want one." I smirk when she glares in my direction.

"That's a very nice offer, Miles, but…"

"You said yourself that you were going to buy these things over the next few weeks anyway. What's the harm in letting me buy them for you and you paying me back? Think of it as an advance from work. People do that sort of thing all the time."

"They do?" She cocks a brow.

"I mean, some people do, yeah." I shrug.

"You're not going to let this go, are you?" She finally concedes, clearly seeing that my stubbornness outmatches even hers.

"Not a chance."

She lets out a dramatic sigh before hoisting her purse up onto her shoulder.

"Fine. I'll let you buy me a couch and a television, but *only* if you swear I can set up the payroll deduction first thing tomorrow and you won't go messing with it later on."

"You have my word." I make a criss-cross motion over my heart.

"You're really frustrating. You know that." She stomps past me, slipping on her flip-flops when she reaches the front door.

"You're just figuring that out?" I tease, snagging her keys from the key hook next to the door before she can grab them herself. "Just relax, this will be fun," I tell her, leading her out into the hallway before stopping to lock the deadbolt.

"Somehow I doubt that," she deadpans, failing to hold a straight face for long.

"Are you sure I need something this big?" Harlow steps back and looks over the sixty-five-inch television mounted on display in front of us.

We've been shopping for nearly two hours. It didn't take her long to pick out a couch once we reached the furniture store, but then I had to spend an additional twenty minutes convincing her to let me buy her the whole set. Now she's been standing in front of the same two televisions for what feels like forever, nibbling on her thumbnail like she can't decide.

"Trust me. You're going to want the bigger screen. It will fit the space a hell of a lot better than the smaller one."

"I guess you're right." She nods. "Let's get the bigger one."

"Wise choice." I grin, kissing her on the temple before going in search of a floor associate to help us.

Not able to find anyone available, I decide to go to the customer service desk where the young girl working promises to send someone over.

Just as I turn to head back to Harlow, a familiar voice washes over me, and I turn to see Delia just a few feet behind me in line.

"I thought that was you." She abandons her spot and comes to stand next to me.

"Hey, D." I nod. "Why aren't you at work?"

"I should ask you the same thing," she counters, her usual sass firmly intact.

"I'm actually heading over soon. I've got two appointments this evening."

"I just came from there. My speaker is acting up again and you know I can't work without my tunes." She holds up the Bluetooth speaker in her hand. "I'm heading back over as soon as I pay for this bad boy."

"Everything going okay today?"

"Smooth as can be. Though Chuck and Tubbs got into a little tiff over an appointment mix up. Apparently one of Chuck's regulars called to schedule an appointment. Tubbs took the call, ended up overbooking Chuck somehow. Anyway, it all got worked out."

"I guess I'll have to talk to him again about the appointment book. This isn't the first time he's done this."

"Trust me, I know. The last time he did it to me." She huffs. "So, what are you doing here?"

"I'm helping Harlow pick out a T.V. for her new apartment," I say, not missing the knowing smirk that instantly appears on her face.

"You've been doing an awful lot with Harlow here recently, boss man. Anything I should know?" She rocks back on her heels.

"If you're asking are we together, the answer is yes," I say, knowing by the way her eyes widen that she didn't expect me to say that, or at least not say it without a little more coaxing from her.

"I just assumed you were fucking her." She nods, seeming almost impressed. "So you're like together, together."

"Together, together," I confirm.

"Huh? Well, will you look at that. There's a woman who can tame him after all," she says more to herself than to me.

"Are you done? I need to get back to Harlow." I shake my head, smiling.

"Oh yes, we don't want to keep your *lady* waiting." She bats her eyelashes dramatically at me.

"You're a fucking handful. Remind me why I employ you again."

"Because you'd be lost without me," she says matter of fact.

"Keep telling yourself that." I laugh, clapping her on the shoulder as I pass her. "I'll see you at the shop in a little bit."

"Yeah you will," she calls after me.

When I finally get back to Harlow, she's still standing in the same spot only this time she's talking to an associate.

"Hey." I step up next to her just as the female associate leaves to make sure they have the television Harlow wants in stock.

"Hey." She leans into me. "What took you so long? I was starting to think you got lost."

"Sorry, I ran into Delia. She couldn't let me slip away without giving me shit for something."

"Uh oh." She grins, knowing how Delia is with me. "What about this time?"

"You." The smile instantly falls from her lips and worry creases her forehead as she turns to face me.

"Me?" she croaks. "You didn't tell her about us, did you?"

"I did." I nod. "You think I'm going to face off with your family but keep it from mine?" I give her a look that tells her she should know better.

"No, I guess not. I just hadn't really thought about it."

"I told you I'm done hiding and that means I'm done hiding. I don't care who knows. Truthfully, the more people that know you're mine, the better. I'll make sure Tubbs gets that message loud and clear." I grin, dropping a kiss to her forehead.

"Tubbs?" She seems confused.

"Don't act like you don't know he's got a thing for you. I think he's made that pretty apparent."

"Oh, he does not." She dismisses the thought. "He just likes picking on me."

"Trust me, Low, I know Tubbs. Every move he's made up to this point has been to try to get you into his bed."

"Men. I swear I don't understand any of you." She rolls her eyes.

"Okay, we do have that model in stock." The associate returns, just as I'm about to respond.

"Great, we'll take it," I say instead, throwing Harlow a wink before following the associate to the sales counter.

"Hey." Harlow raps on the open door of Room B where I'm cleaning up after my first appointment.

"Hey. I didn't know you were coming by tonight." I smile, watching her step inside the room.

She's wearing a different outfit than she was earlier today when we were shopping – having traded in her jean shorts and tank for a short, form-fitting romper that looks insane on her slender frame.

"I met Dad and Jackie for dinner at Rock Bottom. I thought maybe you'd be hungry so I brought you something," she says, holding up a takeout bag that I didn't even notice until now.

"You didn't have to do that," I tell her, crossing the room toward her.

"I wanted to." She turns her face up the instant I reach her, giving me full access to her mouth, where I promptly lay a long, wet kiss.

"You've been drinking," I murmur against her lips, able to taste the remnants of alcohol on her tongue.

"I had a couple of beers," she admits, pressing her lips back to mine.

I groan, tightening my grip on her.

"I've missed you," I say, pulling back just enough to meet her gaze.

"You just saw me." She smiles.

"I still missed you." I rest my forehead against hers.

"Hey, boss." I look up to see Tubbs who falters just inside the door. "Shit, my bad." He shakes his head, realizing what he just walked in on.

"You need something?" I growl, irritated by the interruption.

"Sorry, didn't mean to interrupt. Your next appointment is here."

"Thanks. I'll come out and get her when we're done here."

"Cool. Cool." His eyes dart to Harlow for a split second before he quickly exits the room.

"Well, that took care of that problem." I chuckle, knowing Harlow knows exactly what I'm referring to.

"Men." She shakes her head and steps out of my embrace. "Here." She shoves the takeout bag into my hand. "Eat a little something before you start your next appointment, okay?" She takes my face into her hands.

"Yes, ma'am." I grin, breaking into a full blown smile when she pushes up and drops a kiss to the corner of my mouth. "I'm coming by your place when I'm ready for dessert," I tell her as she backs away.

"I already feel sorry for my neighbors." She giggles, blowing me a kiss before exiting the room.

I close the short distance between me and the door and quickly hang my head out into the hallway so I can watch her walk away. I bite my lip to suppress the groan that works its way into my throat at watching her perfect hips sway.

As if sensing my eyes on her, Harlow turns right as she reaches the mouth of the hallway. She gives me a knowing smile and a small wave before disappearing into the lobby.

Fuck me. I am so far gone it's not even funny.

Chapter Twenty-four

Harlow

"I was starting to think you'd forgotten you owned a phone." I huff the instant Winston's voice comes on the line.

"Some of us have actual lives and don't live on our devices," he kicks back, the familiar sounds of my dad's car shop filtering in through the background.

"Yeah, I know. I'm one of them," I remind him. If anyone avoids technology, it's me. I don't do social media, and I'm rarely on my phone outside of sending a quick text or making an actual phone call. "Sounds like you're in a mood," I point out.

"Not in a mood, just busy."

"Well, I won't keep you. I just haven't talked to you in a couple of weeks, and I feel like you're avoiding me."

"I'm not avoiding you."

"So you just conveniently decided to stop answering my calls the day Miles came to talk to you?"

"That's not true."

"It absolutely is true," I tell him. "You avoided your apartment like the plague the last week I was there, and you didn't even help me move like you promised you would."

"I gave you a bed."

"Yeah, that you made our father deliver."

"I told you, I've been busy," he clips, irritation clear in his voice.

"You're an awful liar, Winston." I shake my head even though he can't see me.

"Harlow."

"Look," I cut him off before he can say more. "I get that this Miles situation is not ideal for you, and I'm sorry that we didn't come clean as soon as we realized there was something between us, but we're happy. Doesn't that count for something?"

"It would if I thought there was any chance in hell it would last."

"Why are you so sure that it won't?"

"Because I know Miles."

"And I don't?" I question.

"Not nearly as well as you think you do."

"So tell me."

"I'm not getting in the middle of this, Low. I'm just telling you straight up, don't get too comfortable. It's only a matter of time before this ends."

"That's your opinion. I guess we will just have to prove you wrong."

"I hope you can." He pauses, sliding his hand over the phone as he talks to one of the other guys at the shop. "Hey, Low, I gotta go."

"Okay, but you're having dinner with Miles and me tomorrow."

"I don't know if I can."

"You can. I've already checked with Stella, and she promised you two would be there. Preston's. Seven o'clock. No excuses."

"I'm not sure how I feel about you going behind my back with Stella."

"I'm not sure I really care," I counter playfully. "Seriously, Winst, Miles and I are together. It's time you wrap your head around that so we can all move on with our lives. He loves you, I love you, and we just want things to go back to normal. Or as normal as they can."

"You're very pushy. You know that?"

"I do because you are too." I smile. "Wonder where we get it from," I say, knowing we both already know.

"Dad," we say in unison, both of us laughing directly after.

"So tomorrow. Seven o'clock?"

"Fine, I'll be there." He tries to hide it, but I can hear the smile in his voice.

"Love you," I sing into the phone.

"Love you too," he grumbles, promptly ending the call seconds later.

"You seem nervous." Miles slides his hand under the booth and squeezes the top of my thigh.

"I am nervous," I admit, jumping slightly at the contact.

"Don't be. It's Winston. He'll come around." He gives me a reassuring smile.

"I know." I blow out a slow breath. "I just can't help but feel a little guilty."

"You have no reason to feel guilty."

"But I do. I feel like I blew in and disrupted his whole life. First, by invading his apartment and being there a lot longer than I intended. Then by hooking up with his best friend."

"He's your brother. You didn't invade or mess anything up. Things happen, and we adjust."

"When did you become so sure of everything?" I question. Knowing when this first started he was questioning things way more than I was.

"I'm in love with you, Harlow Cabell. Of that, there's nothing to feel unsure about."

I suck in a breath, the weight of his words settling down over me like a warm blanket, cocooning me in their safety.

"I…" I start to respond, but my words die off when I look up and catch sight of Stella and Winston heading our way.

"Hey, you two." Stella smiles, sliding down into the booth directly across from me.

"Hey." I look up at my brother as he takes the seat next to her, settling in across from Miles.

"This place is really cool." Stella looks around the dimly lit restaurant. "I can't believe I've never been here before."

"There food is incredible too," I interject. "I had forgotten how good it was until Delia and I came here after work last week."

"Delia?" my brother questions, his gaze falling to me. "Now that's a pairing I didn't see coming."

"Delia is amazing," I tell him, having grown quite fond of the girl over the last few weeks. It's an unlikely friendship. I'll give him that. But once you get past Delia's hard exterior, it's impossible not to like her.

"I'm not arguing with you there." Winston opens his menu, turning his gaze downward. "I just never pictured you two as friends. You're so different."

"Sometimes being different is a good thing," I argue, feeling Miles' eyes on the side of my face seconds before his hand finds my leg again under the table.

"It absolutely is," Stella agrees. "Look at me and this one." She hitches her thumb toward Winston. "We

272

couldn't be more different, and yet we just make sense." She smiles adoringly at him.

"Because you're both batshit crazy," Miles jokes, garnering a playful elbow to the ribs from me. "What?" He smirks at me. "It's true."

"That doesn't mean you have to say it out loud," I tell him, unable to contain the smile that spreads across my face every time I look at him.

"This is fucking weird," Winston grumbles under his breath, drawing our attention in his direction.

"Well, for the record, I think you two look super cute together," Stella says, dropping her chin into her hand as she rests her elbow on the table, instantly drawing my gaze to the large diamond perched on her ring finger.

"Um…" I point to her hand, my gaze bouncing to my brother.

"Oh yeah, about that." A slow smile forms on Winston's face. "So, Stella and I have decided we're gonna get hitched."

"What!" I blurt, not able to contain my excitement over the news. "Since when?"

"Since last night." Stella beams, holding her hand out so I can get a better look at the gorgeous princess cut diamond on her finger.

"And no one called me?" I huff.

"I wanted to, but Winston wanted to wait and tell you guys in person. Surprise!" Her smile widens.

"It's about damn time." Miles grins across the table at Winston.

"That's what I said." Stella giggles. "Took him long enough." She nudges her fiancé playfully.

"Do Dad and Jackie know?" I ask my brother directly.

"Told them this morning." He nods, his earlier unease seeming to dissipate a bit as a lazy smile pulls at his lips.

"You guys." I sigh, so happy I could cry.

"We've decided not to wait," Stella informs us. "We're going to do a small ceremony at the end of August and make it official already."

"That's only two months away," I gawk. "That soon?"

"Neither one of us wants a big wedding, and honestly, I'm ready to be Mrs. Winston Cabell already. Ahhh, just the sound of it makes me all tingly inside."

"Women." Winston chuckles under his breath.

"You love me so shut it." Stella lays a light smack to his bicep.

"That I do." He grins at Stella, and I swear my heart melts inside my chest.

It's one thing to find happiness for yourself; it's something else entirely when the people you love find it too.

"So, as I was saying," Stella continues. "We've decided not to wait. And, we were hoping that you two would stand up with us when we say I do."

"Seriously?" I squeal, practically bouncing in my seat.

"Seriously." She nods. "You two are so important to the both of us, and we can't imagine two better people to stand next to us on the most special day of our lives."

"I don't know what to say." I flatten my palm to my chest, feeling an overwhelming rush of emotion wash over me. Of all the friends Stella has, the fact that she chose me means more than I could ever vocalize into words.

"Say yes." Winston smiles, and it's like everything that's happened over the last couple of weeks has disappeared, and things feel oddly okay in the world again.

"Yes!" I practically scream.

"What about you, Miles?" My brother turns his attention to the man at my side. "Think you can squeeze some time out of your busy schedule to be my best man?"

"Are you kidding?" He grins. "It'd be a fucking honor, man."

"Then it's settled." Stella claps her hands together. "Now where's that waiter? I think champagne is in order."

The remainder of the dinner went by in a blur of good food, bubbly drinks, and busy conversation. If you were an outsider looking in, you would have never guessed that my brother had pretty much avoided Miles and me like the plague over the last couple of weeks.

Walking out of the restaurant, I knew that all was in the past. Miles and Winston laughed and joked like they always have. While Stella and I did our best to keep up with whatever it was, they were talking about. Those two have always spoken their own language of sorts.

And while I know that things can change on a dime, for the first time in a very long time I feel like everything is exactly as it should be.

My brother is marrying the girl of his dreams – who I adore. My divorce from Alan should be final soon so I can finally put that chapter of my life behind me. My dad and stepmom are in good health and doing well. And as for me, well, I'm falling madly and deeply in love with a man who makes me happier than I've ever felt in my entire life.

It finally feels right. All of it feels right. Every aspect of my life seems perfect right now. And even though deep down I'm secretly waiting for the other shoe to drop, I still can't stop myself from enjoying every second of the ride.

"You awake?" Miles nuzzles his face into my hair, his arm tightening around my middle.

"Yeah." I snuggle deeper into his embrace.

"So I was thinking, maybe at the end of the summer we could take a few days off and take the bike up north. There's this incredible lake in northern Michigan. The water is so blue you'd almost swear you were looking at the ocean, and they have these amazing cabins. We could rent one for the week."

"Really?" I roll onto my back and turn my head toward him. Even though the room is dark, I can still see the outline of his handsome face.

"Really." He hitches his hand around my waist and turns me the rest of the way so that I'm lying on my side, our faces inches apart.

"I'd love that," I whisper.

"Me too." I can sense his smile even though I can't see it. "Maybe after Winston and Stella get married. That should give me enough time to rework my schedule. I might have to push up some appointments which will make my schedule a little tighter over the next few weeks, but it will be totally worth it to get to have you all to myself for an entire week."

"I'll have to see if my boss can give me some time off," I tease, running my fingers through his chest hair.

"Approved." He chuckles, rolling on top of me, bracing his arms on either side of my head before lowering his face down to mine. "You've completely obliterated me, Harlow. I hope you know that."

"Obliterated doesn't sound like a good thing," I counter, wrapping my arms around the back of his neck.

"I haven't decided if it is a good thing yet," he teases, nibbling gently on my bottom lip. "But I don't ever want you to stop either." He presses down on top of me, and I salivate under the weight of him.

"Then I won't stop." I groan when he grinds his arousal into my lower belly. Seconds later his fingers flutter down the side of my stomach. "As long as you don't stop." I pant when he shifts his weight and his hand dips between my thighs.

"Never, baby." He kisses me deep, applying more pressure as his fingers glide along my most sensitive area. "I'll never stop." He nips my jaw, withdrawing his hand as his lips work their way down my body.

I come alive under his touch. Each brush of his fingers singes every nerve ending to life. Every touch of his lips makes my heart beat faster. Every murmur and kiss makes me feel on the brink of exploding into a million tiny pieces.

I've never had anyone affect me the way Miles Hollins does. And not just physically, but emotionally as well. He makes me feel things I've only ever dreamt about. He makes me want things I never thought I'd want again. He makes me see the world that was once so black and white, now in bright, vivid color. He doesn't just make me feel alive, he makes me want to *live.*

"Miles." I urge his face back up to mine, needing to feel him inside me. "I need you," I plead.

"I'm right here," he soothes, somehow sensing that I need the reassurance that he's actually here. That this is real life.

I press up, finding his lips in an instant. The familiar zing that I always feel every time we kiss is even more prominent now. Maybe because I know that what I feel for Miles is the real thing.

"I need you," I repeat, this time the words coming out even more desperate.

"Baby." He groans, pressing his forehead to mine as he lines himself at my entrance.

Our eyes meet in the darkness as Miles enters me with one powerful thrust.

Chapter Twenty-five

Harlow

"Hey."

I look up from the paperwork in front of me to see Winston standing in the doorway of the office, a stack of envelopes in his hand.

It's been two weeks since the night we went to dinner, and he and Stella announced their engagement. Since then things have returned to normal for the most part. I mean, Winston still acts a little strange when Miles holds my hand or touches me in front of him, but the more time that passes, the less he seems to react.

"Hey." I smile, pushing back in my chair. "I didn't know you were stopping by today."

"I had a few errands to run, and I wanted to bring this to you," he says, crossing the office. "I'm assuming this is the last of your mail." He drops the envelopes on the desk before plopping down in the chair across from me.

"It should be," I tell him. "I updated my address with everyone I could think of and stopped by the post office last week to have anything I might have missed forwarded."

I grab the mail and start shuffling through it, pausing on a thick white envelope with my attorney's name on it.

My heart rate picks up speed as I quickly tear open the flap and pull out a stack of papers. Tears instantly prick the back of my eyes as I scan the front page.

"It's over," I croak.

"What is?" I look up to find Winston studying me curiously.

"My marriage," I say, barely processing the words as I say them. "I knew this was coming. Monica called me the other day to tell me that the courts would be filing the finalized paperwork in the next couple of days, but seeing it, knowing that it's really over, I can hardly believe it. I'm free." A stray tear rolls down my cheek, and I quickly move to wipe it away.

"This is what you've been waiting for, Low." He leans forward, resting his elbows just above his knees. "So why the hell are you crying?"

"I'm just so happy." I let out what sounds like a mix between a sob and a laugh. "It's finally over."

"Come here." Winston quickly stands, pulling me from my chair to wrap me in a tight hug.

"It almost feels like a dream," I say in disbelief, burying my face in my brother's chest.

"Everything okay?" comes the familiar rasp of Miles' voice and I turn my head to see him standing in the doorway.

"Everything's great," Winston replies first, pulling back to smile at me. "I'll let you give him the good news." He winks before heading for the door, clasping Miles on the shoulder on his way out of the office.

"What good news?" Miles cocks his head to the side and studies my face.

"Here." I hold out the stack of papers still clenched in my hand.

He crosses the office and takes the documents, scanning the top one briefly before his gaze comes back up to mine.

"Does this mean what I think it means?" he asks, a slow smile forming on his lips.

"I'm officially divorced." I nod, still not able to fully wrap my head around it.

"Thank fuck," he sighs, dropping the stack of papers onto the desk before closing the distance between us. "This is exactly what I needed today," he tells me, dipping his face down so that we're standing eye level. "Why do you look like you're on the verge of crying?" He tips my chin up, forcing me to meet his gaze.

"I think I'm in shock," I tell him honestly.

"This is what you wanted," he reminds me.

"I know. And I'm beyond happy. It's just. I don't know. For as relieved as I feel, a part of me feels a little sad too." I shake my head. "That probably sounds crazy." I let out a loud sigh.

"It doesn't sound crazy at all. That was ten years of your life." He points toward the desk in the vicinity of where my finalized divorce papers lie. "Of course you're going to feel a little sad. But this is a chapter of your life that you can finally close the door on. You can move on and start a new life…with me," he whispers the last part.

"I love you," I blurt, not actually meaning to say the words.

A wide smile lights up his face.

"And I love you." He leans forward, laying a light kiss to my mouth before pulling back. "We should celebrate," he announces.

"We should?" I state more as a question than an agreement.

"We absolutely should." He nods enthusiastically. "There's a festival going on this weekend just a few blocks from here. It started today. Let's go. We can eat too much food, drink beer, and listen to music. How's that sound?"

"Are you sure you have time for that?" I question, not able to hide the hint of excitement in my voice.

"My last appointment is at six. It's a pretty easy piece. I should be done by eight. That will give us plenty of time. What do you say?"

"Okay." I smile, feeling the relief I should have felt the moment I opened that envelope finally sweep through me.

"Okay." He grins. "Why don't you take the rest of the day off and meet me back here a little before eight."

"You sure?" I hesitate. "I still have a few things to get done."

"I'm sure. Besides, I'm pretty certain you weren't even supposed to work today," he reminds me.

"Maybe I just like my job," I smirk.

"Or maybe you just like your boss." He winks.

"That too." I laugh, pressing up on my tip toes to kiss his jaw.

"Get out of here. Go home, have a glass of wine, and take a long bubble bath. In the meantime, I'll be here, wishing I could be there to help you wash your back." He gives me a cheeky smile.

"I'm sure you'd be doing a heck of a lot more than washing my back," I counter, giving him a knowing look.

Since this whole thing started, we've pretty much been incapable of keeping our hands off each other. You'd think that as the weeks have passed, it would have died down some, but the truth is I think it only gets worse as time goes on.

I'm addicted to Miles in the most consuming and utterly fantastic way. He makes me so insanely happy that some days I have to pinch myself just to make sure I'm not dreaming.

"You know me so well." He leans forward and kisses me. "Now go, before I take you in the storage room and we start this celebration early." He turns, smacking my backside.

I squeal and jump forward, managing to snag my purse off the desk as Miles ushers me toward the door.

"Tell me something about you that I don't know." I sip the craft beer that Miles purchased for us as we weave through the crowd gathered for the festival.

"How about you just ask me something you want to know?" he suggests, snagging my hand before pulling me toward a vacant stone bench a little off the main path.

He takes a seat and pats the space next to him.

"I'd rather you tell me something I might not think to ask," I challenge, crossing one leg over the other before taking another small sip of beer.

"Okay." He thinks for a long moment. "I think you're the most beautiful woman I've ever laid eyes on." He laughs when I roll my eyes.

"Not what I meant, and you know it." I shake my head, feeling nothing short of perfect in this moment.

Today has been the most incredible day. As promised, Miles was finished by eight when I arrived back at the shop. We walked to the festival hand in hand and spent the last two hours tasting different beers and eating our weight in fried foods from the various food trucks lined up and down the street. We've laughed so much that my cheeks ache. And I swear every time he turns and kisses me, my stomach hits the ground somewhere at my feet.

Miles Hollins hasn't just changed my life. He's making it a life I want to live. I'm reminded of that more and more with each moment that passes.

"Okay, let's see." He taps his chin dramatically. "I got it," he announces after a long pause.

"Well spit it out already." I laugh when he makes no attempt to tell me whatever it is that he's thought of.

"Do you remember when we were younger, I think you had just turned sixteen when I was visiting home before my first tour overseas. I was hanging out with Winston in the living room when you came home from a party, and I heard you in the bathroom slamming shit around. When I knocked on the door and asked if you were okay, you swung it open and screamed in my face."

"I told you to mind your own business," I say, remembering the night he's referring to. It was the night I went to Sarah Burton's birthday party and caught the boy I liked making out with one of my best friends. "What about that night?"

"Well, what you don't know is that when you pulled that door open and squared your shoulders at me, it took every inch of willpower I had not to kiss you right there."

At the moment of his admission, I took another sip of my beer, causing it to go down the wrong hole. After spending the next thirty seconds in a coughing fit, I croak, "What?"

Miles laughs, patting my back until I can breathe.

"Say that again," I request now that I'm not choking.

"You heard me." He grins down at me.

"But you hated me. Why would you want to kiss me?"

"I didn't hate you. You pissed me off, that's for sure. But I never hated you."

"You sure fooled me," I snip playfully.

"Pot meet kettle." He taps me on the nose, instantly pulling a smile to my face.

"Okay, so keep going. Tell me how much you wanted to kiss me." I lean forward, eager to hear the rest of the story.

"It was the weirdest thing. I had always looked at you like a little kid, but in that moment you suddenly weren't a kid anymore. Your cheeks were red and blotchy, and you had dark red rims under your eyes like you'd been crying. Every single thought left my brain, and I swear for a moment I really was going to kiss you. Thank god I didn't." He shakes his head, smiling when he catches the insulted look on my face.

"Ouch," I say dramatically, holding my chest.

"It's not like that." He chuckles. "Can you imagine what would have happened if I had actually done it? You were sixteen, and I was twenty-one. Besides being illegal, I'm pretty sure your brother and father would have both killed me. Not to mention the fact that I wasn't a guy you would want to kiss you back then."

"Why? Because you were such a slut." I laugh at myself.

"Not the wording I would have used, but yes, I guess that's fair." He shakes his head, his smile firmly in place. "The point is, I realized way back then that I was attracted to you. Of course, I never thought it would be anything I'd act on because you drove me fucking nuts. I never really gave it much thought again until you walked into my office with your brother all those years later. One look at you and I knew I was in trouble."

"So I don't drive you nuts anymore?" I ask, purposely being overly sweet.

"Oh no, you still drive me nuts." He chuckles when I swat at him. He catches my hand effortlessly and tugs me toward him. "But it's a completely different kind of nuts. As in the kind of nuts where I feel like I'm going out of my mind every minute I'm not with you. All I want to do is touch you." He slides his hand down my bare arm. "Kiss you." He lays a light peck to my mouth. "Smell you." He moves his face down to my neck and inhales deeply. "And I wouldn't change it for anything in the world." I feel him smile against my skin.

"Keep talking, and you might not make it through that beer," I warn him, already feeling my skin warm and tingly in all the right places.

"Why's that?" He chuckles, pulling back to meet my gaze.

"You know why." I bite down on my bottom lip and give him a knowing look.

"Fuck the beer." He abruptly stands, pulling me to my feet. Taking my cup, he turns, dropping both of our still half full beers in the trashcan behind him.

"Miles," I object, my hands instantly going to my hips.

"Would you rather have the beer or me?" He arches a brow.

"You already know the answer to that."

"That's what I thought." He snags my hand and begins pulling me down the street.

"But we could have at least finished our drinks."

"Sure, if you don't mind that I rip your clothes off in front of every single person at this festival." He throws me an evil smile over his shoulder.

"Shut up." I laugh.

He stops so abruptly that I end up running into the back of him. He turns so quickly to face me that I nearly lose my balance.

Grabbing my face in both of his hands, he dips down so were standing eye level. "If you don't believe I'd do just that then you clearly have no fucking clue how crazy you make me," he tells me matter of fact, causing heat to spread across my cheeks before slowly making its way through the rest of my body.

"You're right. We should go," I say, suddenly feeling just as desperate for him as he seems to be for me.

"Wise choice." He plants a hard, close-mouthed kiss to my lips before he's once again pulling me through the crowded festival in the direction of my apartment.

"Do you see yourself ever having kids?"

I snuggle deeper into my robe, pulling my feet up on my chair as Miles and I sit out on my balcony enjoying the warm night breeze.

"I don't know. I've thought about it, obviously, but it's not something I really ever saw coming to fruition." He scratches his beard as he looks out over the vacant street below my building. "What about you?"

"I would have had five by now if Alan would have agreed," I admit truthfully.

"Really?" He turns his gaze toward me.

"Does that surprise you?"

"A little." He nods. "I mean, now that I think about it, I guess it doesn't. You're a very giving, nurturing person by nature. It makes sense that you'd want children to care for." He pauses and shakes his head.

"What?" I ask when he doesn't say anything else.

"Nothing. I was just thinking about what I just said. When you were a teenager, I thought you were such a spoiled, selfish little shit. I think maybe I misread you. Hell, I think I misread a lot of things."

"No, I was a shit," I say, laughing. "Being with Alan changed me in a lot of ways. As much as I grew to resent him over the years, not everything that came out of that marriage was bad. I think we all take the path we need to take to become who we're meant to be in the end."

"Yeah." He turns his gaze up to the sky. "I guess."

"Can I ask you something?"

"Anything."

I wait until his eyes come back to me before continuing. "Do you regret joining the Army?"

"Yes and no." He shrugs.

"Can you explain that answer?"

"I don't regret serving my country. I don't regret the people I met or the relationships I formed. But I do regret things that happened."

"If you had the decision to make all over again, would you make the same one?"

"If I knew how it would all turn out you mean?"

I nod.

"If I could go back, I'd do every single thing differently - except for you."

"Will you tell me more about what happened over there?" I ask, knowing I don't need to explain the question. He knows what I want to know. It's a subject I've broached many times but have never gotten very far into before he shuts down.

"You know what happened."

"I know about the friends you lost, yes. But that's all I know."

"That's all there is to know."

"We both know that's not true."

There may be a lot I still don't know about Miles, but I know him well enough at this point to know when there's something he's purposely not telling me. I can sense it in his demeanor. In the way his entire mood shifts whenever the subject is brought up. I just don't know why.

He gives me a sad smile before pushing to a stand. "I'm really tired. I think I'm going to call it a night."

I watch him cross the balcony and slide open the door before standing and following him inside. "Miles." He stops at the stairs leading up to the loft and turns toward me.

"I'm sorry if I pushed. I just want to know everything about you."

He holds open his arms, and I immediately go into them.

"You didn't push." He kisses the top of my head. "And you have a right to know anything you want to know. I just can't go there right now. We've had such an amazing day. I don't want to ruin it by digging up ghosts that have long since been buried."

"I understand," I say, even though deep down I really don't.

I know that he went through something terrible over there and my heart breaks that he lost his brothers in arms the way he did. I can't even imagine the guilt he carries knowing they died and he lived. But shouldn't that be something he should share with me? Isn't that what having a partner is for? Leaning on them and sharing that burden. How can I help him when he won't stop shutting me out?

Instead of voicing any of this to him, I follow him up the stairs and into bed without saying another word about it.

Chapter Twenty-six

Miles

He's on top of me, screaming words I can't understand. My hands shake. My heart thuds violently in my chest.

I have to get out of here! It's the only thought in my mind.

They're dead. All of them. My brothers. All dead. He screams louder, pounding his fists violently against my chest.

"I didn't do this," I say in a fog. "I didn't do this. You did." Suddenly I'm on top of him, anger boiling out of every word.

This is his fault. He did this.

His nails dig into my wrists as my hands tighten around his throat. I'm choking him, squeezing so hard his eyes bulge as he fights to find air.

And then I hear her voice...

Harlow.

My eyes snap open, and I see her. My beautiful girl pinned beneath me, my hand splayed across her throat, her green eyes wild with panic.

I rip my hand back, and she immediately gasps for air, clenching her throat where my hand just was. I take one look at her before throwing myself out of bed. I drop to my knees, feeling like the room is closing in on me.

I need air, and yet I feel like I can't get any.

"Miles." Her voice is soft, yet hesitant.

I can't look up. I can't face what I've done.

"Miles," she repeats more forcefully.

"Fuck," I cry out, the remnants of the nightmare still with me. The image of what I woke to even more terrifying.

What used to plague me every single night had never happened when Harlow was in bed with me. Not until tonight.

"Miles. Look at me." Harlow sets her hand on my shoulder, and I instantly jerk back, stumbling to my feet. "Miles." Before I know what I'm doing, I'm running down the stairs two at a time, feeling like if I don't escape this apartment, I might suffocate.

I hear Harlow's voice behind me, but I keep moving. My shoes are barely on before I push my way out the front door and barrel down the street.

Tell me what happened?
Please talk to me.

Harlow has called and text me countless times since I left her apartment in the middle of the night. I haven't answered a single one. She even showed up at my door just after one this afternoon, but I pretended I wasn't here and eventually she went away.

Thank fuck it's Sunday; otherwise I'd be screwing my entire schedule because there is no way in hell I could go into the shop today. I can't even bring myself to get out of bed let alone think of work. My headspace is worse than it's probably ever been and I'm not even sure how the fuck it all manifested. I feel like all the progress I've made over the last eight years went up in a pile of smoke and I'm back right where I started.

I don't even know *how* it happened. One minute I'm in the same nightmare I've had more times than I can count. The next the nightmare is suddenly my reality, only my hands are around the wrong person's throat.

I can still see the panic on her face, her wide green eyes staring up at me in absolute terror. I don't know how I'll ever face her again after that.

Chapter Twenty-seven

Harlow

It's just after seven in the evening. I'm standing outside of Miles' apartment for the second time today, praying that he opens the door this time.

Today has been nearly impossible to get through. I've been trying to reach Miles since he ran out of my apartment last night, but have been unsuccessful up to this point. I've called, texted, shown up at his door. All of which has gotten me nowhere.

I'm worried about him to the point that I feel physically ill, and I know that the only thing that will make me feel better is seeing him.

He was a wreck when he left last night. I don't think I've ever seen anyone so distraught in my entire life. And while the whole ordeal was terrifying for me, my only real focus has been on Miles.

I'm not really sure what happened. He was tossing and turning in bed next to me. I turned on the bedside lamp and gently nudged his shoulder to wake him. And the next thing I knew, he was on top of me, his hands around my throat, and I couldn't breathe. His eyes were open, but he wasn't there; the vacant stare on his face a clear indicator of that.

    I instinctively clawed at his arms trying to free myself, but he was solid on top of me. He was saying something but his words were jumbled, and in my panicked state, I couldn't focus enough to put anything together. I could feel myself starting to lose consciousness the longer my airway was constricted. Spots filled my vision, and for a moment I truly believed I was going to die, but before I blacked out, Miles blinked and in an instant, his hands disappeared from my throat.

    It was probably one of the scariest moments of my life, and yet when it was all said and done, it wasn't me I was worried about.

    Taking a deep breath in and letting it out slowly, I lift my hand and lightly rap on Miles' door. At least thirty seconds pass, and I hear nothing inside the apartment. No movement, no attempt to answer the door. Nothing.

    I adjust the infinity scarf around my neck, using it to hide the fingerprint bruises. It's in the nineties today, and so humid the air feels thick around me. I'm sure my attire seems completely out of place, but I didn't know what else to do. I couldn't risk running into someone I know or worse – Miles seeing what he did to me.

I still can't wrap my head around the fact that any of this actually happened. One minute I felt like I was living a fairytale and now it's like I've been thrown into some terrible nightmare.

"Miles." I knock again, a little louder this time. "Miles, I know you're in there, and I'm not leaving until I see you," I yell into the crack of the door like that will somehow make my words easier to hear inside the apartment.

I lift my hand to knock again right as the door jerks open without warning. I jump backward, startled by the sudden and unexpected movement before my eyes dart upward and find Miles' face.

My stomach twists violently at the sight of him. His hair is standing up in every which way, and there are dark circles under both of his eyes. My gaze jumps from his shirtless torso to his fitted blue jeans that are unbuckled at the waist before finally noticing the half empty bottle of whiskey dangling from his fingers.

"Why are you here?" His voice is thick, his eyes distant. Like he's looking through me, not at me.

"I wanted to make sure you were okay," I start, unable to say more before he cuts in.

"You shouldn't be here," he slurs, clearly intoxicated.

"What is going on, Miles? Why haven't you answered my calls or my texts?"

"Because I didn't want to talk to you," he bites harshly.

"Why? What did I do?" My voice goes up an octave as panic starts to rise in my chest.

"What did you do?" He lets his head fall back, a malicious laugh echoing from his chest. "You're really fucking funny. You know that." His head lulls forward, and his eyes go to the space behind me.

"Miles, what is going on?" I soften my approach, even more, reaching out to touch his forearm.

The instant the contact is made he rips his arm back as if I've just touched him with a hot branding iron.

"Don't!" he bites out violently.

"Will you please talk to me? Let me come inside, and we can talk this out. About what happened last night. I'm not upset with you. I know you would never hurt me."

"But I did fucking hurt you!" he explodes, rearing back and punching the open door so hard I swear there's no way he didn't break something.

"It wasn't you," I start, a clear shake in my voice.

"But it was me, Harlow. It was me." He pounds on his chest, angry tears filling his eyes. "I could have fucking killed you."

"But you didn't." I reach for him again.

"Don't fucking touch me!" he screams, stumbling backward in the doorway.

I look from side to side, a little surprised that not a single neighbor has poked their head out to see what the commotion is all about.

"Miles, please, just let me come in, and we can talk this out."

"There's nothing to talk out. I knew better than to do this. I knew that pretending with you wouldn't make it just all miraculously disappear."

"You weren't pretending. Don't say that."

"I was pretending, Harlow. I've been pretending for the last eight years. I'm fucked! Don't you see that?"

"No, you aren't."

"You have no idea what you're talking about. You don't know the things I've done. What more do I have to do to show you I'm not the guy you want me to be?"

"But you are that guy, Miles. One night doesn't change that. I love you."

"Don't say that to me," he grinds out.

"Don't say what? I love you? Well newsflash, Miles, I do! I love you. And you love me."

"No, I don't."

I take a full step back as if his words were a physical attack.

"Yes you do," I croak, emotion rising in my throat. "And you are not fucked," I insist, my own tears stinging the back of my eyes.

"But I am," he insists, his head shaking back and forth slowly. "I'm so fucked up."

I put my hands on both sides of his face and try to get him to focus on me. "Look at me," I plead. "Miles, look at me," I say more forcefully, surprised when he does as I ask and doesn't immediately push me away. "Whatever this is, whatever is going on, we will figure it out."

He wraps his hands around my forearms and stares at me for a long moment, his eyes darting to the scarf around my neck and then back up to my face.

"It's over."

Pulling my hands away from his face, he takes a full step backward into the apartment.

"Miles!" I cry.

"I'm sorry, Harlow. I can't do this anymore. I should never have done this with you. I'm sorry."

I stick my foot in the doorway right as he attempts to close the door in my face, then push forward with all my might. It does me no good. Even in his drunken state, he's still way too strong for me.

"Miles, please!" I push again, but the door doesn't budge.

"Go home, Harlow." He pulls the door open and steps directly into me, forcing me backward.

"You can't do this to me. You can't promise me the world and then rip it away for no reason."

"For no reason?" Anger flares behind his eyes and he takes another step, forcing me further out into the hallway. "In case you need reminding, I almost killed you last night."

"No, you didn't," I argue.

"Yes, I did," he growls, fingering the scarf around my neck. "And for the record, I never promised you anything."

I rear back, fear and sadness morphing into hurt and anger.

"So that's how you want to play it?" I snip, my hands shaking violently as I clench them at my sides.

"I'm not playing anything. I told you it's over. You're the one who refuses to leave."

"You want me to leave?" I square my shoulders and take a deep breath in through my nose, trying to muster every ounce of strength I have.

"I do," he says, his expression hard and stoic.

Seconds ago he was on the verge of breaking down, and now he's so cold that I can physically feel the chill coming off of him.

"Fine. I'll leave. But don't for one second think I'm ever coming back."

"Good. That's what I want."

"Then you've got it." I spin on my heel, making it all of two steps before turning back to Miles. "You wanna know what I think?" I ask, continuing before he can even think to answer. "I think you're a coward. I think you're so scared of letting someone in that you'd rather spend your life alone than share your burden with another person."

"You can think whatever you want. It doesn't change the fact that this is over."

"No, it certainly doesn't. Goodbye, Miles." I whip back around and take off down the hallway, dipping into the stairwell moments later.

Tears stream down my face before I reach the parking lot, but somehow I manage to make it nearly a full block before completely melting down.

As if Mother Nature is feeling my mood, it begins to rain, the warm droplets of water mixing with my tears like the heavens are crying with me.

I know there are dark parts of Miles' past that I still don't know about. Things that prompted what happened last night and into today. I know there are things that he has seen and gone through that a normal person can't even fathom, but that doesn't excuse his behavior. It doesn't make it okay for him to make me feel like I did something wrong or that I'm not good enough.

I spent years with a man who made me feel that way every single day. I promised myself the day I got out that I would never let someone make me feel that way again. And that's a promise I intend to keep.

Chapter Twenty-eight

Miles

"Damn, you look like shit," Delia says the instant I walk in the front door of Ink*ed*. I'm half a mind to tell her to fuck off, but truthfully I don't have the energy to do even that.

After what happened with Harlow, and quite possibly breaking my hand punching the front door, I polished off the remainder of my whiskey before passing out with my head in the toilet. That's where I stayed until a few short hours ago. I haven't really had time to process anything outside of trying to rid myself of this hangover.

"Thanks," I grumble, heading through the lobby into the main area of the shop.

"She's not here," Delia calls behind me right as I reach the mouth of the hallway that leads back to the office.

"Who?" I question unnecessarily, turning back toward her.

"You know who." She crosses her arms in front of her chest and leans against the doorframe on the other side of the room.

"When is she coming in?" I ask, trying to keep my voice even and unphased.

"She's not." She shakes her head slowly, giving me a small frown. "She called this morning and quit."

"She what?" The words tear from my throat and bounce off the walls around us.

"You heard me." Delia gives me a pointed look. "Whatever you did, you must have fucked up really bad considering she just signed a year lease on that apartment two weeks ago."

"Fuck." I run my hands through my hair and tug on the ends in frustration.

I was so convinced that I was doing the right thing by pushing her away that I didn't even consider what that meant for her. Of course, she'd quit. Why would I think for one second that she'd ever want to see my face again after what I did to her?

I can still see the hurt in her eyes, the desperation on her face. All she wanted was for me to let her in and I couldn't do it. She tried to comfort me, to help me, and I couldn't let her. She wanted to love me, and I threw that love back in her face like it didn't mean a fucking thing.

What kind of person does that to another person?

Apparently, you do.

"So, what did you do?" Delia asks, pulling me out of my own mind and back to the conversation.

"It's over. That's all you need to know," I tell her.

"So it was your fault then." She nods. "I knew you'd find a way to fuck it up."

"Are you done?" I practically growl, my frustration level doubling tenfold in a matter of seconds.

"Yep." She holds her hands up in front of herself and slowly backs out of the room without another word.

"I fucking knew it!" Winston bursts into my office just after six, slamming the door closed behind him. "I knew you'd find a way to fuck it up. Fucking hell, why couldn't you keep it in your fucking pants for once?"

"Winston," I start, ready to try to explain myself the best I can without telling him the real truth.

"Do you have any idea what you've done to her? She's devastated. Like hasn't stopped crying for hours, devastated. I've never seen her like this before. What the fuck?"

My stomach knots at his words and I have the sudden urge to go to her. I push the thought down and quickly refocus.

"You're right. I should have listened."

"That's it? I'm right?" he clips. "How about you tell me how the fuck you guys went from one hundred to zero overnight?"

"I, uh, realized that things were getting a little too serious and I needed to back away." I stand, squaring my shoulders.

"A little *too* serious?" He snorts, unconvinced. "Just weeks ago you showed up at my dad's shop pronouncing your love for her, or did you forget that part?"

"I remember," I say, doing my best to keep my voice calm.

"So was it just a game to you? Make everyone believe you actually care so you can run around fucking her whenever you want without judgment? Fuck, dude, just fuck her and leave it at that. Why did you have to tell her you loved her?"

"Because I fucking do," I burst out, not able to listen to him talk about Harlow like she was just sex to me. She was never just sex. "I do love her." My voice falters.

"Then explain to me what the hell is going on?" Winston grips the back of the chair in front of him and leans forward slightly.

"It just wasn't working out."

"Bullshit." Winston rocks back. "Tell me the real fucking reason."

"I just did."

"And that's why you clearly punched something and fucked up your hand?" he asks, pointing to my right hand that's bruised and swollen around my knuckles. "Because it just wasn't working out."

"Why the fuck do you care why anyway? It didn't work out. Let's leave it at that." I shove a stack of papers across the desk in frustration.

"Why do I care?" He looks at me in disbelief. "Why do I care?" he repeats. "Are you fucking kidding me right now?" He shakes his head. "You have been like a brother to me since we were kids. I warned you that this wouldn't work, but you didn't consider the position it would put me in. Nope. You had to have her, and whatever Miles fucking wants, Miles gets."

"This was never about you," I argue.

"Clearly, otherwise it wouldn't have happened. But now I have to find a way to comfort my sister after my best friend ripped out her heart and fucking stomped all over it."

"I never meant to hurt her, Winston. You have to know that."

"Well what you meant to do isn't really relevant anymore now, is it? The damage has been done. I hope you're happy with the outcome." He turns and rips the door open.

"I almost killed her," I blurt, not able to let him walk away believing what he's currently thinking.

He turns slowly back toward me, his eyes wide with confusion.

"I was having a nightmare. The same nightmare," I say, having shared small pieces of the dream with Winston over the years. "I don't know what happened. One minute I was in the dream with my hands around his neck and the next I was looking down at Harlow. My hands around *her* neck." I collapse back into my chair and drop my face into my hands. "You should have seen her face." I rub my eyes with the balls of my hands.

"That's why you ended things so abruptly." I look up just in time to see him close the door and slide down into the seat across from me.

"I love your sister. I love her like I've never loved a woman before. So much so, that I'm willing to let her go if it means keeping her safe from me."

"Did you ever think of telling her this?"

"She wouldn't listen if I did. She'd try to find a way to fix it. She'd convince me we could work it out. And I'd probably let her. And then what? What if next time it's worse? What if next time I don't wake up before it's too late? I could never live with myself."

"Fuck, man." Winston lets out a slow sigh and leans back in the chair.

"I think maybe this was a sign. You know? Maybe after everything I've done I don't deserve to be happy."

"I don't believe that for one second," Winston disagrees. "You were at war, Miles. You can't blame yourself forever for the things you did to survive or the decisions you made in an impossible situation. You have to find a way to forgive yourself, man. Because until you do, you're right, I don't think you can be with Harlow and not put her at risk." He pauses for a long moment. "I know you don't want to hear this, but you need help. Like real help. Otherwise, this brutal cycle will never end, and you're going to keep coming out on the other side with more casualties at your feet. Maybe not in the literal sense but you know what I mean. If you love Harlow the way you say you do, you'll find a way to make this right. If not, that's on you. Either way, you've got to make a choice."

"You want me to go to therapy. I've told you already, it won't help."

"And you know that how? Because you went twice right after you got home? You never even gave it a chance, Miles. You were so convinced that you knew better and who the hell could tell you differently? It was one thing when you were only hurting yourself, but now you've pulled Harlow into your fucking mess. If you can't do it for yourself, do it for her."

"I'll think about it," I tell him truthfully, knowing deep down there is not one damn thing I wouldn't do to get Harlow back into my arms.

"I really hope you do. In the meantime, stay away from my sister. She's been through enough. You said you were done, so be done. At least until you get your shit sorted out."

"I can do that." I nod, my chest tightening at the thought.

"I love you. You know that. But until this blows over, you know where I stand."

"I know." I nod once.

Winston pushes to his feet.

"You know I've got your back. Always. Do yourself a favor and get the fucking help you need. No matter what you think, you do deserve to be happy."

"Thanks, man."

With that, Winston turns and quickly exits the office.

Chapter Twenty-nine

Harlow
Seven weeks later

"You look beautiful," I exclaim when Stella walks into the room dressed in a white, knee-length, fitted lace dress and sparkly white heels.

Her blonde hair is pinned back on the sides with a long sheer veil attached to a silver and white headpiece, hanging down the back. She kept her makeup light with pale pinks and nudes, accenting her natural features beautifully.

"You don't think it's too tight?" she asks, stepping in front of the floor length mirror at the back of the room before running her hands down the front of her dress.

After much deliberation, Winston and Stella decided to get married on the river. Winston's buddy owns a small restaurant with an outdoor deck that looks out over the water. It's the perfect location, especially since there will only be about thirty people in attendance. Jon – who owns the place – closed the restaurant down for the occasion and has a small staff working that will serve dinner directly after the ceremony.

"I think it's perfect," I tell her, walking up behind her to fluff the back of her hair. "Are you nervous?"

"Not even a little bit." She smiles at me in the mirror. "Is that weird?"

"I don't think so. I think when you know it's right; there's nothing to be nervous about."

"Were you nervous when you got married?" she asks, turning to face me.

I think back to the day I married Alan. Even though it feels like a lifetime ago, I can still remember everything in perfect detail. The flowers his mother insisted on tying to the end of every pew even though I thought they were hideous. The candlestick centerpieces placed on every table. My dress, how it sashayed around my feet when I walked. The way my hand shook when Alan slipped the ring on my finger.

"Extremely," I answer. "Then again, look at who I was marrying. Perhaps that should have been my first clue."

"It wasn't all bad though, was it?"

"I guess not at first." I shake my head. "Lucky for you, you know exactly what you're getting with Winston. I don't think you have to worry about things changing too dramatically. Your relationship will evolve with time, but that's to be expected."

"I'm so happy to have you as a sister." She pulls me in for a tight hug.

"Me too," I admit, fixing her veil as I pull back.

"I wish your mom could be here. Then this day really would be perfect."

"She is here. Just like she was with me on my wedding day and every day since the moment she died. I know Winston feels that way too."

"That's a good way to look at it. I just wish I could have met her."

"Well, I can tell you without a doubt that she would have adored you."

"Thanks, Harlow. That really means a lot." She pauses for a long moment. "How do you feel about today? You think you'll be okay?" Her question brings my reality back to the forefront of my mind. I've been trying really hard not to think about seeing Miles, even though I've known this day was coming for a while.

We haven't spoken since that night at his apartment. There are a lot of things I wish I could have said and I'm sure that he feels the same, but it was easier to cut ties and walk away. But it hasn't been easy and truthfully the last thing I want to do is walk out on that deck in a few short minutes and have to see him standing there.

Winston was prepared to tell him not to come, but I couldn't allow that. He deserves to have his sister *and* his best friend with him on his wedding day, no matter how painful it might be for me.

"Yeah, I think I'll be fine," I finally answer, forcing a carefree smile.

"You're about as bad of a liar as your brother." Stella gives me a sad smile, reaching out to briefly touch my forearm.

She's right, of course. Anyone who cares to look can see I'm barely holding my emotions in check. I thought I was doing okay until this morning, but even then I know that's not the truth. I haven't been okay since everything fell apart. I've just been trying really hard to make everyone think I am, including myself.

If I thought starting over after Alan was hard, it was nothing compared to moving on after Miles. As much as I loved my job at Ink*ed*, there was no way I could stay there. The couple weeks that followed were the hardest. Not only was I battling one hell of a broken heart, but I had to put myself back out in the world without skipping a beat. Enduring interview after interview when all I really wanted to do was curl up in my bed, consume thousands of calories in ice cream and watch sappy romance movies while I cried.

I didn't have enough money saved to get me through more than a month, so I really didn't have a choice in the matter. Sitting there, forcing a smile when all I wanted to do was fall apart proved harder than I think even I realized going into it. But I made my way through, and after less than three weeks, I had lined up a job at Fifth Third Bank in their accounting department.

It's not Ink*ed*, but the pay is excellent, and I like most of my co-workers. And most importantly, it's allowed me to keep my apartment. Though, I find myself more times than not wishing I had chosen something a little further from Miles. I swear every time I step out of my front door I'm afraid I'll see him. Or maybe I'm hoping I will. My emotions kind of all bleed into one another these days.

As much as I wish I could say I'm doing better and that time has helped, the truth is I'm still the same mess I was seven weeks ago when the rug was abruptly pulled out from underneath me. I think part of it is because I was one hundred percent invested in Miles and losing him has been a difficult thing to process. But more so I think it's because I've never really gotten any closure. I've never gotten the answers I truly need.

It went from him being there, to him not being there, without any real explanation as to why. That's been the hardest part of all.

"I don't know if Winston has already said this, but thank you for what you're doing," Stella interrupts my thoughts, pulling my attention back to her. "Your brother was prepared to tell him not to come, but I know it would have killed him to do it."

"I would never have asked him to do that. I made my choice. I knew there was a possibility things wouldn't work out and I'd be forced to see him regardless, yet I still went there anyway." I shrug.

"Yeah, but not everyone would be so selfless and levelheaded about it." She smiles. "Now if we can just keep Jackie away from him, we might get through the day unscathed."

We both chuckle at that.

Jackie has made it her mission to see that Miles and I get back together. She insists we're made for each other and refuses to accept that things are over, even all these weeks later. She's not the only one who was upset to hear of the split. I could tell my father was disappointed, though he was more worried about making sure I was okay. Not that Jackie wasn't worried about me, but her comfort came more in the form of reassuring me everything would work itself out, and we'd find our way back to each other. Not really what you want to hear when it's the furthest thing from what you believe.

"She promised she wouldn't interfere. I can't see her risking making a scene today of all days. She'll just whisper about it to my dad all day and drive him crazy."

"Better him than you." She winks, turning her attention to the door when a soft knock comes from the other side. "Yeah?"

"It's me, hon." Stella's mom peeks her head inside the door. "They're just about ready for you."

"Okay." Stella takes a deep breath in and lets it out slowly.

"You ready?" I grab her bouquet off the chair to my left and hold it up to her.

She takes the flowers from my hand and gives me a wide smile. "Let's do this."

I follow Stella and her mother out of the back room and down a long hallway that opens up into the main dining area of the restaurant. We can see the guests that are gathered outside through the wall of windows along the back, but they're tinted in a way that the people outside can't see in.

I spot Winston instantly, standing at the far side of the deck, the river glistening behind him. Then my eyes slide to his right, and all the air leaves my body.

I knew he was going to be here. I knew I was going to see him. But nothing could have prepared me for what I feel like laying eyes on him again after all these weeks.

He looks even more handsome than I remember and I swear my chest constricts so tight I feel like a thousand pound weight has settled down on top of it.

Every memory hits me like a flash. The way he used to say my name. The sound of his laughter. How he smells. The way he'd always kiss my temple whenever he was standing near. It all comes knocking through me one after the other until every single emotion I've buried over the last two months has boiled its way to the surface.

I fight back the onset of tears that build behind my eyes and try to refocus, but once my sights are set on him, it's like I can't look away.

His hair is combed back away from his face, and he's wearing a dark suit with a purple tie – something Stella coordinated to match my purple, empire dress. He also has a white flower pinned to his chest while I have a small bouquet of the same flowers tied together in my hand.

Nervous butterflies flap wildly in the pit of my stomach, and I have the sudden urge to turn and take off running in the opposite direction.

A few words are exchanged between Stella and her mom, but I'm too fixated on the man on the other side of the glass to listen to them.

Miles rocks back and forth on his heels, glancing around the room like he's waiting for something. For a split, second I allow myself to believe it's me he's waiting for, but I quickly push the thought away.

If Miles had any interest in working things out, he would have done so already. If he wanted to see me, he could have walked down the street rather than wait weeks until my brother's wedding.

No, he's here for Winston and so am I. I just need to get through the next couple of hours, then I can go back to pretending Miles Hollins doesn't exist.

"Harlow." I glance up to see Stella watching me with a funny look on her face. "You have to go." Her gaze slides to the door and only then do I realize that her father is there, holding the door open for me so that he can come in and accompany his daughter down the aisle.

I hesitate, not really sure how to make my feet move. I take a deep breath in to try to calm the sudden wave of nausea that washes through me.

You can do this, Harlow.
Just put one foot in front of the other.

I manage to take one step and then another, my entire body shaking by the time I reach the doorway. I keep my gaze turned downward as I step out onto the deck, trying to focus on the soft music playing in the background and not on the sound of my heart thudding violently against my ribcage.

Taking another deep breath, I raise my head up my line of sight going straight to my father who's sitting in the front row with a warm smile on his face. I smile back, feeling a tiny portion of the weight lift.

I then look toward Winston, purposely avoiding looking in Miles' direction. If I pretend he's not here then maybe, eventually, it will feel like he isn't.
And while I know that forgetting that Miles is here is never going to happen, that doesn't stop me from trying to convince myself of it just the same.

Winston meets my gaze as I reach the end of the makeshift aisle. He gives me an excited smile as I take my place to the left of where Stella will stand.

I pivot, facing the direction I just came from as the wedding march sounds through the restaurant's speaker system. I flip my eyes to the door as it swings open and Stella steps out, arm in arm with her father.

Tears instantly prick the back of my eyes, and even though every fiber of my being is telling me not to, I chance a look in Miles' direction.

The moment I do, the entire world shifts beneath my feet.

Chapter Thirty

Miles

She's so fucking beautiful it hurts to look at her. I've spent weeks waiting for this moment. Every single thing I've done has been leading up to this, and damn if it hasn't been worth every second now that she's here, standing in front of me. Reminding me of exactly what I've been fighting for.

She avoids my gaze as she makes her way down the aisle. I can tell that she's purposely looking anywhere but at me, but that doesn't stop me from looking at her.

She looks stunning in her knee-length purple dress and silver heels. She has her hair pulled back away from her face, and long silver earrings hang low from each ear.

I memorize every detail.

The pale pink of her lips. The way the sun heightens the red hue in her strawberry blonde hair.

How her slender fingers grip the flowers in her hand so tightly, it's like they are the only thing keeping her feet on the ground.

She takes her place next to where Stella will be and turns back toward the door, but even as the bride starts to come down the aisle, there's only one woman I care enough to look at.

And then her eyes sweep to me. The instant our gazes lock I swear I feel my knees physically shake beneath me.

There's so much behind those brilliant green eyes of hers. Pain. Uncertainty. Doubt. Anger. Things I never used to see when I looked at her. It damn near guts me knowing I put that there.

When Stella and her father reach the end of the aisle, I have no choice but to turn my focus to the bride, but that certainly doesn't stop me from glancing Harlow's way countless times throughout the short ten-minute ceremony.

I can't get enough of her. It's like I've been walking around blind and all of a sudden I can see again. Everything looks brighter, more vibrant and colorful, more beautiful.

The ceremony flies by in a blur. It feels like one minute Stella's father is giving her away and the next the minister is introducing the new Mr. and Mrs. Cabell.

As soon as the announcement is made, everyone immediately erupts in a cloud of applause, standing as

Winston and Stella make their way back up the aisle hand in hand.

I quickly move to stand next to Harlow just as she starts to follow them out. She glances up at me and then to the arm I extend to her. I watch about twenty different emotions dance across her face before she finally links her arm with mine and allows me to lead her across the deck and back into the restaurant.

It's been two hours since Stella and Winston exchanged their vows. Two hours of family, friends, good food, and lots of laughter. Two hours that I've sat here wishing I could sit next to Harlow. That I could hold her hand. That I could be the reason for the smile on her face.

I was hopeful when she allowed me to escort her back into the restaurant that maybe we'd have a brief moment to talk, but she was swept away moments after we stepped inside and I haven't had the chance since.

It's been torture – being this close to her and yet feeling the limitless distance that stretches between us.

I watch from my seat as she crosses the deck and slides onto a stool at the outdoor bar. My eyes travel down to where her dress opens up, revealing nearly her entire back. I remember what it feels like to run my hands down that back, how her skin would always prickle under my touch.

"Are you just going to sit there all night staring at her or are you going to talk to her?" Stella plops down in the chair next to me, taking a gulp out of her champagne flute before setting it on the table.

"I'm not staring." I shake my head, lifting the beer bottle to my lips.

"Yeah, and I'm not wearing white." She snorts.

"Don't you have a new husband you can aggravate?" I smirk at her.

"Why yes, I do. But aggravating you is so much more fun."

"And why is that?" I cock a brow.

"So what? You're just going to sit here all day pining over her but never actually make your move?" She leans back in her seat, completely ignoring my question.

"I'm waiting for the right time," I tell her pointedly.

"Well I hate to tell you this, Miles, but there isn't going to be a right time. You're just going to have to suck it up and do it."

"Is that so?" I smirk.

"It is. And I'm married now, so that means I know things." She giggles.

"Pretty sure that's not how it works." I shake my head at her.

"How would you know? Have you ever been married?" She curls her nose at me, clearly feeling the effects of the champagne she's been throwing back for the last two hours. "Oh wait, you haven't," she answers her own question.

"Are you about finished?"

"Nope. I'm going to sit here and bother you until you get your ass up and go talk to the woman you're clearly still in love with."

"That obvious, huh?" I finish off the remainder of my beer.

"Painfully." She laughs.

"Well, in that case." I push to a stand, taking my empty beer bottle with me. "If you'll excuse me."

"Go get her," she says moments after I start to walk away.

Shaking my head, I take a deep breath in and let it out slowly as I approach the bar. Sliding up next to Harlow, I set my empty beer bottle on the counter before signaling the bartender for another.

"I haven't had the chance to tell you how beautiful you look tonight," I say, keeping my eyes forward.

She tenses next to me, but to my surprise, she doesn't make any attempt to leave.

"Thank you," she responds as the bartender slides a fresh beer across the bar to me. "You look very nice as well."

"It's been a long time since I've worn a suit. I kind of feel foolish," I admit, taking a long pull of my beer as I turn in her direction.

"Well you don't look foolish," she says, hesitating for a long moment before her gaze finally slides to mine.

"I've missed you." I hadn't meant to admit that to her. It's true, but not how I was intending on starting this conversation.

"Me too." She gives me a sad smile. "Well, I should probably get back to my family." She slides off her stool and quickly turns.

"Harlow, wait." I wrap my hand around her bicep to keep her from walking away.

"I can't do this right now, Miles," she says, her face still turned away from me.

"Can we go somewhere and talk?" I ask, releasing her arm as I step directly in front of her, giving her no choice but to look at me.

"I shouldn't," she starts, but I immediately cut her off.

"Please, Harlow. Just give me five minutes."

"Miles, I…"

"Five minutes, Low. After I'm done, if you never want to speak to me again, I promise you'll never have to ."

She holds my gaze for what feels like a full minute before she finally nods.

I take her hand, feeling her tense at the contact, before pulling her to the opposite side of the deck. I lead her through a wooden gate and down the small staircase that leads down to the ground level.

"Where are we going?" Harlow asks when I pull her in the opposite direction of the parking lot.

"You'll see." I smile, leading her down toward the water.

Within minutes we reach the concrete pathway that lines the river and eventually circles up to the bridge.

"I didn't know there was a path down here," she says, looking out over the water.

"They've redone a lot of this in the last few years." I nod my head, gesturing for us to keep walking.

"It's really nice." She pauses, letting out a slow breath. "So what did you want to talk about? I really don't want to be gone long."

"We're almost there," I tell her, veering left off the path and up a small hill to where there's a massive rock sitting at the top.

"You brought me to a rock?" She looks at me like I have five heads.

"It's not just any rock." I laugh, taking her by the shoulders and turning her back toward the water. The sun has begun to set, casting an orange glow across the sky which makes for an incredible view over the river.

"Wow. The river looks beautiful from here." She lets out a slow exhale.

"Me and Winston used to come up here and get high," I tell her, laughing when she turns, wide eyes in my direction.

"You didn't?"

"Oh, we did." I chuckle. "But over the last few years, it's become more of a quiet escape for me. A place I like to come when I feel like I need to get away." I hold out my hand to her. "Come here." I wait until she takes my hand before helping her up onto the rock. Once she's settled, I hop up next to her, my heart feeling like it might beat out of my chest at any moment.

We sit in silence for a long moment. I open my mouth to say something a hundred times but I can't seem to find the right words to start with. I guess there's no easy way to ease into a conversation that has the magnitude to be life-changing.

Depending on how this goes, I could walk away from here today with the woman I love, or I could truly lose her forever. I guess there's only one real way to find out where my future lies.

Chapter Thirty-one

Harlow

"When I first stepped off the plane in Iraq, it felt like I'd entered a different world," Miles begins, his eyes locked on the river that stretches out before us. "It was like the person I was before no longer existed and I was forced to become something else. To be someone else. Most of the time I didn't even recognize myself. Other times I didn't want to." He pauses, letting out a slow breath. "I told you a little bit about my friends that were killed. What I didn't tell you was how it happened."

"Miles." I hold up my hand to stop him, sensing how hard this is for him.

"No." He shakes his head. "Just let me get this out. I was too afraid to tell you the truth before, but you deserve to hear it now."

"Okay." My voice quiet.

"We were searching a building. My team was to go in first. Make sure the field was clear, floor by floor. Something we had done countless times before. When we reached the second floor, there was a boy, maybe early teens. He caught one look at us and took off running. I sensed that something was off, but we had our orders and I made the call to keep going. It wasn't uncommon for us to encounter regular civilians." He takes a long pause. "We were ambushed minutes later. They came at us from all sides. We got separated in the chaos. Me and Tripp were pinned down on the third floor, and we'd lost contact with the rest of our group. Then the whole building exploded. It blew out the entire side of the building where Tripp and I were huddled. I got hit with debris and blown back a few feet. Tripp, uh, he took the full force of the blow. There was nothing I could do for him."

My heart thuds violently in my chest as Miles goes on. As hard as it is to hear, I hold onto every single word he says.

"It's all kind of a blur after that. I couldn't hear anything. There was dust and rock everywhere. And then I saw him. The boy. The one who had spotted us. I didn't think. I just lifted my gun and pulled the trigger." The words catch in his throat and he takes a couple deep inhales to calm himself. "Seconds later, a man and a woman came around the corner with two much smaller children, clearly trying to escape the war zone they had found themselves in. I still had my gun raised and my finger on the trigger. I was prepared to kill them all if I had to. But then the woman looked down at the boy I'd shot, and I knew instantly that he wasn't to blame for what happened. He didn't run away to tell the enemy we were here. He ran away to warn his family, and I killed him for it." His shoulders shake as a sob runs through him.

"Miles, you couldn't have known." I try my best to soothe him, but there are no words that can possibly help what I'm sure he's feeling right now.

"I should have known." He looks at me, tears welling in his eyes. "I should have known."

"You did what you thought you had to do to protect yourself."

"Did I?" he questions like he's really not sure. "I've asked myself that very same thing millions of times over the last eight years. What could I have done differently?" He pauses for a brief moment. "I watched that mother mourn over her dead son. I stood there with my gun pointed at them and saw first-hand what I had done." He blows out a breath. "I think I was in a state of shock by the time the boy's father thought to act. I pulled the trigger as he approached, but I was out of ammunition without any time to reload. He knocked me back to the ground. Before I had even processed what was happening, he was on top of me with his hands around my throat."

My fingers instinctively slide across my neck, remembering how it felt when Miles' fingers had bit into my skin that night.

"All I remember thinking was there was no way I was going to die there. I somehow managed to get the upper hand. The next thing I knew I was on top of him. I remember choking him so hard. I was prepared to kill him and for doing nothing more than trying to escape. The woman was screaming. I couldn't understand what she was saying, but it was enough to get my attention. That's when I realized the two children were still standing there. They were over the body of their dead brother, watching their dad die too. Even then I couldn't bring myself to stop. Tripp was dead. I had no idea where any of my other brothers were, and as far as I knew, I was going to die in that building. Being that certain of death does something to a person."

"Did you kill him?" I ask when he stops talking and turns his gaze back out to the water.

"Another team arrived, otherwise I would have. I don't know what happened to him. I was ushered out so quickly I don't know what happened to any of them. I thought when I got home things would get better, but honestly, it was harder being here most days than it was being there. At least there I didn't have to face the monster I'd become. But here, being home – around my family and friends – having to live with what I'd done. The innocent boy I had killed. I couldn't even bare to look at myself in the mirror most days. I've dreamt of that man and his son nearly every night for the last eight years. That is until you."

He reaches over and takes my hand.

"You quieted the demons. You gave me a sense of peace I didn't think I would ever find. And I thought that was enough. But then I woke up… And my hands," he chokes on his words. "They were around your neck."

"Miles." I slide from the rock and reach for his hands, pulling him down with me. "Look at me. I'm fine."

"I almost killed you too." Tears brim his eyes, and it takes everything I have not to resolve into a puddle on the ground.

"But you didn't kill me. And what you did to that boy…I can see why that haunts you. But Miles, you have to find a way to forgive yourself. You aren't that person. You have to know that."

"But I don't know that. Or at least I didn't for a very long time. After that night at your apartment, I panicked. I was so afraid of hurting you again that I pushed you away which only hurt you more. I never wanted that. It killed me to let you go, Harlow. It gutted me." He cups one side of my face in his hand. "People have been telling me for years to get help, but I never listened. I let the pain and guilt fester until it was eating me from the inside out. It wasn't until my demons were passed to you that I realized they were right. The next day all I wanted to do was run to you and beg for your forgiveness, but I knew if I did, and you took me back, it was only a matter of time before we ended up right back there again and I couldn't do that to you. I couldn't come to you until I was sure."

"Sure of what?"

"That I wouldn't hurt you again."

He slides his hand down the side of my neck and onto my shoulder before letting it fall away.

"I started seeing a therapist twice a week and joined a local veterans' support group. It's amazing how hearing stories like your own, seeing what other people have gone through and overcome, will do for a person. I've been sleeping at night and just generally feel better. Relieved even. Because instead of holding it in and obsessing over it, I'm finally letting it go. I'm freeing myself of something I've carried with me for far too long. I'm not miraculously healed, but I feel stronger every day. It won't happen overnight, but eventually, maybe I'll even find the strength to forgive myself."

"You will," I tell him, taking his hands in mine. "Because despite what *you* think, despite what *you* see, *I* see the real you and I wouldn't change one single thing about the incredible person you are."

"You've always managed to see past the darkness. Even when it was right in your face, all you saw was the light. I think that's one of the reasons I fell in love with you so hard and so fast. Because you made me see it too. I never meant for things to happen the way they did, and I can't change that I hurt you, but what I can do is promise that I'll spend the rest of my life trying to make it up to you if you'll let me."

"What are you saying?" I ask, fearful to allow myself to be hopeful.

"I'm saying I'm sorry. I'm saying I promise to continue to get the help I need. I'm saying I swear I will never hurt you again. I'm saying that I'm so deeply in love with you that the thought of living without you makes it hard to breathe."

I blink back the tears that are building behind my eyes, feeling overwhelmed with a million different emotions all at once. A part of me is ready to throw caution to the wind and jump right back in. The other part of me is terrified even to consider it.

Miles didn't just hurt me. He completely leveled my entire world in a single blow. I'd be crazy not to be a little hesitant at least.

"I miss you, Harlow. I miss your smile and your laugh. I miss the way you make me feel. I miss how my heart nearly pounds out of my chest every time you walk into a room or how with one look you can bring me right to my knees. You are my light at the end of the tunnel, Harlow. You didn't just save my life. You *are* my life. Tell me I can still fix this. Tell me it's not too late." He takes my face in his hands and lowers his forehead to mine.

"It's not too late," I whisper, knowing there's no sense in fighting it.

Miles pulls back, and despite the tears swimming in his eyes, he's wearing the widest smile I think I've ever seen.

"I love you, Miles. It wouldn't matter if it was seven weeks ago or a year from now, all you had to do was say the words."

"I promise never to hurt you again."

"Don't make that promise because you *will* hurt me again. And I will hurt you. It's part of being in a relationship. Instead, promise me that you'll always stand and fight by my side, no matter how tough things get. And that you'll always share with me how you're feeling. That you won't ever shut me out again. That's all I really want."

"I swear it," he says, leaning in to press his lips to mine.

The instant the contact is made my entire body flutters to life. It feels like I've been holding my breath for nearly two months and suddenly I can breathe again.

I drink him in, revel in his taste and his smell, wondering how I was able to go so long without feeling the way I feel in this moment. The way only Miles can make me feel.

I knew when this all started it wouldn't be easy, but then again most good things never are. It's the things you have to fight for that mean the most. And I will fight for Miles until my last breath, even on the days he won't fight for himself.

"I love you." I feel his breath against my lips.

"I love you too," is my only response and it's the one I mean the most.

Epilogue

Miles
One year later

"What the hell are you doing here?" Delia storms into the back office with her hands flailing wildly in the air.

"I have a couple of things I needed to do really fast," I retort.

"Do you have any idea what time it is?"

"Would you relax? I've got plenty of time." I shake my head at her.

"I swear to god if you're late to your own wedding, Harlow will never forgive me. She left me in charge of you."

"Did she now?" I chuckle, pushing to my feet. "Well, that was her first mistake."

"No, her first mistake was agreeing to marry your ass," she tells me, hands firmly on her hips.

"But thank god she did." I smile.

"Well, she might have a change of heart when you don't show up for the ceremony."

"Would you relax? I'm leaving now, okay?" I grab the paper in front of me and quickly slide it into a large white envelope. "I just had a few things to finalize for Harlow's present."

"Well for marrying your ass it better be something good," she quips.

"Think a house will do?" I ask, watching her eyes go wide.

"You bought her a house?" She gapes at me.

"Not just *any* house. I bought the house that her mom and dad lived in when she and Winston were kids. A two-story farm house right outside of town. The perfect place to raise a family."

"Who are you and what have you done with Miles?" She looks around like maybe the real me is hiding in a corner somewhere.

"What can I say? When you meet the one, everything changes."

"Clearly." She snorts. "But if I come in one day and the beard is gone, I'm going to have you admitted for testing because then I'll know you're under some weird sort of mind control." She laughs.

"Harlow loves my beard." I run my hand down the front of it. "Meaning, it's not going anywhere."

"Well thank god for that. The last thing I want to do is have to stare at that face of yours all day. At least the hair kind of masks the ugly," she jokes, sticking her tongue out at me.

"Are you just about finished? I've got a wedding to get to."

"Well then let's go already." She throws her hands up.

"If we're late, I'm telling Harlow it was your fault." I playfully shove her shoulder on the way toward the back door.

"Man, I never imagined that when I stood up as your best man, it would be my sister you're marrying," Winston whispers over my shoulder as I anxiously wait for the doors at the back of the room to swing open.

"I never imagined you being my best man," I counter, throwing him a sideways glance. "Because I never thought I'd get married."

"Yeah, that's true too." He grins, his gaze going to the back of the room.

I follow his line of sight, sucking in a hard breath when I look up and see Harlow standing in the doorway, her arm linked with her father's.

Her gaze instantly comes to me and a wide smile spreads across her face. It's enough to damn near bring me to my knees.

The last year hasn't been the easiest for us. We've had our fair share of ups and downs, but we've always come out on the other side better for it. She is my rock. The one constant that never falters no matter what happens.

I feel like I've been waiting my whole life to make her my wife and today I finally get to.

"What's going on inside that pretty little head of yours?" I reach over the center console of the car and take Harlow's hand, squeezing it.

"I'm just trying to figure out why you're driving south when we're supposed to be going north." She eyes me skeptically. "Last time I checked, Michigan is that way." She points behind us.

"We've got the cabin for the next two weeks. It can wait another hour," I tell her, lifting her hand to my lips and laying a light kiss to her knuckles.

"What are you up to, Mr. Hollins?"

"You're about to find out, Mrs. Hollins." I wink, turning left down yet another winding back road.

It's already nearing midnight, and while I'm more than a little eager to get our honeymoon started, there was one thing I knew I had to do first.

I slow slightly, still not familiar enough with the road to know exactly where the driveway is. Harlow sits up straighter in her seat and starts looking around, clearly trying to place where we are.

Once I catch sight of the old rusted red mailbox, I whip the car into the driveway, the front end bouncing when we hit a dip in the gravel.

It isn't until the headlights illuminate the house when we reach the end of the driveway that I hear Harlow take a sharp inhale. She has the door open and is climbing from the car before I've even put it in park.

Quickly killing the engine, I climb out after her, joining her at the front of the car.

"This was my house," she says, her eyes pinned on the old farmhouse with chipped white paint and a sunken in front porch.

"It's your house again," I tell her, feeling her eyes on the side of my face.

"What?" she blurts.

I turn, smiling when I catch her shocked expression.

"I bought it for you. Well, for us. It needs a lot of work, but I thought we could fix it up together. Make it a home we can raise a family in."

"I don't know what to say." She looks from me to the house and then back to me.

"Do you like it?" I ask, suddenly feeling a bit uncertain.

"Miles, you bought my childhood home. Every memory I have of my mother is in this house. I don't just like it…" Her eyes well with tears. "I can't believe you did this." She shakes her head, her hand coming up to cover her mouth.

"You have made me the happiest man on this earth, Low. I can't match that, but I sure as hell can try." I step directly in front of her, bending down so that we're standing eye level. "Welcome home, Mrs. Hollins."

Harlow squeals and throws her arms around my neck. "I love you. I love you. I love you," she chants, bouncing in my arms.

"And I love you," I tell her, pulling back to press my lips to hers.

The road we take isn't always the smoothest, but it's the bumps along the way that show us what really matters in this life.

Harlow is my perfect match. In finding her, I found myself.

She taught me it's okay to be imperfect.

It's okay to be hurt and angry.

That obsessing over a past I can't change only limits the future I can.

We are so much more than the sum of our mistakes.

And that one thing, that one moment – no matter how terrible or tragic – does not define *all that we are*.

I may not have deserved my happy ending, but I got it anyway. And there isn't a day that will go by where I won't look at Harlow and know…

This is the girl who not only saved my life but gave me a life worth living.

The End

Acknowledgments

Thank you so much for taking the time to read ALL THAT WE ARE. I truly hope you enjoyed Miles and Harlow's story.

So much goes into writing a book. I feel like I leave a piece of myself inside each and every one I write and this one was certainly no exception. Miles' story was such a personal one for me and I would just like to take a moment to thank everyone who is currently serving or has served in the military. You truly are heroes.

To everyone who helped make this book possible- thank you.

Rose, you've been such a blessing and I'm so happy to have you as part of my team.

Angel, I'm so glad to have met you. Thank you for being someone I can always count on to give it to me straight. But most importantly, thank you for being my friend.

Sommer, your covers are out of this world. You are so talented and I'm so glad to have gotten to work with you a second time!

To all the bloggers that spend hours promoting authors simply because they love books that much- THANK YOU! We don't say it enough but never doubt how truly appreciated you are.

To my readers- thank you. If I could hug each and every single one of you in person I would. It's because of you that I'm able to live my dream and I will forever be grateful. From the bottom of my heart- thank you.

XOXO

-Melissa

Made in the USA
Columbia, SC
04 May 2023